"Gorgeous!"—Elizabeth Strout

"King captures the agita of an early-life crisis and the eccentricities of a writer's life, spiking the narrative with wit, sumptuous imagery and hilarious skewerings of literary elitism."—*People*

"*Writers & Lovers* is exactly the book we need now. Witty and heartfelt . . . I could not stop reading." —Judy Blume

"I loved this book . . . from the first paragraph." —Curtis Sittenfeld, *London Evening Standard*

"Dangerously romantic, bold enough and fearless enough to imagine the possibility of unbounded happiness."—*Washington Post*

"Wonderful, calming, and romantic." —Ann Patchett on *PBS NewsHour*

"Fantastic."—Emma Roberts

"King has created a woman on the cusp of personal fulfillment and strong enough to stand on her own, someone akin to Sally Rooney's Frances in *Conversations with Friends*." —*Boston Globe*

Praise for *Writers & Lovers*

"*Writers & Lovers* reminded me so much of my youth that I asked Lily if she had been reading my mail in the 1990s. It's all about love and being broke and trying to make art. It's a very tender and enveloping book."

—Ann Patchett, Parnassus Books

"Romance isn't the point for Casey. Love is the gravy; words are the filet. Finding a way to build a life around work she loves, finding a way to support herself as a writer—this is the line connecting all three corners of the love triangle at the heart of this novel."

—*New York Times Book Review*, Group Text Book Club

"This smooth, deliberate chronicle of creation keeps the men in their place and Casey firmly rooted at the center of her own story." —*Los Angeles Times*

"King's gift is to suspend the reader, to make the wait for resolution fascinating." —*Minneapolis Star Tribune*

"Intimate and vulnerable." —*Entertainment Weekly*

"[*Writers & Lovers*] shares with [*Euphoria*] a fascination with the difficulty of defining the worth of one's life when the familiar markers of adult achievement are slow to materialize. With wit and what reads like deep insider wisdom, Ms. King captures the chronic low-level panic of taking a leap into the artsy unknown and finding yourself adrift, without land or rescue in sight." —Maureen Corrigan, *Wall Street Journal*

"A down-to-earth saga of an extremely bright and likable single woman wrestling with sexual desires, emotional dreads . . . An engaging portrait of a woman confronting modern hardships."

—Associated Press

"The best readership for this novel may be those most fascinated by the real or imagined lives of artists, a journey that King has portrayed effectively and compassionately with well-crafted prose, evocative descriptions, and spot-on dialogue."

—*New York Journal of Books*

"Funny and romantic and hard to put down, full of well-observed details of restaurant culture and writer's workshops. It's hard to imagine a reader who wouldn't root for Casey."

—*Library Journal* (starred review)

"King is one of those rare writers who can entwine sadness, hilarity and burning fury in the briefest of moments."

—*BookPage*

"An extraordinary novel . . . King beautifully documents every aspect of Casey's character. Casey's insights into the world of writing are fascinating and often humorous . . . The prose [is] linguistically sophisticated, but clean and uncluttered."

—*Midwest Book Review*

"This novel will become a defining classic for struggling young writers."

—*Vulture*

"A knowing look at the pursuit of a life in the arts, with a protagonist you'll root for."

—*Marie Claire*

"A breath of fresh air, with characters that leap off the page."

—*Amazon Book Review*

"Masterful . . . You can't put it down, and you'll feel larger and more connected once you finish it. Plus, it's funny as hell."

—*Dead Darlings*

"Seemingly light and breezy, the novel has an impressively steely core . . . *Writers & Lovers* has one of the most completely satisfying endings around, both surprising and solidly in character."   —*Columbus Dispatch*

"[R]emarkably funny . . . full of moments of keen observation, of wry remarks about the challenges of writing and the awkwardness of early love."   —*Bookreporter*

"King leaves no barrier between readers and smart, genuine, cynical, and funny Casey. A closely observed tale of finding oneself, and one's voice, while working through grief."
                                              —*Booklist* (starred review)

"[A] charmingly written coming of age story."
                                        —*Kirkus Reviews* (starred review)

"Lily King's novel follows a deeply relatable protagonist navigating a whole menu of crises surrounded by a cast of genuine, vivid characters . . . The book occupies a small space, but packs it to the brim with humanity."   —*Entertainment Weekly*

"Elegant, droll . . . This meditation on the passing of youth is touching and ruefully funny."   —*Publishers Weekly*

"*Writers & Lovers* is a puzzling and beautiful novel about writing and love . . . Reading the book feels like waiting for clouds to break—a kind of gorgeous agony."   —*Guardian*

"King's writing is spirited, clever and funny, and her novel is better than most others you'll read this year."
                                              —*London Evening Standard*

"An easy and light-hearted read . . . Its examination of the female psyche shines a light on the complexities and emotions that underpin our decisions at pivotal times in life's sometimes arduous journey: it's a tale of doubt, self-discovery and reinvention."
                                                            —*The Lady*

"Lily King is one of our great literary treasures and *Writers & Lovers* is suffused with her brilliance. It is captivating, potent, incisive, and wise, a moving story of grief, and recovering from grief, and of a young woman finding her courage for life."

—Madeline Miller

"*Writers & Lovers* is a portrait of the artist as a young woman. Lily King writes masterfully about desire and loss, creativity and inspiration, and how each overlaps and influences the other. I found myself reading slowly, underlining phrases, wanting to linger in the world of this novel. Her insights about love—how it is elusive and ineffable—and about grief—how it is something that you live inside—took my breath away."

—Christina Baker Kline

"*Writers & Lovers* made me happy. Even as the narrator grieves the loss of her mother and struggles to make art and keep a roof over her head, the novel is suffused with hopefulness and kindness. Lily King writes with a great generosity of spirit."

—Ann Patchett

"My favorite of Lily King's books so far. Exuberant and affirming, it's funny and immensely clever, emotionally rare and strong. I feel bereft now I've finished."

—Tessa Hadley

"If you loved *The Friend* but wish it had had more sex and waitressing, get ready for Lily King's *Writers & Lovers*. Delicious."

—Emma Straub

"*Writers & Lovers* stole my heart from its first pages. I am in love with this book. In. Love. This deep dive of a novel will stay with me forever."

—Elin Hilderbrand

Writers
& Lovers

Writers
& Lovers

A NOVEL

Lily King

Grove Press

New York

Printed in the United States of America

First Grove Atlantic hardcover edition: March 2020
First Grove Atlantic paperback edition: February 2021

This book was set in 11.5-pt. Bembo
by Alpha Design & Composition of Pittsfield, NH

ISBN 978-0-8021-4854-4
eISBN 978-0-8021-4855-1

Grove Press
an imprint of Grove Atlantic
154 West 14th Street
New York, NY 10011

Distributed by Publishers Group West

groveatlantic.com

21 22 23 24   13 12 11 10 9 8 7 6 5 4 3 2 1

For my sister, Lisa,
with love and gratitude

I have a pact with myself not to think about money in the morning. I'm like a teenager trying not to think about sex. But I'm also trying not to think about sex. Or Luke. Or death. Which means not thinking about my mother, who died on vacation last winter. There are so many things I can't think about in order to write in the morning.

Adam, my landlord, watches me walk his dog. He leans against his Benz in a suit and sparkling shoes as I come back up the driveway. He's needy in the morning. Everyone is, I suppose. He enjoys his contrast to me in my sweats and untamed hair.

When the dog and I are closer he says, 'You're up early.'

I'm always up early. 'So are you.'

'Meeting with the judge at the courthouse at seven sharp.'

Admire me. Admire me. Admire *judge* and *courthouse* and *seven sharp*.

'Somebody's gotta do it.' I don't like myself around Adam. I don't think he wants me to. I let the dog yank me a few steps past him toward a squirrel squeezing through some slats at the side of his big house.

'So,' he says, unwilling to let me get too far away. 'How's the *novel*?' He says it like I made the word up myself. He's still leaning against his car and turning only his head in my direction, as if he likes his pose too much to undo it.

'It's all right.' The bees in my chest stir. A few creep down the inside of my arm. One conversation can destroy my whole morning. 'I've got to get back to it. Short day. Working a double.'

I pull the dog up Adam's back porch, unhook the leash, nudge him through the door, and drop quickly back down the steps.

'How many pages you got now?'

'Couple of hundred, maybe.' I don't stop moving. I'm halfway to my room at the side of his garage.

'You know,' he says, pushing himself off his car, waiting for my full attention. 'I just find it extraordinary that you think you have something to say.'

I sit at my desk and stare at the sentences I wrote before walking the dog. I don't remember them. I don't remember putting them down. I'm so tired. I look at the green digits on the clock radio. Less than three hours before I have to dress for my lunch shift.

Adam went to college with my older brother, Caleb—in fact, I think Caleb was a little in love with him back then—and for this he gives me a break in the rent. He shaves off a bit more for walking his dog in the morning. The room used to be a potting shed and still has a loam and rotting leaves smell. There's just enough space for a twin mattress, desk and chair, and hot plate, and toaster oven in the bathroom. I set the kettle back on the burner for another cup of black tea.

I don't write because I think I have something to say. I write because if I don't, everything feels even worse.

At nine thirty I get up from the chair and scrub at the sirloin and blackberry stains on my white pleated shirt, iron it dry on the desk, slip it on a hanger, and thread the hook of the hanger through the loop at the top of my backpack. I put on my black work pants and a T-shirt, pull my hair into a ponytail, and slide on the backpack.

I wheel my bike out of the garage backward. It barely fits because of all the crap Adam has in here: old strollers, high chairs, bouncy seats, mattresses, bureaus, skis, skateboards, beach chairs, tiki torches, foosball. His ex-wife's red minivan takes up the rest of the space. She left it behind along with everything else except the kids when she moved to Hawaii last year.

'A good car go to waste like that,' the cleaning lady said one day when she was looking for a hose. Her name is Oli, she's from Trinidad, and she saves things like the plastic scoops from laundry detergent boxes to send back home. That garage makes Oli crazy.

I ride down Carlton Street, run the red at Beacon, and head up to Comm. Ave. Traffic thunders past. I slide forward, off the bike seat, and wait with a growing pileup of students for the light to change. A few of them admire my ride. It's an old banana bike I found at a dump in Rhode Island in May. Luke and I fixed it up, put on a new greased-up chain, tightened the brake cables, and shimmied the rusty seat shaft until it slid up to my height. The gearshift is built into the cross bar, which makes it feel more powerful than it is, as if there's a secret engine somewhere. I like the whole motorcycle feel of it, with the raised vertical handlebars and the long, quilted seat and the tall bar in back I lean against while coasting. I didn't have a banana bike as a kid, but my best friend did and we used to swap bikes for days at a time. These BU students, they're too young to have ridden a banana bike. It's strange, to not be the youngest kind of adult anymore. I'm thirty-one now, and my mother is dead.

The light changes, and I get back on the seat, cross the six lanes of Comm. Ave. and pump up and over the BU Bridge to the Cambridge side of the Charles River. Sometimes I don't make it to the bridge before cracking. Sometimes it starts on the bridge. But today I'm okay. Today I'm holding it together. I glide down onto the sidewalk on the water side of Memorial Drive. It's high summer, and the river seems tired. Along its banks a frothy white scum pushes against the reeds. It looks like the white gunk that collected in the corners of Paco's mother's mouth by the end of a long day of her incessant complaining in the kitchen. At least I don't live there anymore. Even Adam's potting shed is better than that apartment outside Barcelona. I cross at River Street and Western Ave. and veer off the concrete onto the dirt path that runs close to the river's edge. I'm all right. I'm still all right, until I see the geese.

They're in their spot near the base of the footbridge, twenty maybe thirty of them, fussing about, torquing their necks and thrusting their beaks into their own feathers or the feathers of others or at the few remaining tufts of grass in the dirt. Their sounds grow louder as I get closer, grunts and mutterings and indignant squawks. They're used to interruptions on their path and move as little as possible to get out of my way, some pretending to nip at my ankles as I pedal through, a few letting their butt feathers swish through my spokes. Only the hysterical ones bolt for the water, shrieking as if under attack.

I love these geese. They make my chest tight and full and help me believe that things will be all right again, that I will pass through this time as I have passed through other times, that the vast and threatening blank ahead of me is a mere specter, that life is lighter and more playful than I'm giving it credit for. But right on the heels of that feeling, that suspicion that all is not yet lost, comes the urge to tell my mother, tell her that I am okay today, that I have felt something close to happiness, that I might still be capable of feeling happy. She will want to know that. But I can't tell her. That's the wall I always slam into on a good morning like this. My mother will be worrying about me, and I can't tell her that I'm okay.

The geese don't care that I'm crying again. They're used to it. They chortle and squall and cover up the sounds I make. A runner approaches and veers up off the path, sensing I don't see her. The geese thin out by the big boathouse. At the Larz Anderson Bridge, I turn right, up JFK toward Harvard Square.

It's a purging of sorts, that ride, and usually lasts me a few hours.

* * *

5

Iris is on the third floor of a building owned by a Harvard social club, which began renting out the space a decade ago to pay off nearly a hundred thousand dollars in back taxes. There aren't many students around in the summer, and they have a separate entrance on the other side of the big brick mansion, but I hear a few of them rehearsing sometimes. They have their own theater where they put on plays in which men dress up as women and their own a cappella group that flashes in and out of the building wearing tuxes day and night.

I lock my bike to the metal post of a parking sign and climb the granite steps and open the big door. Tony, one of the headwaiters, is already halfway up the first flight, his dry cleaning draped over his arm. He gets all the good shifts, so he can afford to have his uniform professionally cleaned. It's a grand staircase, covered with a greasy beer-stained carpet that must have once been a plush crimson. I let Tony reach the top and circle around to the next set of stairs before I start up. I pass the portraits of the presidents who have been members of the club: Adams, Adams, Roosevelt, Roosevelt, and Kennedy. The second flight is narrower. Tony is moving slowly, still only halfway up. I slow even more. The light from the top of the stairs disappears. Gory is coming down.

'Tony, my man,' he shouts. 'How's it hanging?'

'Long, loose, and full of juice.'

Gory cackles. The staircase shakes as he comes toward me.

'You're late, girl.'

I'm not. It's what he says to women instead of a greeting. I don't think he knows my name.

6

I feel the stair I'm on sink when he passes me.

'Busy night ahead. One eighty-eight on the books,' he says over his shoulder. Does he think it's the afternoon already? 'And the on-call just called in sick.'

The on-call is Harry, my only friend at Iris. He isn't sick, though. He's on his way to Provincetown with the new busboy.

'Strap on your long iron,' he says.

'Never leave home without it,' I say.

Somehow in my interview he wheedled the golf stuff out of me. He plays croquet, it turned out. Not at garden parties but professionally, competitively. He's supposedly one of the best croquet players in the country. He opened Iris after a big win.

Below me, he sniffs loudly three times, hacks it up, swallows, gasps, and goes out into the street with all the cash from last night in a pouch with CAMBRIDGE SAVINGS BANK in big letters. Someone has pressed a Post-it to his back that says: 'Mug Me.'

'Casey fucking Kasem,' Dana says when I get to the top of the stairs. 'No one's fired you yet?' She's bent over Fabiana's hostess podium, making the seating chart. It's barely legible and guaranteed to be unfair.

I go down the hall to the bathroom and change into my white shirt and wrangle my hair into the required high tight bun. It makes my head hurt. When I come back, Dana and Tony are moving the tables around, putting the large parties in their sections, making sure everything is to their advantage, the big tables, the regulars, the restaurant's investors who don't pay but tip astronomically. I don't know if they're friends outside of the building, but they work every shift together like a pair of evil skaters, setting each other up for another dastardly deed, then preening around the room when it comes off. They definitely aren't lovers. Dana doesn't like to be touched—she practically broke the new busboy's arm when she said she had a crick and he reached up to knead her neck with his thumb—and Tony never stops talking about his girlfriend, though he paws at all the male waiters through every shift. They have Gory and Marcus, the manager, completely snowed or at least compromised. Harry and I suspect it's the drugs that come through Tony's brother, a dealer who is in and out of jail and who Tony talks about only when he's wasted, demanding vows of silence as if he's never told you before. We call Dana and Tony the Twisted Sister and try to stay out of their path.

'You've just taken two tables out of my section,' Yasmin says.

'We have two eight-tops,' Tony says.

'Well use your own bloody tables. These are mine, you fucks.' Yasmin was born in Eritrea and raised in Delaware, but she's read a lot of Martin Amis and Roddy Doyle. Unfortunately she doesn't stand a chance against the Twisted Sister.

Before I can band with Yasmin, Dana points a finger at me. 'Go get the flowers, Casey Kasem.'

She and Tony are the headwaiters. You have to do what they say.

* * *

Lunch is amateur hour. Lunch is for the new hires and the old workhorses working doubles, working as many hours as management will give them. I've waited tables since I was eighteen, so I went from new server to workhorse in six weeks. The money at lunch is crap compared to dinner unless you get a group of lawyers or biotech goons celebrating something with rounds of martinis that loosen the bills from their wallets. The dining room is filled with sunlight, which feels unnatural and changes all the colors. I prefer dusk and the windows slowly blackening, the soft orange light from the gilt sconces that masks the grease stains on the tablecloths and the calcium spots we might have missed on the wineglasses. At lunch we squint in the blue daylight. Customers ask for coffee as soon as they sit down. You can actually hear the music Mia, the lunch bartender, is playing. It's usually Dave Matthews. Mia is obsessed with Dave Matthews. Gory is often sober and Marcus is mellow, doing whatever he does in his office and leaving us alone. Everything at lunch is backward.

But it's fast. I get slammed with three deuces and a five-top before the clock in Harvard Yard strikes noon. There isn't time for thought. You are like a tennis ball knocked from the front of the house to the back over and over until your tables are gone and it's over and you're sitting at a calculator adding up your credit card gratuities and tipping out the bartender and the bussers. The door is locked again, Mia is blasting 'Crash Into Me,' and after all the tables are broken down, glasses polished, and silverware rolled for tomorrow's lunch, you have an hour in the Square before you clock back in for dinner.

* * *

I go to my bank next to the Coop. There's a line. Only one teller. LINCOLN LUGG, the brass plate reads. My stepbrothers used to call poop Lincoln Logs. The youngest one used to pull me into the bathroom to show me how long he could make them. Sometimes we all went in there to look. If I ever see a therapist to talk about my childhood and the therapist asks me to remember a happy moment with my father and Ann, I'll talk about the time we all gathered round to gaze at one of Charlie's abnormally large Lincoln Logs.

Lincoln Lugg doesn't like my expression of amusement when I step up to the counter. Some people are like that. They think anyone's amusement must be at their expense.

I put my wad of cash in front of him. He doesn't like that, either. You'd think tellers could be happy for you, especially after you'd graduated to dinner shifts and doubles and had $661 to put in your account.

'You can use the ATM for deposits, you know,' he says, picking up the money by the tips of his fingers. He doesn't enjoy touching money? Who doesn't enjoy touching money?

'I know, but it's cash and I just—'

'No one is going to steal the cash once it's inside the machine.'

'I just want to make sure it goes into my account and not someone else's.'

'We have a strictly regulated systemized protocol. And it's all recorded on videotape. This, what you are doing right here, is much less secure.'

'I'm just happy to be depositing this money. Please don't rain on my picnic. This money is not even going to be able to take a short nap before it is sucked out by federal loan sharks, so just let me enjoy it, okay?'

Lincoln Lugg is counting my money with his lips and does not respond.

I'm in debt. I'm in so much debt that even if Marcus gave me every lunch and dinner shift he had, I could not get out from under it. My loans for college and grad school all went into default when I was in Spain, and when I came back I learned that the penalties, fees, and collection costs had nearly doubled the original amount I owed. All I can do now is manage it, pay the minimums until—and this is the thing—until what? Until when? There's no answer. That's part of my looming blank specter.

After my encounter with Lincoln Lugg, I weep on a bench outside the Unitarian church. I do it somewhat discreetly, without noise, but I can no longer stop tears from drizzling down my face when the mood strikes.

I walk to Salvatore's Foreign Books on Mount Auburn Street. I worked there six years ago, in 1991. After Paris and before Pennsylvania and Albuquerque and Oregon and Spain and Rhode Island. Before Luke. Before my mother went to Chile with four friends and was the one who didn't come back.

The store seems different. Cleaner. The stacks have been rearranged and they've put the register where Ancient Languages used to be, but it's the same in back where Maria and I used to hang out. I was hired as Maria's assistant in French literature. I'd just moved back from France that fall and had this idea that even though Maria was American we'd be speaking French the whole time, speaking about Proust and Céline and Duras, who was so popular then, but instead we spoke in English, mostly about sex, which I suppose was French in its way. All I remembered now from eight months of conversation with her is a dream she had about Kitty, her cat, going down on her. Her rough tongue felt so good, she'd said, but the cat kept getting distracted. She'd lick a bit then move on to her paw, and Maria woke herself up screaming, 'Focus, Kitty, focus!'

But Maria isn't in back. None of them are, not even Manfred the cynical East German who went into a rage when people asked for Günter Grass, because Günter Grass had been in strong opposition to reunification. We've all been replaced by children: a boy in a baseball cap and a girl with hair to her thighs. Because it's Friday at three, they're drinking beers, Heinekens, just like we used to do.

Gabriel comes out from storage with another round. He looks the same: silver curls, torso too long for his legs. I had a crush on him. He was so smart, loved his books, dealt with all the foreign publishers on the phone in their own language. He had a dark, dry humor. He's handing out the bottles. He says something under his breath, and they all laugh. The girl with the hair is looking at him the way I used to.

I wasn't broke when I worked at Salvatore's. Or at least I didn't think I was. My debts were much smaller and Sallie Mae and EdFund and Collection Technology and Citibank and Chase weren't hassling me yet. I sublet a room in a house on Chauncy Street with friends, eighty dollars a month. We were all trying to be writers, with jobs that got us by. Nia and Abby were working on novels, I was writing stories, and Russell was a poet. Of all of us, I would have bet that Russell would stick with it the longest. Rigid and disciplined, he got up at four thirty every morning, wrote until seven, and ran five miles before he went to work at Widener Library. But he was the first to surrender and go to law school. He's a tax attorney in Tampa now. Abby was next. Her aunt convinced her to take a realtor's exam, just on a lark. Later she tried to tell me she was still using her imagination when she walked through the houses and invented a new life for her clients. I saw her last month outside an enormous house with white columns in Brookline. She was leaning into the driver's window of a black SUV in the driveway and nodding profusely. Nia met a Milton scholar with excellent posture and a trust fund, who handed her novel back after reading fifteen pages, saying first-person female narratives grated on him. She chucked it in the dumpster, married him, and moved to Houston when he got a job at Rice.

I didn't get it. I didn't get any of them then. One by one they gave up, moved out, and got replaced by engineers from MIT. A guy with a ponytail and a Spanish accent came into Salvatore's looking for Barthes's *Sur Racine*. We spoke in French. He said he hated English. His French was better than mine—his father was from Algiers. He made me a Catalan fish stew in his room in Central Square. When he kissed me he smelled like Europe. His fellowship ended, and he went home to Barcelona. I went to an MFA program in Pennsylvania, and we wrote each other love letters until I started dating the funny guy in workshop who wrote gloomy two-page stories set in New Hampshire mill towns. After we broke up, I moved to Albuquerque for a while, then ended up in Bend, Oregon, with Caleb and his boyfriend, Phil. A letter from Paco found me there, and we resumed our correspondence. Enclosed in his fifth letter to me was a one-way ticket to Barcelona.

I poke around in the Ancient Greek section. That's the next language I want to learn. Around the corner, in Italian, the only other customer sits cross-legged on the floor with a small boy, reading him *Cuore*. Her voice is low and beautiful. I started speaking a little Italian in Barcelona with my friend Giulia. I come to the long wall of French literature, divided by publishers: rows of red-on-ivory Gallimards, blue-on-white Éditions de Minuit, dime-store-like Livres de Poche, and then the extravagant Pléiades, set apart in their own glass case, leather bound with gold print and thin gold stripes: Balzac and Montaigne and Valéry, their spines glistening like jewels.

I shelved copies of all these books, cut open the boxes, stacked them on the metal storage racks in back, and brought them out a few at a time, usually arguing with Maria all the while, about *À la recherche*, which I adored and she said was as boring as *Middlemarch*. She had to give herself eighteen hand jobs, she told me, to get through *Middlemarch* the summer she was seventeen. That book made my nethersphere sore, she said.

I see a copy of *Sur Racine*, which we didn't have the day Paco came looking for it. I had to special order it for him. I touch the bit of glue at the top of the spine. I don't ever cry about Paco. Those two years with him rest lightly on me. We went from French to a sort of hybrid of the Catalan and

Castilian that he taught me, and I wonder if that's part of the reason I don't miss him, that everything we ever said to each other was in languages I'm starting to forget. Maybe the thrill of the relationship *was* the languages, that everything was heightened for me because of it, more of a challenge, as I tried to maintain his belief in my facility with languages, my ability to absorb, mimic, morph. It was a trick no one expected of an American, the combination of a good ear, a good memory, and an understanding of the rules of grammar, so that I appeared more of a prodigy than I was. Every conversation was a chance to excel, to frolic, to amuse myself and to surprise him. And yet now I can't remember what we said to each other. Conversations in foreign languages don't linger in my head like they do in English. They don't last. They remind me of the invisible-ink pen my mother sent me for Christmas when I was fifteen and she had gone, an irony that escaped her but not me.

I slip out before Gabriel recognizes me or one of his employees comes out from behind the reference desk to assault me with help.

I didn't mean to move back to Massachusetts. I just had no other plan. I don't like being reminded of those days on Chauncy, writing stories in my dormer window on the third floor, drinking Turkish coffee at Algiers, dancing at the Plough and Stars. Life was light and cheap, and if it wasn't cheap I used a credit card. My loans got sold and sold again, and I paid the minimums and didn't think about the ballooning balance. My mother had moved back to Phoenix by then, and she paid for my flights to see her twice a year.

The rest of the time we talked on the phone, talked for hours sometimes. We'd pee and paint our nails and make food and brush our teeth. I always knew where she was in her little house by the noises in the background, the scrape of a hanger or the chime of a glass being put in the dishwasher. I'd tell her about people at the bookstore, and she'd tell me about people at her office in the state house in Phoenix—she was working for the governor then. I'd get her to retell some of her stories from Santiago de Cuba, where she grew up with her American-born, expat parents. Her father was a doctor, and her mother sang show tunes at a nightclub. Every now and then she'd ask if I had done my laundry or changed my sheets and I'd tell her to stop being maternal, it wasn't in her nature, and we'd laugh because it was true and I had forgiven her for that. I look back on those days and it feels gluttonous, all that time and love and life ahead, no bees in my body and my mother on the other end of the line.

Up on the street the heat pools just above the hoods of the parked cars, making the brick buildings squiggly. The sidewalks are packed now, packed with out-of-towners creeping along with their crêpes and iced lattes, their children sucking down milkshakes and Mountain Dews. I walk in the street to avoid them and cross over to Dunster and back up to Iris.

I go up the stairs, past the presidents, directly to the bathroom even though I'm already wearing my uniform. It's empty. I catch myself in the mirror over the sink. It's tilted away from the wall for people in wheelchairs so that I'm at a slightly unfamiliar angle to myself. I look beat up, like someone who has gotten ill and aged a decade in a few months. I look into my eyes, but they aren't really mine, not the eyes I used to have. They're the eyes of someone very tired and very sad, and once I see them I feel even sadder and then I see that sadness, that compassion, for the sadness in my eyes, and I see the water rising in them. I'm both the sad person and the person wanting to comfort the sad person. And then I feel sad for that person who has so much compassion because she's clearly been through the same thing, too. And the cycle keeps repeating. It's like when you go into a dressing room with a three-paneled mirror and you line them up just right to see the long narrowing hallway of yourselves diminishing into infinity. It feels like that, like I'm sad for an infinite number of my selves.

I splash my face and pat it down with paper towels from the dispenser in case someone comes in, but as soon as I get it dry my face crumples up again. I put my hair back into the tight bun and leave the bathroom.

I'm late by the time I enter the dining room. The Twisted Sister is back in action.

Dana glares at me. 'Deck. Candles.'

The deck, past the bar and through the French doors, is humid and smells of roses and lilies and the peppery nasturtiums the chefs use to garnish the plates. All the flowerpots are dripping dirty water and the floorboards around the edges are soaked. It smells like my mother's garden on a rainy summer morning. Helene, the pastry chef, must have just watered. This rooftop oasis is her creation.

Mary Hand is in the far corner with a tray of tea lights, a water pitcher, and a trash can, knifing out the old wax from the night before.

'The three and fourpence,' Mary Hand says. She has her own vernacular. She's been waiting tables at Iris longer than anyone else.

I sit down beside her. I pick up the rag on the tray and wipe out the insides of the glass holders she has voided, pour a few drops of water in each, and drop in a fresh tea light.

It's hard to know how old Mary Hand is. She's older than I am but by three years or twenty? She has straight brown hair without a fleck of gray, which she pulls back with a beige elastic, a long face, and a spindly neck. All of her is long and lean, more colt than workhorse. She's the best waitress I've ever worked with, flat calm but fast and efficient. She knows your tables as well as she knows her own. She saves you when you forget to fire the entrées for the six-top or you leave your wine opener at home. At the height of the night, when everyone's losing their shit, when your plates have been left so long under the heat lamp they've gotten too hot to carry even with a cloth and the sous chefs are slandering you and the customers are waiting for their apps, their checks, their water refills, their extra jus, Mary Hand will be speaking in a slow drawl. 'Simple as toast and jam,' she might say, loading up every one of your entrées along her long arms without flinching.

'C'mon, little homunculus,' Mary Hand coos at a burned-down tea light. No one ever calls her just Mary. She twists the knife and it comes out with a satisfying pop and a spray of wax water that hits us both, and we laugh.

18

The deck is pleasant like this, empty of customers, the sun behind the tall maples dappling the tables with light but not much heat, raised up high above the hot, loud chaos of Mass. Ave., Helene's plants, hundreds of them, in boxes along the short stone walls and in planters on the ground and hanging from trellises, all flowering, the leaves dark green and healthy. The plants all seem satisfied, thriving, and it makes you feel that way, too, or at least that thriving is a possibility.

My mother had a green thumb. I want to tell Mary Hand this, but I haven't mentioned my mother at the restaurant yet. I don't want to be the girl whose mother just died. It's bad enough that I'm the girl who's just been dumped on her ass. I made the mistake of telling Dana about Luke during my first training shift.

'Is it like this every year, so fecund?'

'Mmmm hmmm,' Mary Hand says. I can tell she likes the word 'fecund.' I knew she would. 'She has a gift.' She pronounces it *gyift*, very slowly. She means Helene. 'A gyift for flora.'

'How many years have you been here?'

'Since about the Truman administration.'

She's squirrely about the details of her life. No one knows where she lives or with whom. It's just a question of how many cats, Harry says. But I'm not sure. The story is that she used to go out with David Byrne. Some say it was in high school in Baltimore; some said it was at RISD. Everyone says he broke her heart, that she never recovered. If the Talking Heads ever come on when the music is cranked before or

19

after service, whoever's closest to the stereo at the bar will switch stations fast.

'How'd you get this job?' she says. 'You're not one of Marcus's usual hires.'

'What do you mean?'

'You're more like us, the old guard.' She means people hired by the previous house manager. 'Cerebral.'

'I'm not sure about that.'

'Well, you know what cerebral means, so case in point.'

Tony comes out on the deck to give us the breakdown. Only one large table out here, a party of ten for an anniversary. Mary Hand and I push two tables together, cover it in several cloths, lining up the points of the corners of the top layer with the straight hem of the bottom. We do the same to the rest of the smaller tables, then set them, shining the silver and polishing the glasses with small cloths as we go. We put a candle on each table and get the flowers I arranged for lunch out of the walk-in. The chef calls us all to the wait station where he tells us the specials, explaining each preparation and ingredient. The chefs I've worked with before were high strung and volatile, but Thomas is calm and kind. He never lets things in his kitchen get out of hand. He doesn't have a temper or a vile mouth. He doesn't hate women, not even waitresses. If I make a mistake, even on a busy night, he just nods and takes the plate and slides back what I need. He's good, too. We're always trying to get our hands on an extra carpaccio or seared scallops or Bolognese. The high shelves in the wait station are full of finagled food, pushed to the back where Marcus can't see and eaten surreptitiously throughout the night. I have to eat at the restaurant—I can't afford more than cereal or noodles at the grocery store—but even if I weren't broke I would sneak that food.

Thirty minutes later every seat in my section is filled. Mary Hand and I fall into a groove. The French doors to the deck have to be kept closed because the AC is on in the dining room, and when our meals are up and loaded we hold the door for each other. She brings my drinks to one of my fours, and I deliver salmons to her deuce when she's opening bottles of champagne for the rowdy ten.

I like going from the hot kitchen to the cool dining room to the humid deck. I like that Craig is working the bar because no matter how many orders he has, he always makes it to your tables to talk about the wines. And I like the mindless distractions, the way there is no room to re-member anything about your life except that the osso bucco goes to the man in the bow tie and the lavender flan to the birthday girl in pink and the side cars to the student couple with the fake IDs. I like memorizing the orders—aren't you going to write it down, the older men will say—punching them in on the computer in the wait station, collecting my food in the window, stabbing the dupes, serving on the left, clearing from the right. Dana and Tony are too busy with their big tables to insult anyone and after I bring out Dana's salads while she's taking an order, she garnishes my vongoles.

I have a table from Ecuador and speak to them in Span-ish. They hear my accent and make me say a few sentences in Catalan. The feel of that language in my mouth brings back Paco, the good parts, the way his whole face crumpled when he laughed and how he let me fall asleep on his back. I tell them one of our dishwashers is from Guayaquil, and they want to meet him. I get Alejandro, and he ends up sitting and smoking with them, talking about politics and grinning madly, and I get a glimpse of who he is when he isn't engulfed in spray and steam and food waste. But things pile up in the kitchen and eventually Marcus storms out to the deck and sends him back to his station.

The only conflict comes at the second seating when Fabiana puts a deuce that was supposed to be Dana's in my section.

'She just got the five,' Dana says. 'What the fuck?'

Fabiana comes all the way around the wait station, a place she avoids for its chaos and potential for stains. She wears silk wrap dresses and is the only woman allowed to keep her hair down. She is clean and showered and never smells of salad dressing.

'They asked for her, Dana. You're getting the seven at eight thirty.'

'The fucking *teachers* from Wellesley? Oh thanks. I'll probably get a fiver off their ice water and the side salad they split three ways.'

I lean past the tall shelving to peer through the doors to the deck. A tall woman and a balding man. 'You can have them. I don't even know who they are.'

Marcus is coming toward us from the bar.

'Why are you still here?' Fabiana snaps at me for his benefit. 'Get out there, Casey.'

I think they've started sleeping together.

22

I go out to the deck.

'Casey!' They both get up and give me tight hugs. 'You don't recognize us,' the woman says. The man looks on benevolently, red cheeked and mellow, a few cocktails already in him. She's large, boobs angled like the prow of a boat, a short gold chain with a turquoise stone around her neck. It looks like something my mother would wear.

'I'm sorry.'

The table behind them needs their check.

'We used to work in Doug's office. With your mom.'

It was her first job after she left my father, in a congressman's office. The Doyles. That's who they were. Liz and Pat. They hadn't been married then.

'She fixed us up, you know. She told Pat that I wanted him to ask me out. And she told me he was going to, even though he'd never said such a thing. The cheek! And here we are.' She takes my hand. 'We're so sorry, Casey. We were devastated to hear. Just devastated. We were in Vero, or we would have been at the service.'

I nod. If I'd had some warning I might be able to handle it better, but this is a surprise attack. I nod again.

'We wanted to write you, but we didn't know where on the globe you were at that point. And then we ran into Ezra, who'd heard you were back here and at Iris!' She puts a warm hand on my arm. 'I've upset you.'

I shake my head, but my face betrays me and my eyebrows go all funny.

'She gave me this necklace.'

Of course she did.

'Excuse me,' the man behind them says, waving his credit card.

I nod to him and to everyone who stops me on my way back to the wait station. I unroll a place setting from the lunch bin and put my face in the napkin as I print out the check.

'Get a grip, will you,' Dana says, but she puts the slip on a tray with chocolates and brings it out to my table for me.

I push through the swinging door into the kitchen. The cooks are busy, their backs to me and to the food that's waiting for me under the heat lamp. I go into the walk-in. I stand in the dry cold, looking at the dairy shelves in back, the bricks of butter wrapped in wax paper and cartons of heavy cream. Cases of eggs. I breathe. I look down at my hand. Caleb let me have her ring. She wore it my whole life, a sapphire and two small diamonds. The sky and the stars we called it when I was little. Her friend Janet had thought to take it off her finger afterward. My hand looks like hers when I wear it. I can do this, I say to the glinting blue-black eye. And I go out to take the order of Liz and Pat Doyle.

When I bring their pinot grigios and their apps they're still somber with me, but by the time their swordfish and risotto comes out Pat is talking animatedly, using words I don't understand like equities and the Shiller PE, and by coffee they're chuckling about someone named Marvin doing the hustle at their daughter's wedding and have nearly forgotten they know me at all. They leave me their business cards, though, on the tray with their merchant receipt and cash tip. Sixteen percent. They both own their own businesses. Neither of them works in politics anymore.

Table by table, people vanish, leaving behind their soiled napkins and lipstick markings. The tablecloths are disheveled and crusted, wine bottles turned upside down in their watery holders, a sea of glasses and coffee cups and smeared dessert plates. Everything left for someone else to clean up. We work slowly now, getting the room and the deck back in order. Only Yasmin and Omar, who have dates waiting for them at the bar, are still moving quickly.

The last thing is drying glasses and rolling more silverware for lunch. Alejandro brings out the steaming green racks of glasses. At first they're too hot to touch without a cloth. Omar and I do the roll-ups: napkin folded into a triangle, spoon on top of fork on top of knife laid alongside the long edge, two side points folded in then everything rolled to the pointed tip. Craig is laughing with Omar's skinny date at the bar, so he's rolling them faster and faster. We have to have a hundred of them in the bin before we can leave.

By the time I get on my bike, it's nearly one in the morning. My body is depleted. The three miles to my potting shed feels far away.

The dark, the heat, the few people paired up on the sidewalks. The river and the moon's quivering reflection. You taste like the moon, Luke said out in that field in the Berkshires. Fucking poet. On the path a few people are holding hands, drinking from bottles, lying in the grass because they can't see all the green goose poop. He took me unawares. I didn't have time to defend myself.

In the morning I ache for my mother. But late at night it is Luke I mourn for.

The BU Bridge is empty, silent. I arc up and over the water. There's a tightness, a rasp in my breathing, but I do not cry. I sing 'Psycho Killer' in honor of Mary Hand. I reach Adam's driveway, and I have not wept. This is a first. I roll my bike into the garage. This is a small victory.

Two past-due notices and a wedding invitation have been slipped under my door. A message is flashing on my machine. My blood leaps. Old reflex. It's not him. It's not him, I tell myself, but my heart slams anyway. I hit Play.

'Hey.' Pause. Long breath like a roll of thunder into the receiver.

It's him.

My mother died six weeks before I went to Red Barn. I called to ask if I could change the dates, if I could come in the fall or next winter. The man who answered gave me his deepest sympathies but told me I'd been offered the longest artist's residency they had. Eight weeks. April 23 to June 17. The Red Barn calendar, he said, was inalterable.

A long silence spread between us.

'Are you calling to forfeit your spot?' he asked.

The last time I'd used the word 'forfeit' must have been at recess in fourth grade. *If you show your teeth or tongue, you must pay a forfeit.*

'No, I don't want to forfeit.'

I flew from Bend to Boston and took a bus to Burrillville, Rhode Island. Early spring. New England. I stepped off the bus and smelled my childhood, smelled the thawing earth in our yard and the daffodils at the end of the driveway. I was given a dorm room to sleep in and a cabin to work in, and when I stood on the porch of my cabin the first morning I remembered my mother's fawn-colored jacket with the white wool cuffs and collar and the smell of her wintergreen Life Savers in the left zip pocket. I heard her say my name, my old name, Camila, that only she called me. I felt the slippery seat in her blue Mustang, cold through my tights.

At Red Barn, my mother was both dead and resurrected.

In the dining room hung a framed letter from Somerset Maugham, who'd been one of the early fellows there.

'Red Barn is a place out of time,' he'd written in the letter.

Luke was tall and scrawny, like one of my brother's goofy friends from middle school. Before he was anything else, he was familiar.

It started the fourth night I was there. One of the fellows was showing her film in the art shed. I'd gotten there too late for a seat and stood in back. Luke came in a few minutes later. Onscreen, a power tool was drilling a screw into a raw egg. In very slow motion.

'What'd I miss?' he said in a fake whisper. 'What'd I miss?'

He slipped in behind me. I'd been seated at his table once for dinner—there was a new seating chart for dinner every night—and passed him in the hallways of the farm-house a few times. I hadn't thought much. I wasn't registering other people well at that point. Nor was I writing. I had eight weeks to devote to my novel, but I couldn't focus. The cabin I'd been given had a funny smell. My heart beat too fast and under my skin it felt mealy, like an old apple. I wanted to sleep, but I was scared of dreaming. In my dreams my mother was never herself. Something was always off. She was too pale or too bloated or wearing heavy velvet clothing. She was weak, she was failing, she was fading from view. I was often trying to persuade her to stay alive, long soliloquies about what she needed to do differently. I woke up exhausted. Animals rustled outside my window.

When Luke stood behind me, I became animal myself: alert, cautious, curious. More people came in and he was pushed in closer and there were long moments when my shoulder blades rested against his chest. I felt him breathing in and out, felt his breath in my hair. I'm not sure what happened in the movie after the nail went through the egg.

When it was over, I staggered out of the room and onto the porch. It was still light out. The sky was violet, the trees dark blue. The frogs had started up in the pond across the road, louder and louder the closer you listened. I stood against the railing while behind me people creaked into the old rocking chairs and passed out beers and raised their bottles to the filmmaker, who was giggling psychopathically, the way you do when you've exposed yourself through art.

Luke came up beside me. We looked out at the fields. The back of his hand brushed up against the back of mine and stayed there.

'Wanna go somewhere?' His eyes were washed out, pale as dawn.

We got in his truck and headed for Pawtucket because we saw a sign and liked saying the name, dragging out the 'Paw' and clipping off the 'tucket,' over and over. Pawwwww-tckt. It was on the border of Massachusetts, where we'd both grown up, an hour apart. He lived in New York now. In Harlem. He asked where I lived.

'Oh, I have this little cabin in Burrillville, Rhode Island.'

He laughed.

'I've still got seven weeks to come up with a plan.'

'You could always move in with Duffy,' he said.

Duffy was six foot six, the director's grown son, who dropped our sandwiches off on our porches at noontime. He tied love notes around heart-shape rocks and left them in women's lunch baskets.

There was a gazebo on the town green in Pawtucket. I had a deck of cards in my backpack, and we sat up there cross-legged and played Spit in the dark. It got heated and we shouted at each other and a cop came up the stairs. His flashlight lit up the piles of cards spread out between us, and he chuckled.

He'd never heard of Spit so we showed him how to play, and he said he'd have to teach his grandson. He took care of his grandson on Thursday nights, he told us.

He had a bad hip and moved slowly back to his cruiser.

'Not much happening in Pawwwwww-tckt,' I said.

'Just a small dustup down at the gazebo.'

On the way back to Red Barn we called out all the funny names of Massachusetts towns we could remember.

'Billerica.'

'Belchertown.'

'Leominster.'

We spoke in the accent we'd both lost long ago.

He drove with his left hand on the wheel and his right tucked under my arm, his fingers curving slowly around the outline of my breast.

* * *

It was strong, whatever was between us, thick, like the wet air and the smell of every green thing ready to bloom. Maybe it was just spring. Maybe that's all it was. We took our lunch baskets and ate ham sandwiches by the pond near our cabins. We walked into a cluster of cattails, some of their pods new and green and some, maybe left over from fall, long and brown and tall as us. Luke called them bulrushes and yanked me close. We both tasted of mayonnaise. Our heads knocked against the brown pods. The sun felt warm for the first time.

'You kissed me in the bulrushes,' I said.

He pointed to a pair of swollen eyes floating just above the water's surface. 'While the bullfrogs looked on, misunderstanding everything,' he said and pulled me down to the ground.

I told him the things that were coming back to me about my mother when I was little: her lemon smell and her gardening gloves with the rubber bumps and her small square toes that cracked when she walked barefoot. Her tortoiseshell headbands that were salty at the tips if you sucked on them.

'I can feel her. I can feel her right here.'

He kissed where I was touching, just below my collarbone, in that place where all my feelings got caught.

I believed she'd sent him to me, a gift to help me through.

We ran to the lake, swam across it, ran back to the dorm and took a bath together in the tub with the clawed feet and two taps and a rubber plug on a chain. Water sloshed all over the wood floor. We lay damp on his bed laughing, our chests pumping at the same time, knocking together, making us laugh even harder. When I looked at him I hid nothing.

I understood then how guarded I'd been before with men, how little of me I'd let them see.

He was married once, he said. They'd lost a child, he said later. It was a long time ago. He didn't say more.

I couldn't sleep beside him. It was too strong. I wanted him too much. It never went away. And I needed sleep to write. I wasn't getting much done. During the day I mooned at my window, waiting for his steps on my porch.

Pull yourself together and do your work, I could hear my mother chide me. But I was too far gone to listen.

Luke was writing. He wrote five poems that first week, eleven the next.

'I wrote a poem about bees.'

'I hate bees.'

'It just came out of me whole this morning.' His face was lit up. He lay down on the cot in my cabin. 'How can you hate bees?'

'I don't like the hive concept, the way the drones are crawling all over each other, programmed to serve the queen. I don't like the gooey larvae or the idea of royal jelly or the way they swarm. It's one of my biggest fears, being covered in bees.'

He was impressed by my quick list of grievances. 'But they are also life giving. They impregnate flowers, and they give us our food supply. They work as a collective. Plus they are responsible for the line: "And live alone in the bee-loud glade."'

'What is a glade anyway? Is it a stand of trees or the open space between them?'

'A glade is a glade.' He spread his arms out, as if a glade were appearing before us.

'God, you poets are full of shit. You have no idea what half the words you worship mean.'

He caught my arm. 'Get your bee-loud glade over here,' he said, and I slid on top of him.

He wrote eight more bee poems then took me to the Berkshires in his truck to see his friend Matt, who kept hives. It was the first hot day in May, and we stopped for mocha frappes and found a seventies station that played songs like 'Run Joey Run' and 'Wildfire' and 'I'm Not in Love.' We knew all the words and belted them out the open windows. When 'I'm Not in Love' came on, with that line about how he keeps her picture 'upon' the wall because of a stain that's lyin'. there, we were laughing too hard to sing along. I peed a little and had to change my underwear at a rest stop, and he called me Betsy Wetsy the rest of the trip.

We arrived in the late afternoon. From what Luke had told me about Matt, I was picturing a guy in a shack with piles of garbage in the back, but he lived in a bright red house with window boxes full of flowers. His wife, Jen, came out first, and she and Luke bear hugged, swaying with exaggeration and affection.

'Caliope was so angry when I told her you were coming,' she said. 'She's at sleepaway camp for three nights.'

'A big three-night camp?' Luke said.

'It's an experiment. She said you could sleep in her tree house, which is not an invitation she extends very often.'

Luke nodded and there was a sudden silence, broken by Matt when he came out holding a small boy, who sat erect and vigilant on his father's arm. I didn't know many couples. My friends seemed to get married and disappear. Or maybe I disappeared. Nia and Abby had stayed in touch until they had babies. I'd tried to see Abby in Boston before taking a bus to Rhode Island, but she never returned my call. I had the gift I'd bought for the baby in my suitcase at Red Barn. When people have babies they stop calling you back.

We went inside and they fixed us drinks—cranberry juice and seltzer—and the boy, who'd just learned to walk a few weeks ago, staggered around the black-and-white tile floor. When he made his way to me he held up a knitted brown goat with tiny white horns. I squatted down to have a look, and he squeaked in surprise. Instead of backing up he put his face unnaturally close to mine.

'Well hello, little fellow,' I said.

Another squeak.

I touched the goat's soft horns: one, two. He did the same. He smelled faintly of poop and Desitin. I was surprised how quickly that word 'Desitin' came to me. How did I even know it?

One, two on the horns. Three on his nose.

He opened his mouth—a dark toothless cavern—and after a few seconds a loud cackle came out.

I imitated him—the open mouth, the delay, the laugh—and he took it as an invitation to sit on my lap, which, because I was squatting, had to be created quickly. We dropped down onto the floor at the same time.

Jen shot me a grateful smile. She was talking to Matt and Luke about their plans for creating a neighborhood CSA and protesting against the Starbucks that had bought out the local doughnut shop.

Matt took us out back to see the bees. They didn't have a yard. They had meadows and woods beyond the meadows. We followed a path that had been cut through the long grass and wildflowers to the white boxes of bees. Matt picked up a can and stuffed it with a burlap cloth and lit the cloth on fire and pumped air into it from a bellows on the side, and smoke started coming out of the nose at the top of the can. He lifted up the lid of a white box and set the smoker nearby then pulled up one of the trays of combs. It was covered in layers and layers of bees, and they clung on as he raised it high, every bee moving on top of other bees. As he continued to hold it up, the whole mass of them began to change shape and sag with gravity, some dribbling off like drops of liquid back into the box. It was revolting. I had to work hard to not imagine a sudden swarm.

Luke was mesmerized. I didn't understand what the bees meant to him. The grass we were standing in was itchy and I just wanted Matt to lower the lid so I could go back into the kitchen and sit back down on the floor with their squeaky little boy, but we stayed out there a long time, going from box to box, though they were all the same, always a huge churning drooping clump of bees.

Dinner was to be an herb pasta and salad. Jen brought in basil, rosemary, sage, red lettuce, and a bowlful of misshapen tomatoes from their greenhouse. Matt, Luke, and I were put to chopping, and the kitchen smelled like we were still outside. They were the kind of people who were only inside when they had to be. We ate on the back patio at a table that Matt had made from an old door. Luke sat beside me, but not close to me, on a long bench.

The three of them spoke of people they'd known when they all lived in a house on the Cape in their twenties. Matt and Jen had disguised it well when we'd arrived, but I understood now that despite several phone calls over the course of the last month Luke had not told them about me or that I was coming along on this visit. They asked me a few questions, and I kept my answers short. I could tell they weren't trying to retain the information. I knew that I would remember them and their child and their bright-red house and their boxes of bees and that they wouldn't recall anything of me. They were kind people doing their best to be welcoming, but they did not want me there and I did not know why.

The baby got passed around. He nursed and reclined in his mother's arms. He sat for a while upright in his father's lap, and every time Matt laughed he would look straight up at his father's chin and laugh, too. Matt passed him to Luke, and they got quiet. They didn't know if I knew that he'd had a child. Luke held him up to his face, and the boy plucked at his glasses until he noticed me beside Luke and lunged at me with both arms. I caught him and we all laughed and Luke looked relieved.

He got strangely buoyant then and told a story about how when he was four he walked a mile to the penny candy store naked. The police brought him back home. I could tell Matt and Jen had heard the story before but laughed as if they hadn't.

After another long hour around a fire pit, Luke and I walked in the dark to the treehouse. I wanted to talk about the weirdness of dinner, but once we were alone in the meadow I didn't care about words. I needed to touch him, press against him and relieve my heaviness, my swollen ache for him. Lightning bugs flashed everywhere, for hundreds of feet in every direction. We kissed hungrily and pulled apart our clothes and pushed hard against each other in the thick spring grass. Everything else vanished into my desire for him.

We lay there a long time afterward, and the lightning bugs came closer and closer and flashed so near we could have touched them.

'I think for the rest of my life lightning bugs will make me horny,' I said.

He gave a half laugh, but he was gone somewhere else by then.

There was only one thin mattress and one pillow in the treehouse. He moved the flashlight around the room, and it lit up a box of Legos and a couple of board games and two dolls in chairs having a tea party. Luke got under the blankets and I curled up close, but even his skin felt plastic and closed off.

He reached up to touch the corner of a drawing stuck on the wall with a thumbtack. It was hard to tell what it was, a house or a dog. 'Our daughters were nearly the same age,' he said. 'Caliope is seven weeks older than Charlotte.'

Charlotte.

'How old was she when she—' I didn't know if he was a person who said *died* or *passed* or *was taken*. 'When you lost her.'

'Four months and twelve days.'

He let me hold him, but he was rigid in my arms all night.

He was gone when I woke up. In the house Jen told me he'd helped Matt move a few of the hives, then gone to the hardware store. Jen left her boy with me while she took a shower. Luke and Matt came back and ate egg sandwiches outside. By the time we got in the car to leave I was shaking with hunger and confusion.

I made him stop at the Dunkin' Donuts before the highway. We drove an hour after that, barely speaking. Then he said, 'What if,' and stopped.

'What if what?' I forced myself to ask. I knew it wasn't a good 'what if.'

'It's not reliable.'

'What?'

'All this.' He waved his hand back and forth over the gearshift. 'Between us.'

'All what?'

'This attraction.'

'Not reliable?'

'Not meaningful. Not good.'

'I think it's pretty good,' I said, playing dumb.

'What if it's the Devil?'

'The Devil?'

'Bad. Evil.'

It was like something very loud had started blaring in my ears.

By the time we got back to the Barn he had decided we shouldn't touch each other. It was too confusing, he said. It was too much. It was too unbalanced. There was a disconnect between our souls and our bodies, he said.

I skipped dinner and stayed in my cabin. I lit a fire and stared at it. He found me there. He was inside me before the screen door had stopped shaking.

We lay on the old rug sweating, all the tension and misery of the day washed away. I felt loose and weightless. We looked at the signatures on the wall of all the writers and artists who had stayed in my cabin.

'They all definitely wrote more in here than I have,' I said. 'But I think I'm in the running for the most orgasms.'

Caleb called me on one of the phone cabinets outside the dining room. He said his friend Adam had a place I could rent cheap in Brookline. I said I might move to New York, and I told him everything, even the part about the Devil, which I'd planned to leave out.

'Stay away from him, Casey. Write your book.' He sounded like my mother. He never had before.

I wondered if I did, too. 'Do I sound like Mom to you?'

'No, you do not sound like Mom. You sound like a fool who is sabotaging an amazing opportunity. Get ahold of yourself.'

I worked on the same chapter the whole time I was there. Two months. Twelve pages. While poetry poured out of Luke. Poems about lightning bugs, bullfrogs, and, finally, a dead child. The one about the bullfrogs he taped to the seat of my banana bike. The one about the dead child he read to me early one morning, then shook in my arms for an hour afterward. I never showed him any of my novel.

His last week there he gave a reading in the library. He was nervous walking over. He gripped the pages and told me they were all for me, about me, because of me. But when he was at the podium and I was in the first row, he never looked at me. When he read a poem about eating a peach on an overturned rowboat, the peach I'd brought, the rowboat where we'd sat together, he said it was for his mother, who loved peaches. He read the poem about the dead child, and everyone wept.

He got a standing ovation, the only one I'd seen there. People leapt to their feet without thinking about it. Women flocked around him afterward, women who'd arrived in my month and women just arriving and discovering him.

*   *   *

40

On his last night, we took a walk down a road lit blue by the moon. A cow in a field lumbered beside us, the wire fence invisible. We turned down the dirt road to the lake and dropped our clothes in the grass and swam in silence toward the middle. The frogs, which had stopped their singing, resumed full throttle. We came together, cool and rubbery, and we sank as we kissed. We lay on our backs and the moon had a thick milky caul around it. It blotted out all the stars nearby. The water dripped from our raised arms back into the lake. He said we'd have to find a way into each other's lives. He did not say how.

The next day he got in his truck and rolled down the window. He put his palm flat to his chest. 'You're deep in here,' he said, and drove away.

The number he gave me rang and rang. No person. No machine. I had a week left at Red Barn, and I tried that number from the wooden phone cabinet before every meal. On my last night there I sat next to a painter. She'd arrived a few days before Luke left, and he'd introduced me. He knew her in New York. Her eyes were kind. She passed me the mashed potatoes. She said, 'You know he's still married, right?'

On my machine he breathes another long breath into the phone. 'I need to see you,' he says.

I wait at the Sunoco station. He's late, and I sit on the cement border of a bed of garish marigolds. My legs begin to shake.

His truck slides up beside me, and he gets out, scrawnier than I remember. His hair is longer. It looks dirty. We hug. I can't feel him. There's churning under my skin, and my heart is going so fast that I'm not sure I'll be able to remain conscious. He swings my banana bike into the back of the truck without comment, without recognition.

We get into the cab, our old positions.

'This is hard, isn't it?'

I nod.

'I've just been moving very slowly,' he says, pulling out onto Memorial Drive.

We head west to Route 2. He wants to go swimming at Walden Pond.

'Loraine told me she told you.' Loraine was the painter. 'It's only on paper, Casey. It's not like . . . I've had other girlfriends and she's had . . . other men. For all intents and purposes—'

'Do you have a girlfriend now?'

42

'No.' He shifts into fourth too early and the truck shakes and he shifts back down. 'Not really.'

The whole drive to Concord I want to get out of the car, but when we park and stand on the hot tar I just want to get back in. There's an ice-cream truck rumbling in the lot and a cluster of kids with their heads slanted up to the sliding window. Their bodies are bouncing, their bathing suit butts drooping from the water and the sand. We step into a shady stand of pines and I nearly crash into Henry Thoreau. He's in bronze, a diminutive man, the size of a twelve-year-old boy. Behind him is a replica of his cabin. The door is open. I step up into it.

It's just one small room with an army cot to the right covered with a gray wool blanket and a sloped desk to the left, painted green. On the far wall is a brick hearth and a potbellied stove in front of it. All I can feel is the effort of reproduction. Nothing of Thoreau is here.

Luke takes my hand and tugs me to sit on the bed with him. There's a dead spider on the blanket whose legs look woven into the wool. He would like that. It would probably end up in a poem. I take pleasure in not showing it to him.

'We always seem to end up on a cot in a cabin in the woods.' He smiles and looks at me in the old way and I know if I lean toward him the slightest bit he will kiss me and I won't be able to control anything after that.

I get up and step down onto the yellow pine needles.

We cross the street and join a stream of people walking down the path. Below us on the small beach, bodies swarm. Children cry.

'It's so crowded,' I say.

'It's better than usual. Last month there was an hour wait just to get into the lot.'

Last month. He was here last month. The month he did not call me. I'm so heavy I can barely move. It takes so much effort just to follow him around the bathing beach to a trail in the woods around the pond. A wire fence runs along the water side of the path, and there are signs prohibiting people from going off the path and destroying the fragile ecosystem. But people have disobeyed, and all the small patches of sand you can see through the trees are taken so we keep walking. We find an empty little beach and crawl between the wires and down the steep embankment to it. We spread our towels a few feet apart. He gets up after a few minutes and sits on mine with me. He brushes some sand off my knee and bends his head down and puts his teeth on my kneecap like it's an apple.

I don't touch the pale back of his neck or the boyish bolts of his spine.

My body aches from my throat to my groin. I want him to slide his fingers into my bathing suit and make all the heaviness and misery go away. I feel like a hag in a fairy tale, waiting to be made young and supple again.

I get up and walk into the water. It's warm and clear. I've never been to Walden Pond before. I read the book in high school, when I lived less than an hour from here, but I never thought of it as a place that still existed. I drop into the water and push out from the shore on my back. He stays on my towel and gets smaller and smaller in his white T-shirt.

The shirt smells. I remember knowing that he smelled when I first met him. Then I stopped noticing.

'You smell,' I call back.

'What?' he says, but I kick out farther. The trees are so tall from this angle, dark, with their hardening summer leaves. The sky is cloudless, and directly above me its deep blue enamel thins and I can see the black of space behind it.

When I get out he watches my body and the water rushing off of it. He's still on my towel, so I sit on his.

'You're not going to swim?'

'Come here.'

I know how he wants it to go. I stay where I am. A swimmer, a woman with strong mottled arms in a bright-blue bathing cap, cuts a diagonal line across the pond.

'It's like there's this gristle between me and the world,' he says. 'I'm trying to work my way through it. I'm just moving really slowly. It's hard work. It's tough gristle.'

When my skin is dry and taut I tell him I have to get back. I am the on-call that night.

In his truck I smooth out my skirt. It's pretty, sage green with small ivory flowers. I know I'll never wear it again.

'Don't look at me like that,' he says.

'I'm not looking at you.'

'I know.'

He says he can bring me home to Brookline but I say the Sunoco station is fine.

'Don't close up,' he says.

The truck glides along Memorial Drive. I see my path by the river, the geese at the base of the Western Ave. Bridge.

45

All your life there will be men like this, I think. It sounds a lot like my mother's voice.

He pulls up next to the marigolds. I tell him not to get out, and he doesn't. I see his forehead resting on his hands on the steering wheel as I pull my bike out of the back.

I wheel it around to his window and ring my bell out of habit. It is the sound of me coming to his cabin at the end of the day. I want to take that sound and stuff it into a bag with rocks and throw it in the river. He smiles and rests both elbows along the side of his truck. My body is fighting me. If I get closer, he will put his fingers in my hair. I squeeze the handlebars and stay in place.

'Off you go,' I say.

I sit on my banana bike as he backs up, shifts, and pulls out. I stay there beside the marigolds on the side of the Sunoco station until his truck disappears around the bend where the river turns west.

I have one writer friend left who's still writing. Muriel's been working on a novel set during World War II for as long as I've known her. We met here in Cambridge six years ago, in line for the bathroom at the Plough and Stars, and hung out for a while before we both moved away for grad school. We crossed paths once at Bread Loaf, but I would never have known she was back here if I hadn't overheard one of my customers at Iris talking about her niece Muriel, who was writing a book set in a Jewish internment camp in Oswego, New York. I was refilling their waters and said, Muriel *Becker*? I got her number from her aunt.

The day after Walden, Muriel takes me to a launch party of a writer she knows. I ride to her place in Porter Square, and we walk up Avon Hill. The houses get fancier the higher we climb, grand Victorians with wide front porches and turrets.

'I'm spatchcocking my novel,' she says.

I have no idea what she's talking about. I often don't.

'It's what my grandmother did to a chicken when she wanted it to roast faster. Basically you cut out the backbone and sort of compress all the pieces in a pan.' She's had a good writing day. I can tell by the way her long arms are flying all around. I have not. I've been stuck on the same scene for a week. I can't get my characters down the stairs.

I've already told her on the phone about Luke's visit, but we have to go over it again. I have to reenact on the sidewalk the way he bit my knee. I have to say in a lugubrious voice, 'I'm just moving so slowly.' I have to holler the word 'gristle' up the street. But my chest is still burning.

'I'm usually better at protecting myself from this kind of thing.'

'From heartbreak?'

'Yeah.' My throat is closing. 'I can usually get out of the way before it hits me straight on.'

'That's not really heartbreak then, is it?'

The road and the houses with their big backyards grow blurry. 'He just blasted me apart. I don't even know where to find the bolts and screws. I always thought that if ever there came a time when I didn't hold anything back and just laid my heart on the table—' I have to squeak out the rest. 'Which I did. I did that this time. And it still wasn't enough.'

She wraps an arm around me and pulls me in tight. 'I know how you feel. You know I do. It's good to get whacked open at least once, though,' she says. 'You can't really love from inside a big thick shell.'

She turns onto a small lane lined with cars. The party is at the end on the left, a massive house: bow windows, three stories, mansard roof. The doorway is jammed. We stand on the threshold, unable to enter. The other guests are mostly older by twenty or thirty years, the women in stockings and heels, the men in sports jackets. The air smells like a cocktail party from the seventies, aftershave and martini onions.

The party is for a writer who leads a fiction workshop at his house near the Square on Wednesday nights. Muriel's been urging me to join it, but the idea of showing anyone any part of my novel is too painful to consider right now. I can't look back at it. I have to keep moving forward. She insists I won't have to show my work, that I can just check out the scene there, meet some other people who don't make you feel crazy for all your life choices. The writer had been a professor at BU until three years ago when his wife died, and he left teaching to write full-time and be home for his kids. But he'd missed teaching and started the workshop. He doesn't teach exactly, Muriel says. He has people read their work aloud, but he rarely speaks when they're done. They've come to understand that if he likes what he's hearing, his hands will move to his knees. And if he doesn't, his arms remain crossed over his chest. And if he really loves it, his fingers will be laced together in his lap by the end.

Muriel brought me to two other literary events earlier this summer: a reading in someone's basement apartment almost as small as the potting shed during which people read out of notebooks in the dark in quavering voices, and the release of a poetry chapbook called *Shit and Fuck* at a convenience store in Central Square. So this is definitely a step up. We inch our way through the vestibule into a living room, which is slightly less jammed. It's a big room, with floral sofas and end tables, furniture with brass-handled drawers, and large oil paintings, contemporary, abstract, the paint balled like nubs on an old sweater.

Muriel grabs my arm and pulls me through an archway into a smaller room lined with books. There's a guy alone in there, looking at the shelves.

'Hey there,' she says, and I can tell she barely knows him because of the pause before they hug. Usually Muriel mauls people. 'Our newest workshop victim.'

'Silas,' he says to me. He's tall and bent like he's loping, even though he's standing still.

'Casey.' I put out my hand.

He shifts a book from one hand to the other to shake it. His eyes are dark brown and hooded.

Muriel points to the book. 'You got a copy already?'

'I kinda had to. I was one of the first to arrive and he was sitting at the dining room table with a huge stack of books next to him.' He shows it to us. 'He didn't know who I was. From last week. I said my name, but he didn't get it quite right.' He flips to the title page.

Carry on, Alice, it says above the signature.

We laugh.

Two women are waving from the far side of the other room, trying to squeeze their way toward us. Muriel sees them and presses back into the crowd to meet them halfway.

I take the book from Silas's hand. My calves tingle like they do when I'm in a bookstore or stationery shop. It's a beautiful cover, abstract, navy blue with ivory streaks of light. The paper is rough, old-fashioned, like heavy typewriter paper. *Thunder Road* it's called. By Oscar Kolton. I haven't read him. Paco had one of his books I think, and I didn't much like the writers Paco did, men who wrote tender, poetic sentences that tried to hide the narcissism and misogyny of their stories.

I hold the book and imagine I've written it, imagine I'm holding my own book.

'You think he knows the title's already been used?' I say, hoping Silas hasn't seen my hunger.

'Maybe you should go tell him.'

'Set it to music, dude,' I pretend to call toward the dining room. 'It'll be a hit.'

We read the blurb on the front: 'Kolton has always delivered truth and beauty in spades, but here he gives us glimpses of the sublime.'

'I wouldn't mind a few glimpses of the sublime,' Silas says.

I flip to the back flap to see what Oscar Kolton looks like. Silas studies the photo with me. It was taken from the side, one of his shoulders in the foreground, elbow to knee, bicep flexed. He's bearing down on the lens with a menacing look. The contrast between black and white is so extreme his face looks carved out like an Ansel Adams rock face and the backlighting has turned his pupils to pinpricks.

'Why do men always want to look like that in their author photos?'

'My deep thoughts hurt me,' Silas says in a scratchy voice.

'Exactly. Or'—I try to mimic him—'I might have to murder you if you don't read this.'

He laughs.

'Whereas with women'—I take a book off the shelf by a writer I admire—'they have to be pleasing.' The photo backs

51

up my argument perfectly. She has a big apologetic smile on her face. I bounce the photo in front of Silas. 'Please like me. Even though I'm an award-winning novelist, I really am a nice, unthreatening person.'

We pull a few more from the bookcase, and they all support my gender theory.

'So how would you pose?' Silas says.

I sneer and flip him two birds.

He laughs again. He has a chipped front tooth, a clean diagonal cut off one corner.

Muriel is bringing her friends toward us.

'Did you read last Wednesday, to the group?' I say.

'I did.'

'What'd he do with his hands?'

'It was bad I think. Behind his back.'

'What does that mean?'

'No one could tell me. They hadn't seen it before.' He flashes his tooth again. He doesn't seem to care much about Oscar's verdict. 'So what are you working on?'

'I'm a waitress.'

He squints. 'What are you writing?'

'A novel.'

'Impressive.'

'I've been working on it for six years and still don't have a full draft or a title. So maybe not so impressive. Are you going back next week?'

'I don't know. It might be too religious for me. A lot of verbal genuflecting.'

'Really?' Muriel hasn't depicted it this way.

Silas hesitates. 'It's not really a free and open exchange of ideas. People just take down everything he says.' He hunches over and pretends to scribble in a tiny notebook. 'And, like, it was this small thing, but at one point he said that every line of dialogue had to have at least two ulterior motives, and I said what if the character just wants to know what time it is. People gasped. And then silence. I like a little more debate. Or maybe I just don't like a lot of rules.'

Muriel and her friends are hovering behind him. Silas shifts slightly, putting a bit more of his back to them. I don't think it's deliberate. 'You haven't ever gone to it?'

'No, I work nights.'

He looked at me like he knew that wasn't the whole truth and started to say something, but Muriel broke in.

'Look, *real* people from the *real* world.' she says.

She introduces us. One is an infectious disease doctor specializing in AIDS research, and the other heads up a non-profit in Jamaica Plain. They wear makeup and bracelets and dresses that don't come from the T.J. Maxx in Fresh Pond. They have crossed the room for Silas, and they pepper him with questions. I drift out of the conversation, out of the room.

I don't have the money for a copy of *Thunder Road*, but I follow the line from the entryway through the living room and into the dining room. I veer into the kitchen and peer at the writer through the window in the swinging door. His back is to me, and a small stooped woman is leaning over the table toward him, clutching the book he's just signed to her chest. She's still talking when he reaches for the book of the woman behind her. I can only see the back of him, the rim of a blue tie showing beneath his collar and a shoulder blade jutting up through the white dress shirt as he signs his name. I can't see if his face is as chiseled and pissed off as in the photograph.

All the surfaces in the kitchen are covered with baking sheets and trays of hors d'oeuvres. Every few minutes a server comes in for a refill. It feels strange not to be the one wearing a bun and apron.

'Prosciutto-wrapped fig?' she asks, face full of overlapping freckles.

'Oh, thanks so much,' I say, trying to convey my bond with her. I take a fig from the tray and a napkin from her other hand. It bugs me when people don't take the napkin, too. 'Thanks, it looks yummy.' But she's moved on to a group by the breakfast nook.

When I get back to the library, Silas is gone, the women from the real world are gone, and Muriel's in an argument about Cormac McCarthy with three men in moustaches.

The asphalt is purple in the dusk. We walk in the middle of the road down the hill. The sun has sunk but its heat hangs in the air. My ears ring from all the voices at the party. We talk about a book called *Troubles* that I read and passed along to her. She loved it as much as I did, and we go through the scenes we liked best. It's a particular kind of pleasure, of intimacy, loving a book with someone. The short biography on the back page said that the writer, J. G. Farrell, died while angling, swept out to sea by a rogue wave.

'Do you think that's an Irish euphemism for suicide?' I say.

'Maybe. You go out to see a man about a dog. And if he's not there you get swept away by a rogue wave.'

We both love Irish literature. We have a pact we'll go to Dublin together when we have money.

I tell her Silas said that Wednesday nights felt cultish.

She considers that. 'Well, a lot of people there want to *be* Oscar, and a number of others want to sleep with him. Maybe that is like a cult.'

'And where do you fall on that spectrum?'

'To be him. Definitely.'

'Do people sleep with him?'

'No. He wrote this essay for *Granta* last winter about his dead wife and how he can't think about other women and it got some people all hot and bothered.'

We hug goodbye outside her apartment building, talk for another half hour, and hug goodbye again.

The streets are quiet on the way home, the river flat and glossy. The sky is the darkest blue it gets just before turning black. I'm halfway across the BU Bridge before I realize I'm finishing that scene in my head. They're talking and I can hear them and they're finally going down the stairs.

Last fall Muriel's boyfriend told her he needed to be alone in a room with books. They'd been together nearly three years. He said that if they stayed together they'd just get married and reproduce, and he needed to write. So do *I*, Muriel told him. She didn't give a fuck about marriage and kids. But he didn't know *anything,* he said, though he had two graduate degrees. He needed to be alone in a room with books. He went to live on the third floor of his brother's house in Maine. That was ten months ago. They hadn't had contact since.

A week after the book party, Muriel goes to her niece's bat mitzvah and meets a guy.

'I liked him,' she says. 'Christian.'

'Christian?'

'My dad said, "Leave it to Muriel to find a man named Christian at a bat mitzvah."'

She's a little giddy.

The next day David, the old boyfriend, calls her. They say women have intuition, but men can smell a competitor across state lines.

'He wants to see me,' she says. 'He wants to go on a walk.'

'Is he still in his room with books?'

'I don't know.' She's half laughing, half crying. 'Christian was such a good guy. We were supposed to go out Thursday night. Oh, holy crap, I nearly forgot. That guy Silas asked me for your number.'

He calls me the next morning. I can't remember what he looks like. Or I can't match what I remember with the voice. It's low and ragged, like a half-broken engine. An old-man voice. I'm not convinced it's him.

He asks if I'd like to go to the Museum of Fine Arts on Friday night. 'They stay open late. And we could get a bite to eat after.'

Bite to eat. It was something my mother would say.

'Sure.' I feel like laughing. I'm not exactly sure why, but I don't want him to hear it.

'You're laughing.'

'No, I'm not.' I was. 'I'm sorry. It's my dog. He's doing this thing with his ears.'

'What's his name?'

I don't know the name of Adam's dog, and he isn't in the potting shed with me. Do I really not know the name of that dog? 'Adam's dog.'

'Adam's Dog is the name of your dog?'

'It's not really my dog. It's Adam's. My landlord. I take care of him sometimes. I don't know his real name.'

Silence.

I should never answer the phone in the morning. 'I mean, I'm sure I knew it. I'm sure he told me. But I've forgotten it. I have to walk him every morning right in the middle of my

57

writing time and I resent him so much I don't even want to know his name and I only do it for the fifty bucks off my rent.'

'And he's not why you were laughing, either.'

'No, I really don't know why I was laughing.'

Silence.

'It's just that I can't quite match your voice to your body right now.' I wince at the word 'body.' Why was I talking about his *body*? 'And the expression 'bite to eat' reminds me of my mother.' Do *not* tell him your mother is dead. He has called to ask you out on a date. Do not mention a dead mother.

'Huh.' It sounds like he was getting into a different position, reclining, smooshing a pillow under his head maybe. 'Do you get along with her?'

'Yes. Completely. Very simpatico.' But I don't want to pretend she is somewhere that she isn't, like I did with the dog. 'She died though, FYI.' *FYI?*

'Oh shit. I'm so sorry. When?'

'Recently.'

He gets the whole thing out of me, all the bits I know about her trip to Chile. It still burns a bit, coming out. He listens. He breathes into the phone. I can tell he lost someone close somehow. You can feel that in people, an openness, or maybe it's an opening that you're talking into. With other people, people who haven't been through something like that, you feel the solid wall. Your words go scattershot off of it.

I ask him, and he says his sister died, eight years ago.

'I usually say it was a hiking accident,' he says. 'That she fell. But she was struck by lightning. People can get very caught up in that. The symbolism. Or the physical details. Either one. It bugs me.'

'Where were you when you found out?' I don't know why, but I need to picture him at that moment. It's such an awful moment. I heard over the phone at five in the morning in a tiny kitchen in Spain.

'I was home, at my parents' house. I was supposed to be on that trip but I'd gotten mono. That day was the first day I felt okay. I went to the mall to get a pair of sneakers, and when I came back my father told me to sit down. I said I didn't want to sit down. I heard it all in his voice. I already knew. For so long I was so mad he made me sit down. Something like that rips you out of your life and you feel for a long time like you're just hovering above it watching people scurry around and none of it makes sense and you're just holding this box of sneakers—' I hear a voice in the background, a woman. 'Oh shit, Casey, I have to go. My class started twelve minutes ago.'

'You're in school?'

'Teaching. Summer school. God, I'm sorry to hang up right now but that was the head of my department. Can I call you tonight?'

'I'm working. I'll see you at the museum on Friday.' I don't want to spend too much time on the phone, then have it be awkward in person like in that story 'The Letter Writers' about a man and a woman who fall in love through ten years of correspondence, and when they meet their bodies can't catch up to their words.

We hang up. My room comes into focus again, my desk, my notebook. It's still morning. The whole time we were on the phone I didn't worry even once that it would ruin my writing time.

Muriel comes to the potting shed after her walk with David. I make tea and we sit on my futon.

'I thought he'd be different, that he'd have some Jack Nicholson crazy in his eye. All this time, I was scared he'd be different. But he was just the same.' Her voice breaks. 'He was just the same. And I couldn't touch him. He was unappealing to me. We started walking and he put his arm around me and I thought I'd get over it, that feeling, because it was exactly as I'd hoped. He wants me back. He made a terrible mistake, he said. And I just kept thinking, When can I get back in my car. I tried to hide it from him, but he saw and said I was cold, said my eyes were like a snake's. Then he sort of broke down and said we'd had something so perfect, and he'd known it all along and the only reason he'd left was he knew it wouldn't end. He'd panicked. Looking at the rest of his life scared him. But losing me, he said, was even scarier.'

'Where were you?'

'Fresh Pond. We went around and around. For hours. He was so dramatic, leaping around me, throwing out his arms. He actually hit a runner at one point. I kept asking him why he didn't tell me all this before, and he said he didn't know. He cried. I've never seen him cry before, not actual tears. It was awful. I couldn't fake it, though. I couldn't even tell him I'd think about it. It was over. It was so clear. And when he tried to kiss me, I shoved him away. My arms just pushed him away before I knew what I was doing. It was so physical, the repulsion. It felt *biological*. Like I knew I would never have children with this man. It was so awful and weird. I could see all the things I had loved about him, I could *see* them, but I didn't love them anymore.'

She breaks down. She doubles over on my futon, and I hold on to her and rub her back and tell her it's going to be all right, which is what she has been doing for me all summer long. I make more tea and cinnamon toast and we scoot back on the futon and lean against the wall, eating and sipping and looking out my one window at the driveway where Adam seems to be arguing with Oli the cleaning lady.

'Did David write his book?' I ask.

'He didn't even start it.' She blows on her tea. 'And I've written two hundred and sixty pages since he left.'

At lunch, Fabiana seats me two doctors in the corner. They've kept their big laminated name tags clipped to their shirt pockets. They're both internists, their tags say, at Mass General. When I pour their water, they're talking about a laparoscopic liver biopsy, and when I drop their sandwiches they've moved on to giardia.

If they hadn't been talking medicine the whole meal, I wouldn't have said anything. I don't get up the nerve until I'm serving their espressos.

'May I ask you a quick question?'

The one on the left busies himself with a sugar packet. He's on to me. But the older one nods. 'Be our guest.'

'My mother went to Chile last winter. She flew from Phoenix to LA to Santiago. She had a cough left over from a cold but no fever. Apart from that, she was in full health. Fifty-eight years old. No medical issues.' It comes out of me perfectly, like memorized lines. 'They spend five days in the capital then fly to the Chiloé Archipelago where they visit a few islands, and on the island of Caucahué she wakes up feeling cold and short of breath. Her friends get her to a clinic there and they put her on oxygen and radio for an air ambulance and just before it comes she dies.'

Both doctors seem frozen. The younger one is still holding the sugar packet.

'What do you think happened? The death certificate says cardiac arrest, but it wasn't a heart attack. Why did her heart stop? Was it a pulmonary embolism? From the long plane flight? That's what my brother's boyfriend, Phil, thinks. But he's an ophthalmologist.'

The two doctors look at each other, not in consultation but in alarm. How do we get out of here?

'There was no autopsy?' the younger one says, finally releasing the sugar into the demitasse.

'No.'

'I'm so sorry,' the older one says. 'It must have been a terrible shock.'

'Without her history and a full report . . .' the other one says and turns up his hands.

'It was most likely an embolism.'

'Could we get the check when you have a chance?'

They knock back their espressos while I print it out, put down two twenties, and bolt out of the dining room.

My mother's friend Janet was with her at the clinic on the island. She wasn't struggling, Janet told me. She wasn't in pain. She was dozing. Sort of in and out. Then she sat up, said she had to make a phone call, lay back down again, and was dead. It was very peaceful, Janet told me. Such a pretty day.

I tried, in phone calls with Janet, to get more detail than pretty day and peaceful. I wanted everything, my mother's exact words and the smell of the clinic and the color of the walls. Were children kicking a ball outside? Was she holding Janet's hand? Who did she sit up to call? Was there any noise at all when her heart stopped? Why did it stop? I wanted to hear my mother tell it. She loved a story. She loved a mystery. She could make any little incident intriguing. In her version, the doctor would have a wandering eye and three chickens in the back named after Tolstoy characters. Janet would have a heat rash on her neck. I wanted her and no one else to tell me the story of how she died.

Her suitcase arrived at Caleb and Phil's house three days after the funeral. Caleb and I opened it together. We lifted out her yellow rain slicker, her two cotton nightgowns, her one-piece bathing suit with the pink-and-white checks. We pressed our noses to every item, and every item smelled of her. We found gifts in a paper bag, a pair of beaded earrings and a man's T-shirt. We knew they were for us. When the suitcase was empty I slid my hand into the interior elasticized pouches, certain there would be something in writing, a note or a sentence of goodbye, of premonition, in case of. There was nothing but two safety pins and a thin barrette.

The rest of the week goes badly. My writing flounders. Every sentence feels flat, every detail fake. I go for long runs along the river, to Watertown, to Newton, ten miles, twelve miles, which help, but after a few hours the bees start crawling again. I scroll the 206 pages I have on the computer and skim the new pages I have in my notebook since Red Barn. I can't find one moment, one sentence, that's any good. Even the scenes I've clung to when all else seems lost—those first pages I wrote in Pennsylvania and the chapter I wrote in Albuquerque that poured out of me like a visitation—have dimmed. It all looks like a long stream of words, like someone with a disease that involves delusions has written them. *I am wasting my life. I am wasting my life.* It pounds like a heartbeat. For three days straight it rains, and the potting shed starts to smell like compost. I arrive at Iris soaked through and barely dry off before I have to ride back home. I try to fold my white shirt carefully into my knapsack but it wrinkles, and Marcus scolds me for it. Each way I pass the Sunoco station on Memorial Drive, the ugly marigolds in their concrete bed, and hot tears mix with the rain. The date at the end of the week with Silas, for which I have swapped a lucrative Friday night for a Monday lunch, fills me with dread. But when I am not paying attention, I remember his voice on the phone and his chipped tooth, and a ripple of something that might be anticipation passes through.

Harry and I have two doubles together, Tuesday and Thursday. I'm not an efficient waitress when Harry is working —we get lost in conversation and cajole the sous chefs into making us BLTs or crab cakes and smoke cigarettes with Alejandro out on the fire escape and are never around when Marcus is looking for us—but I am a cheerier waitress. Harry's charm rubs off on me. My service is worse, but my tips are always better.

'He's not panna cotta, is he?' he says on Thursday lunch over vichyssoise and iced coffees in the wait station while Marcus interviews someone in the office.

Harry asked me to dinner after the first shift we worked together. He was handsome and hilarious, with a sexy British accent and a flawlessly hetero shield. He told me he'd been born in Lahore, but moved when he was three to London.

'Northeast London?' I asked, because he sounded exactly like a friend I'd had in Paris from there.

'Yeah, Redbridge. Who are you, Henry Higgins?'

He said he became English at age nine when he switched schools and changed his name from Haroon to Harry. 'My skin magically lightened. It was quite a trick. After that I was just one of the lads.'

Over dessert I planned to tell him about Luke, tell him that I wasn't ready to date yet. But when the panna cotta arrived he mentioned an ex, named Albert. I was floored. Later we called it the panna cotta revelation.

'Who?' I say now.

'This Silas fellow.'

'Shit, I hope not. You can have him if he is.'

'A writer? No thanks.'

'What do you mean?'

'I don't want someone who's all up in here all the time.' He waves his fingers around his glossy black hair. 'I like a thruster. Writers aren't thrusters. Not the good ones. And I couldn't be with a bad writer. God, that would be awful.' Ooful is how he says it. He goes off to drop a check at his deuce. 'Plus,' he says when he comes back, '*I* want to be the wordsmith. I like to dominate, verbally. Your three-top wants hot tea. Tell them it's ninety degrees outside and their lips are going to melt like wax.'

Marcus comes out of the office while I'm dropping the tea and Harry's taking an order and finds our bowls of vichyssoise. 'I'm not ever scheduling you two together again.' He always says that. It makes us feel about six years old. We make faces at each other behind his back.

When I get home that night, late—there was an anniversary party for sixty-one in the downstairs dining room— Silas is on my machine.

'Casey, I'm sorry. I had to leave town. For a while. I'm not sure how long.' His mouth is really close to the receiver, cars whipping by behind him. 'I'm sorry to miss our date tomorrow. I really am. It's the one thing that. I don't know. I barely know you. But. I had to. I had to go. Anyway, I'll call you when I get back. Don't. Well, I can't really. Take care of yourself.' There was a pause and then, 'Shit,' and the receiver crashed into the cradle.

'Another fucking flake,' I say to Muriel.

'Could be a family emergency or something.'

'It wasn't. He was like, uh, had to leave town, uh, for a while. No idea how long.'

She looks at me doubtfully.

'I'd like to meet a guy who wants what he says he wants. No more "I'm just moving slowly" or "I just need to go away for a really vague amount of time." Jesus.'

'Don't write Silas off.'

'I'm totally writing him off.'

'I'm going to show you a story he wrote.'

'Don't. I do not want to see it.'

Muriel says she doesn't want my Friday night off to go to waste, and she invites some people over to her place for dinner.

Harry swaps a shift with Yasmin and comes with me. He flirts madly with all the straight guys. He's gone off gay men, he says. It went badly in Provincetown with the new busboy. Muriel serves Moroccan chicken, couscous, and sangria. She's spread a batik cloth over her couch.

'Very multicultural bohème,' Harry says.

Most of Muriel's friends are writers, real writers, not like my old friends who got over it like the flu. She's put the

68

food buffet style on her desk, which she covered with a sari and pulled out from the wall. I fill my plate next to a guy who calls himself Jimbo and had a novel published last year. *Motorcycle Mama.* It received mixed reviews, Muriel told me, but he got a six-figure contract for the next one anyway.

'Beware the murky bowl of unidentifiable forcemeats,' Jimbo says, nudging my shoulder with his. I can tell he doesn't know if we've met—or slept together—before. We haven't done either, and I ignore him. 'Rudy,' he says with unnecessary volume in my ear to a guy on my other side. 'This looks like what we used to get at the A.D. on Pepe's night off.' In case there are people who don't know he went to Harvard. He moves on bellowing through the room.

The only other person there who has published a book is Eva Park. Her short story collection was gorgeous, got a ton of attention last year, and won the PEN/Hemingway. She's perched uneasily on a short stool listening to two of Muriel's colleagues explain to her why her book is a masterpiece of contemporary fiction. I met Eva six years ago, when she was working on the collection. They aren't *stories*, she told me, they're hard little polyps I'm trying to remove from my brain. She was sort of ablaze with a lot of nervous energy then. All the stuffing seems to have gone out of her since. She looks embarrassed, sitting on that stool, to be who she is now. She seems pained by all the compliments Muriel's colleagues are giving her. Success rests more easily on men. Across the room, Jimbo holds up a bottle and hollers that the Grey Goose has flown.

Muriel calls me over and makes me squeeze on the couch between her and her grad school friend George, who turned up unexpectedly that afternoon, which apparently he does from time to time. She's told me about him. He's unhappy and lives in North Carolina. We're pressed together on the couch and have to lean away from each other to be in focus. He has a smooth plump face and gold-rimmed glasses. Big round eyes through the lenses.

Harry is on the other side of Muriel, and they have enhanced the intensity of their conversation to force George and me to talk to each other. I already know part of his story. He and his wife arrived in Ann Arbor together for grad school. He was in the fiction program with Muriel, and his wife was in nonfiction. During their second year there she started getting migraines and was sent to a specialist. At her third appointment, the doctor locked the door and they had sex. On the examining table with the crinkly paper. The doctor remained standing the whole time. I shouldn't know these details, but I do. They're all writers in the chain—his wife, George, and Muriel—so the particulars didn't get lost. Now the wife is migraine-free and living with the doctor, and George is heartbroken and teaching freshman comp at UNC–Greensboro.

'Muriel says your novel's about Cuba,' George says.

It occurs to me that the chain goes both ways, that he may know all about Luke, that those juicy Red Barn tidbits haven't gotten lost, either.

'It's not really about Cuba. It's just set there.'

'Why?'

'My mother lived there when she was a girl. Her parents were American, but after the war her father set up a medical practice in Santiago de Cuba. There was this moment when she was seventeen and had to decide whether to run away with her boyfriend and join the rebels in the mountains, or leave Cuba with her parents. In the book I have her choose love.'

'And the revolution.'

'Yeah.' Love and the revolution. I push some chicken around on my paper plate. I need to change the subject. Talking about my book makes me feel flayed alive. 'John Updike came into the restaurant where I work a few weeks ago, and while I was putting down his salad the woman next to him told him how much she loved *The Centaur,* and he shook his head and said he only wrote it because he didn't have any other ideas at the time. That's kind of the way I feel.' *Love and the Revolution.* I don't hate it.

'Did you tell Updike you were a writer?'

'No.' I laugh. 'God no.' But when that woman who loved *The Centaur* dropped her fork and I bent down to get it, I touched one of the leather tassels of his loafer, for a bit of luck. 'What are you working on right now?'

'Oh.' He looks down at his fingers, which are wringing the neck of his napkin. 'I'm a little stuck.'

'On what?'

'A story.'

'What's it about?'

The question clearly pains him as well. 'A sort of art heist in the Golden Horde in 1389.'

I want him to be joking, but he is not.

'Wow. How long have you been working on it?'

'Three years.'

'Three *years*?' I don't mean for it to come out like that. 'It must be more of a novella by now.'

'It's eleven and a half pages.'

This is a detail Muriel hasn't shared, more peculiar and intimate and, to me anyway, more horrendous than his wife's infidelity. I don't know what to say.

'Are you waiting tables tomorrow night?' he says.

'Yeah.'

'The next night?'

'Yup. Most nights. Why?'

'I'm trying to ask you out.'

But I can't go out with a guy who's written eleven and half pages in three years. That kind of thing is contagious.

August arrives and Iris becomes a wedding factory: re-hearsal dinners, receptions, and an occasional small ceremony on the deck. For these events the restaurant is closed to the public, and we pass around oysters, crab toasts, stuffed figs, and risotto balls along with flutes of champagne on special silver trays. When we finally get the guests seated, we slide salads then entrées then desserts in front of them. We water and wine them. There are long periods of time when we line the wall and watch the wedding party, each with our own particular cynicism.

Our waitstaff isn't young. We're mostly in our late twenties and thirties and however old Mary Hand is. Only Victor Silva is married. Dana thinks all the bridesmaids are snots and tends to pick fights with them. Harry believes every groom is closeted and hitting on him. Mary Hand hangs out with musicians in the corner, making sure they get a full meal and all the drinks they want. I always say the couple is too young. They never seem to know each other very well. They look at each other warily.

Not one of the events in August makes me feel like getting married is a good idea. It was nothing I ever aspired to, anyway. My parents were married twenty-three years and never made it look appealing.

'I liked her hair,' my father told me once when I tried to find out why he cut in line at a golf club on Cape Cod to meet my mother. She was staying with a friend from junior college, and he was in a tournament. He'd been on the minor league tours for nearly a decade, he told her, and if he didn't qualify for the PGA that year, he was going to quit. My mother asked what he'd do then. 'Marry you,' he said.

My mother told me he wooed her with wanderlust. He could teach golf anywhere. He was a better teacher than player, he confessed to her. They could spend a year or two in the south of France, Greece, Morocco. Head over to Asia. There was a lot of interest in golf in Japan, he said. After that maybe Cuba would have opened up again. Maybe he could bring her back there to live, he told her. She quit college to marry him, but he surprised her after the honeymoon by buying a house north of Boston. He got a job at the high school, and they never left. Instead of love and the revolution, instead of traveling the world, she became a radical in our conservative town, distributing flyers and hiring vans to go to protests against discrimination, Vietnam, and nuclear power. Sometimes she and Caleb were the only people in those vans.

She started going to St. Mary's to help her stay married, to remember loyalty, to understand the will of God. But what she found after six months at church was Javier Paniagua. He was the new cantor, twenty-six to my mother's thirty-seven. He played folk songs on the guitar and supervised the playground after mass. I remember his first day, when I was eleven, because I was allowed to play outside longer after Sunday school. Normally my mother called to me from the edge of the parking lot, and I went to her immediately. She was tense and impatient back then and would grit her teeth and try to yank my arm off if I kept her waiting. But that day she crossed the patch of dead grass and sank her heels in the wood chips to ask him about a song he'd played. She told him she'd known that song as a girl in Cuba, and this caught his interest.

At first my father was amused by my mother's church-going. He liked it better than the protesting. He even went to mass with us on Christmas and Easter. After a few years, though, he grew annoyed. He called the church St. Fairy's and made fun of Father Ted, a flushed man in his fifties who looked like Captain Stubing on *The Love Boat*. Father Ted wets the bed, he'd say, trying to get me to laugh. He never understood the real threat was the curly-haired kid with the guitar.

Javier was at St. Mary's for nearly five years—I don't know what he did on the days that weren't Sunday or when their affair began—until he was diagnosed with cancer, the same leukemia that had already taken two pilots he'd dropped chemicals with over South Vietnam. When treatment in Boston failed, my mother drove him to his family in Phoenix and stayed until they buried him a year and a half later.

My mother came back in the late spring of my sophomore year of high school. She rented a small house on the outskirts of town. My father and I had moved in with a woman named Ann by then, and they didn't object when I went to live at my mother's. She wasn't familiar at first. She wore blue jeans and beaded belts and cried a lot.

But she made efforts with me. I'd put up a photo of Lady Di on my wall and when Prince Charles married her that June, she woke me up at six in the morning with raspberry scones and a pot of English breakfast tea. We watched the carriage make its way through London, and she seemed excited, but once they reached the cathedral and the cameras zoomed in on their faces, my mother's mood changed. She's terrified, she said. And look at him, so cold. That poor girl. That poor girl, she said over and over. My mother was the same age as Diana when she married my father. Nineteen. Never put yourself in that situation, she said to me. Never ever, she said as Diana walked slowly up the stairs with the long train behind her. Marriage is the polar opposite of a fairy tale, my mother said.

I went back to bed before they'd said their vows.

At Iris, leaning over to refill a glass or relight a candle, I eavesdrop on the wedding guests.

'She was always in love with the roommate.'

'He got her to add two zeros to the prenup.'

'Is it so hard to find a goddamn Catholic in this town?'

'She said he was like a Cossack in bed.'

'A *what*?'

'You know, like super rigid. Like a doll that doesn't bend.'

And the toasts reveal everything: the rancor between the two families, the promiscuity, the unrequited loves, the bad behavior, the last-minute confessions—all delivered in drunken tangents that end with saccharine platitudes. The rites of marriage are an expensive and dreary business. The only thing that can cut through my skepticism is if the mother of the bride stands up. No matter what she says, no matter how poorly expressed, no matter how icy or bland or clichéd, I cry. Harry holds my hand.

August is endless.

My old friends are getting married, too. The invitations catch up with me eventually, forwarded from Oregon or Spain or Albuquerque.

Unfortunately, sometimes these invitations arrive before the wedding has taken place.

I check the regret box on the small return card and write an apology without an excuse. I do not mention my debt or my work commitments to the weddings of strangers or my bewilderment at why they would participate in a hollow, misogynistic ritual that will only end in misery.

It's easy when it's just a box to check. It's harder when they track you down by phone. Tara from middle school calls and puts me on the spot. She wants me to be her maid of honor. In November. In Italy. She knows my situation. I'm not sure why she's going through the motions of asking.

'I know what you're going to say,' she says. 'But it's going to be easy for you. I got a huge discount on the dresses so they're only three hundred. And they're classic—a soft lilac—you can cut it off and wear it all the time. And we got a super deal on a villa outside of Rome. It's magnificent. Meals included. Only four hundred a night when it's normally like eight. And we bundled the plane tickets—business class. If you get them by the end of the week, it'll only be seven fifty.' She's acting like she's not talking about dollars but something much easier to come by like hairs on my head, like I can just pluck them off and hand them to her.

'You have no idea how out of the realm that is for me.'

'I need you there. You have to be there. This isn't a choice, Casey.' The squeak in her voice reminds me of how she used to wheedle her mother until she got what she wanted. 'You go to your best friend's wedding.'

Best friend? She's a good friend. She's an old friend. Just the smell of her parents' living room would bring back three years of my life, but that was many lives ago.

'I would give anything to be there in that beautiful place watching you marry the man of your dreams.' Brian, an oaf with the energy of a hibernating bear. 'But I don't have eighteen hundred and fifty dollars. I don't even have a hundred and fifty dollars.'

'Well, I can't pay your way. We're already giving a free ride to my sisters.'

'That's not what I was angling for. I would never accept that.'

'You have a job. We played phone tag for two weeks because of all the *shifts* you're working. What else are you going to spend this money on? This is one of those selfish decisions you are going regret the rest of your life. We need to be there for each other. You need to make this happen against all odds and obstacles. You put it on a credit card, and you come to my wedding.'

'I've maxed everything out. I can't accrue more debt. I can barely meet the minimums.'

'Jeez, Casey. At some point, don't you think you have to grow up? You can't expect to be given a pass forever. It's time to be an adult. You can't live in your made-up worlds all your life. People get *real* jobs that make *real* money so that they can be a *real* friend at their best friend's wedding. I flew from my vacation in *Bermuda* to Arizona for your mother's funeral. And it wasn't cheap, buying it three days before.'

The underside of my arms begin to burn.

'Did your mother have any idea how much trouble you were in?'

If she hadn't said this, it might have been okay.

'Did you pay for that ticket, Tara?'

'What do you mean?'

'Did you, yourself, pay for the ticket from Bermuda to Phoenix?'

Silence.

'And if we took away Brian's salary at Schwab and your dad's little allowance, how much money would you have working part-time at that nonprofit? Would you be able to afford Bermuda or your two-bedroom in SoHo? Are you more of an adult because two men are giving you the illusion of self-sufficiency?'

She hangs up on me.

I am hemorrhaging friends with these weddings. Muriel and Harry are nearly all I have left.

* * *

On the last day of August I go to work in the morning and the waiters are all gathered around the bar. I think I've missed a meeting but it's just Mia reading something out loud: 'The Mercedes limo slammed into a wall in the Alma tunnel, on the right bank of the Seine under the Place de l'Alma, the police said.' I wedge my way in-between Mary Hand and Victor Silva to see what she's reading from. 'Shocked eyewitnesses reported that the car was full of blood.'

The front page of the *Boston Globe* is spread out on the counter with an enormous photo of a mangled black car. The headline above: DIANA IS DEAD.

The hardest thing about writing is getting in every day, breaking through the membrane. The second-hardest thing is getting out. Sometimes I sink down too deep and come up too fast. Afterward I feel wide open and skinless. The whole world feels moist and pliable. When I get up from the desk I straighten the edges of everything. The rug needs to be perfectly aligned with the floorboards. My toothbrush needs to be perpendicular to the edge of the shelf. Clothing cannot be left inside out. My mother's sapphire needs to be centered on my finger.

When I was fifteen, my father's girlfriend, Ann, had my sweaters dry-cleaned. My mother used to wash them in Woolite and lay them on a towel to dry, but she was in Phoenix with Javi by then, and my father and I were living at Ann's and she would gather up my sweaters while I was at school. They'd come back a few days later on hangers covered in paper, sheathed in long plastic bags, which she hung on my closet door. I didn't like the shape of these bags, the swollen tops with the sweaters beneath and then the empty length of sheer plastic, dangling like the lower region of a jellyfish. I was scared of those bags. I'd get the sweaters out of them and tie tight knots along the length of each one and shove them to the bottom of my wastebasket. I was scared I'd try to suffocate myself in my sleep.

I didn't want to die. I wasn't happy, living in Ann's big house without Caleb, who was in college and never called, but I wasn't sad. I barely had any emotions at all. But at night I terrified myself with this fear that somewhere inside me someone wanted to die.

When my mother came back from Arizona, she asked if I wanted to talk to someone, a professional, she said. I don't know why she said this, what precipitated it, but it scared me, the idea that this professional might go in and find that other person inside me, the person who was feeling all the things I did not let myself feel. My mother had returned brokenhearted and in the middle of divorce litigation with my father. I heard terrible noises through her bathroom door, sounds I couldn't connect to my mother. She was grieving, but I didn't understand what that felt like then. I told her she was the one who should see a shrink, not me.

In college one of my best friends was a psych major and practiced on me with the Minnesota personality test. She showed me the bar graph of my results. All the bars were in the medium size, normal range except two, which were much taller. One was for a category called Defensiveness to the Test. The other was for schizophrenia. I wondered if that tall schizophrenia bar had anything to do with why I tied those dry-cleaning bags in knots before bed that year my mother was gone, my suspicion that there was someone else inside me. I hadn't had that fear again, and I don't think I've ever exhibited any signs of that illness, but I did start writing fiction the year my mother was gone and maybe that's where I channeled my schizophrenic potential.

During the time my mother was out West, I did some of the same sort of rearranging of objects that I do now after writing sometimes. I always had to put on my right shoe, then the left. I could never leave a shirt inside out. If I followed the rules, my mother would definitely come back from Phoenix. And here I am, making rules again, even though nothing I do now will ever, ever bring her back.

When I was visiting her a few years ago she hugged me and said, 'Tomorrow after you leave I will stand here at this window and remember that yesterday you were right here with me.'

And now she's dead and I have that feeling all the time, no matter where I stand.

A dam comes by with my mail. He sees me at my desk in the window, so I have to open the door. He hands me a postcard and four envelopes from debt collectors, stamped with bright red threats.

'I feel like I'm harboring a fugitive in here,' he says. 'How do you sleep at night?'

'I don't much.'

I can tell he doesn't believe me. He thinks of me as young and somehow protected by my youth.

Adam points to the EdFund envelope. 'Those guys are awful. They get sued left and right for unlawful practices.'

I need to get back to my desk.

'Didn't you get a full ride at Duke? Weren't you ranked one or two in the country at some point?'

'When I was fourteen,' I say.

'But isn't golf one of those sports where if you're good you only get better?'

'Not if you sell your clubs.'

He thinks if he's silent I'll say more.

'Well,' he says finally. 'There's a lot to be said for being unencumbered.' He looks greedily around at the nothing of my life. 'It's the scent of freedom in here, Casey. You won't be able to smell it till you've lost it.'

Actually I could smell it. It was the scent of black mold and gasoline that came in from the garage.

I toss out the envelopes and sit back at my desk with the postcard. One side is a photograph of spiked snow-covered mountains in the background, lower, rounder brown mountains below, and a bright green pasture with wildflowers and a grazing cow. WELCOME TO CRESTED BUTTE, it says at the bottom. Crested Butte?

On the other side, in small ballpoint scrawl:

> For a while now I've needed to get in my car and drive
> west. I've needed to see mountains and the sky. I hope
> I can explain it to you better when I get back. The
> man who sold me this postcard kept a dog behind the
> counter, and I thought of Adam's Dog and my only
> regret about leaving is not going on that date with you.

I drop it in the bin on top of the past-due notices.

That week I make a few trips to the public library to research Cuba. Each time I end up in the biography stacks, reading about writers and their dead mothers.

George Eliot's mother died of breast cancer when she was sixteen. 'Mother died,' are her only preserved words on the subject. She had been called home from boarding school when her mother got sick, and after her death Eliot lost all hope of further education. She became her father's partner in work and home, traveling with him on trips to Coventry, mending his clothes, and reading him Walter Scott in the evening.

D. H. Lawrence told a girl who loved him that he would never love her back because he loved his mother 'like a lover.' He was twenty-five when a tumor was discovered in his mother's abdomen. Lawrence stayed at her bedside for the final three weeks, reading and painting and working on what would become the novel *Sons and Lovers*. During that time a galley of his first novel, *The White Peacock*, arrived at the house. His mother looked at the cover, the title page, and then at him. He felt her doubt of his talents. Her pain worsened and he witnessed her increasing agony. He begged the doctor to give her an overdose of morphia to set her free, but the doctor refused. Lawrence did it himself. He wrote later, 'From the death of my mother, the world began to dissolve around me, beautiful, iridescent, but passing away substanceless. Till I almost dissolved away myself, and was very ill, when I was twenty-six. Then slowly the world came back: or I myself returned: but to another world.'

As a child Edith Wharton had been scolded by her mother for wanting to be alone to make things up, and forbidden to read novels until after marriage. When her mother died, she sent her husband to the funeral. She stayed home to write. She was thirty-nine, and she published her first novel the following year.

Marcel Proust was thirty-four when his mother died. Apart from a year of military service, he had lived with her his whole life. After she was gone he went to a clinic outside Paris for nervous disorders where he was forbidden to write. He considered suicide but believed it would be killing his mother again if he destroyed his own memory of her. When he left the clinic he began to write a critical essay about the writer Sainte-Beuve, fueled by an imaginary conversation with his mother. In the piece he reaches back to memories of his childhood, to saying goodnight to his mother, and it becomes the beginning of *Swann's Way*.

'Hold yourself straight, my Little Goat,' were Julia Stephen's last words to her daughter, thirteen-year-old Virginia. Woolf's mother lay dead in bed for several days after that and when

Virginia was led in to kiss her for the last time, her mother was no longer on her side but on her back, in the middle of her pillows. Her cheek was like cold iron, and granulated, Virginia wrote later. A few days later she went to Paddington to meet her brother's train. It was sunset and the glass dome of the station was lit up a blazing red. After her mother died, her perceptions were more intense, she wrote later, 'as if a burning glass had been laid over what was shaded and dormant.' That summer she had her first breakdown. It lasted two years.

I 'm delivering two blackened bluefish and a Turkish roast pigeon to table 13. They're arguing about Ronald Reagan's legacy, and the woman says he was a Howdy Doody manqué, which I think is a good line, but the two men don't hear it. I slide the pigeon into place and a creepy sound comes from every direction in the room, like an alien invasion.

Ooooooooooooooooooooo.

A lean boy in a tux and floppy red hair comes running into the center of the dining room and people flinch and gasp and the redhead flings out his arms.

'Here's my story, sad but true,' he croons. 'About a girl that I once knew.'

Along the perimeter of the room other boys in tuxes are still ooooing. When the song changes tempo, they switch to 'hey, heys' and 'bop, bops' and 'whoa oh, oh, ohs' and start closing in on the lead in the middle and the dining room erupts in applause that reaches a crescendo when they all come together in a perfectly formed circle and flash their fake fifties smiles.

The Kroks are back in town.

I fire my six-top on the computer in the wait station. Dana brushes past me, kicks through the kitchen door with a stack of cleared plates.

'Anyone got a gun with twelve bullets?' she says to the line cooks before the door swings shut.

The Kroks sing 'Mack the Knife' and 'In the Mood' and 'The Lion Sleeps Tonight.' For 'Earth Angel' they grab an older woman and put her on the floppy-haired boy's knee while the rest encircle her with adoring looks. Then they fling her back where she came from in one motion on the last note of the song. They put their heads down as if in prayer and back away slowly from the smallest of them all, a curly-haired cherub who steps forward, opens his mouth, pauses, and begins singing.

'By yon bonnie banks and by yon bonnie braes. Where the sun shines bright on Loch Lomond' slow and smooth, in a high quavering voice. I'm carrying a pot de crème to my deuce but am no longer moving. It feels like everyone in the dining room has stopped breathing. Even Dana behind the bar now stops stirring the whiskey she's poured into her coffee.

The rest of the Kroks come in at the chorus: 'You take the high road and I'll take the low road' but quietly, a mere rumble to the boy's high bright reed. The boy sings three more verses and the last chorus himself.

For me and my true love will never meet again
By the bonnie bonnie banks of Loch Lomond.

When he stops the silence is long and complete. Then, a tor-rent of applause. The Kroks know this is their showstopper. They wave goodbye and jog out the door.

The dining room remains quiet. I carry my dessert the rest of the way, and my two ladies at 9 are patting their eyes. After I put down the plate and two spoons, I wipe mine, too. Five minutes later the diners have rebounded with more volume and demands than before.

I can't seem to recover. The sound keeps playing in my head. I try to hide in the walk-in but the line cooks have begun their breakdown and keep coming in. I spend the rest of the shift, when I'm not serving, crouched on the floor beside the linen cabinet near the wait station, pretending to straighten the piles of tablecloths and napkins.

When it's finally over and I get out of the building, I unlock my bike but don't get on it. I don't want to get home too soon. I don't want to lie in bed churned up like this. I walk my bike to the river.

The students are returning. For the past two days the streets have been clogged with double-parked station wag-ons piled high with plastic milk crates and comforters. Now they walk in packs in the center of the road, yell to other packs at doorways of bars. Music spills from open dorm windows. The path along the river is busy, too, full of freshmen with nowhere to go yet. I move slowly, my bike wheels ticking.

I pass runners, walkers, and bikers. Two dudes with headbands throw a Frisbee low across the grass. A group of girls lies on the ground and looks up at the moon, which is nearly full. I used to have this path all to myself at this time of night. I'm already nostalgic for summer.

And I'll be in Scotland before ye.

A woman runs by me, sweatshirt hood up, fists clenched. We catch eyes just before she passes. Help, we seem to be saying to each other.

After the footbridge, the people thin out. I look for the clusters of geese, but they're gone. Have they started south already?

I find them just before the next bridge, a wide roiling mass of them, snorting and snuffling like pigs. They're down the embankment in the weeds at the river's edge. Some are half in the water, wings slapping the surface. Others are pecking the ground. I move closer and a few heads lift, hoping for food. I don't have anything for them, but it's the perfect place to sing loudly about bonnie banks and bonnie braes, whatever a brae is, and I do. More heads lift. My mother told me once that I had a beautiful voice. I was singing along with Olivia Newton-John in the car, and I had been trying to get her to say that. I wasn't just absentmindedly singing. I'd been going for the compliment. My voice is nothing special, but when your mother tells you something about yourself, even if you've coaxed it out of her, it's hard not to always believe it.

I sing to the geese. And I feel her. It's different from remembering her or yearning for her. I feel her near me. I don't know if she is the geese or the river or the sky or the moon. I don't know if she is outside of me or inside of me, but she is here. I feel her love for me. I feel my love reach her. A brief, easy exchange.

I finish the song and push my bike back up the embankment. A few geese watch, their heads above the rest. Their necks look navy in the moonlight, their chinstraps pale blue.

A few mornings later I get hit by a car. I was giving myself a pep talk while walking the dog. I'd had a few bad days of writing, and I was tempted to go back a chapter to fix it, but I could not. I just needed to move forward, get to the end. Painters, I told myself, though I know nothing about painting, don't start at one side of the canvas and work meticulously across to the other side. They create an underpainting, a base of shape, of light and dark. They find the composition slowly, layer after layer. This was only my first layer, I told myself as we turned the corner, the dog pulling toward something ahead, his nails loud on the sidewalk. It's not supposed to be good or complete. It's okay that it feels like a liquid not a solid, a vast and spreading goo I can't manage, I told myself. It's okay that I'm not sure what's next, that it might be something unexpected. I need to trust—the leash snaps out of my hand and the dog bolts across the street after a squirrel and I bolt after him and slam into a silver sedan.

I find myself on the ground a few feet away from where I was. It all probably looks a lot worse than it is. The car stops immediately and a woman comes flying out saying 'sorry, sorry, sorry' in a Caribbean accent and lifts me up and holds me in her arms. Someone else brings the dog back. I'm crying

94

but not because I feel any pain. My hip and wrist are a little sore, but that's it.

'I will take you right this minute to hospital,' she says.

But I can't go to the hospital and am relieved I don't need to. She insists, just to make sure, she says. Sometimes there are injuries inside the body. I have to explain I can't afford it.

'I will pay! Of course I will pay!'

When I tell her that without insurance X-rays will cost hundreds of dollars, she grows frightened and gets back in her car.

At work the wrist gets sorer, and by the end of the night the busboy is carrying most of my food. It doesn't feel broken, though. I got lucky. If the accident had been any worse, the cost would have sunk me.

When Liz and Pat Doyle come back a few nights later and tell me about a job, a real job with health benefits, I'm more receptive than I would have been before the accident.

'I thought of you because your mum helped get this organization off the ground,' Liz says. 'And it's a writing job. They need a writer.' She hands me a card: LYNN FLORENCE MATHERS. FAMILIES IN NEED. 'Lynn is a character. You'll love her.'

Muriel makes me wear pantyhose and a pair of her beige pumps to the interview. I blend in with the women I pass on Boylston Street, but I feel like a freak.

Lynn didn't know my mother, but she's the type of person my mother loved: quick, outspoken, a thin but charming layer of femininity covering a masculine confidence and drive.

'Sit, sit,' she says, directing me to a green padded chair. She sinks into the armchair behind her desk. I slide my resume toward her. She scans it and passes it back. 'You're thoroughly overqualified. Hablas español?'

'Sí. Viví dos años a Barcelona con mi novio Paco que era un profesor de Catalan pero me hizo loca y tuve—'

'Whoa. Okay. You lost me back at Barcelona.' She exaggerates the theta.

She gives me a W-9 form and tells me about their health insurance—a gold policy, she says—and other benefits.

Muriel told me I should ask about the 'mission' of the organization, so I do.

'Rich people's unwanted crap transported to poor families who are desperate for it.' She pulls out three blank pieces of paper from her drawer. 'This is just pro forma. I don't know what a master's in creative writing means exactly, but I'm sure you can write circles around all of us here.' She pairs the papers with an index card and stands up. 'Mr. and Mrs. Richard Totman of Weston have donated an old refrigerator that went to a home in Roxbury. I'd like you to write a brief thank-you to them.'

I follow her down the hallway to a windowless room with a chair, desk, and typewriter. 'Just bring it to me when you're done.' She shuts the door behind her.

I look at the card. Both the organization's address and the Totmans' address are on it. I don't know where to put the addresses on a formal business letter. I strain to think of all the business letters I've gotten, the kinder ones before my debts were turned over to collection agencies. I make

96

my best guess and start in. The typewriter's electric, and it takes me a while to figure out how to turn it on. It has one of those balls in the middle with all the letters on it. The keys are sensitive. I go through the first two sheets of paper quickly because it keeps typing letters I didn't mean to touch. I'm careful with the last sheet and manage to get both addresses on without errors, one above the other on the left side of the paper. No idea if that's right. I begin:

Dear Mr. and Mrs. Totman,

Or should I have written 'Mr. and Mrs. Richard Totman'? My stepmother always got mad at me when I addressed a letter to her as Mrs. Ann Peabody instead of Mrs. Robert Peabody. But it's too late.

Thank you very much for your donation of the refrigerator.

I don't know what to say after that. Something about the family in Roxbury. *You have made a lovely family in Roxbury very happy?* Is that true? Already used 'very' above. *It has been installed in the house of a family in need in Roxbury?* Three 'ins' in one sentence. *It was very generous of you?* 'Very' again. My pinky touches a key and six semicolons shoot out onto the page. Fuck. I scan the room for Wite-Out. Nothing. The desk has one thin drawer below the surface. No Wite-Out, but a small stack of white paper. I yank the sheet out of the machine and begin again.

97

It takes me eight drafts and forty-five minutes. Lynn is on the phone when I emerge from the room. She asks me with her eyes what happened and I don't know how to mime the answer and she doesn't signal for me to wait. I set the letter on her desk and leave.

I feel like kissing every step of the staircase as I climb up to the restaurant that night in my comfy black sneakers. I never have to go back to that office on Boylston Street again and sit in uncomfortable clothes and type in a windowless room. I get to move and talk and laugh and eat good food for free. And my mornings, my precious mornings, are saved.

Victor Silva, who recently told me he writes poetry and essays, comes in late in his big black cape and overhears me talking to Harry about the interview.

'Why on God's green earth would you ever think about a *desk job*?'

'Financial security. Health insurance. Fingers that doesn't smell like aioli.'

He bunches my fingers in his hands like a bouquet. 'But I love the smell of your aioli-scented digits,' he says in his wife's Brazilian accent, then, in his best Bard: '"Universal plodding poisons up the nimble spirits in the arteries."' Then back in his own voice: 'You know they have a health plan here.'

'What?'

'It's not bad. We use it. Bia's plan at Polaroid is crap.'

'Are you serious?'

98

'Would I lie to your wounded fawn face?' He goes off with his two pots of tea in long strides.

'He has kind of an asexual writer thing for you, doesn't he?'

'Is that what it is?'

I go to see Marcus about the health insurance. It's a Cambridge Pilgrim plan, and the deduction is manageable.

'Why didn't you tell me about this when you hired me?'

'I don't know. Maybe it was because you looked like Mommy and Daddy took care of all those messy details.'

'Screw you. My mother's dead, and my father's a perv. Put me on that fucking plan.'

Iris is a crude place, but it was better than writing thank-you letters to rich people in Weston.

Three mornings later, after the dog walk but before my cereal and cup of tea, in the middle of my writing morning, in what I believe is the middle of a paragraph, I finish a sentence. I lift my pencil a few inches from the page and read it. It's the last sentence of the book. I can't think of another. That's it. I have my underpainting.

B runch that Sunday is a zoo. It's raining, the deck is closed, and we have to haul a few extra tables downstairs and cram them in the club bar. We're worn out before we open. Harry met a Harvard design student that week, and they've gone off to the deCordova museum for the day. The Twisted Sister is hungover and storms up and down the stairs barking orders as if they are the only people lifting a finger, while Mary Hand and I quietly cloth, set, and flower every table. Yasmin is sick, and Stefano, the on-call, isn't picking up. We keep returning to the reservation book, hoping that the numbers have gone down since we last looked.

People arrive all at once, hungry and cranky. Our clientele are people who don't deny themselves much of anything, but on Sunday mornings they've often foregone all pleasures, and not just the Catholics who can't eat before receiving the host. Sometimes they have even waited to have their first cup of coffee. They arrive at Iris ravenous and jonesing for caffeine.

Brunch also means working with Clark, the brunch chef. For my first few shifts with him I thought he was kind like Thomas. He gave me the extra Romanesco my customer wanted for her crab cakes and replaced an overcooked sirloin without complaint. He said my long neck reminded him of the Road Runner and *beep-beeped* at me when I came in for my orders. At the end of a bad brunch last month, when I'd dropped a benedict and forgotten a niçoise and my body was buzzing like a hive, he found me on a milk crate in the walk-in and when I got up to leave he blocked my way. He touched my hair and breathed all over me. He reeked of the tequila in his Mexican coffees.

'You probably suck dick better than you wait tables.' He grinned, and I could tell this line had actually worked in the past.

'Nope,' I said. 'I don't,' and I ducked under his arm and shoved up the big handle to get out of there.

I came in early the next day to tell Marcus what happened.

He laughed. 'Jesus, Casey. You came in here so fucking serious I thought you were going to tell me you killed someone. He was *teasing* you. Clark has no trouble getting his dick sucked, believe me.'

Later I heard him and Clark laughing hard in the kitchen.

Clark has been punishing me ever since.

I'm slammed out of the gate. Three families of five within fifteen minutes downstairs and two deuces up top, while Dana and Tony share a party of twelve.

Fabiana seats me another three-top. 'You're a sadist,' I whisper to her as I pass by with a tray of samosas and Bloody Marys.

'The rest of us are still wasted from last night. You're taking one for the team.'

Two small boys at the new three-top are looking right at me. Children suffer the most at brunch. Their faces could be used for UNICEF posters. I can't get to them, though. I have to drop the main courses at one of my five-tops downstairs. We aren't allowed to use trays for food, only the small red lacquered ones for drinks. The plates have been sitting in the window under the heat lamp long enough to get hot, but I don't have time to find a cloth. I load up four along one arm and grab the last in my left hand, kick open the kitchen door, and run directly into one of the little boys. Two omelets slide across their plates but stop right at the edge.

''Scuse me, miss,' he says. He's wearing a red bow tie and an orange-and-white-checked shirt. His burly hair has been combed down and is still damp. He's six, maybe seven. 'It's my dad's birthday.' He thrusts out a wad of cash at me. 'Can I pay for our food?'

'You may. But after I take your order. After we know how much it will cost.' The plates are burning the inside of my right arm.

His mouth twists. He's only practiced these words. He doesn't have any more.

'Here.' I put down the plate in my left hand on the counter of the wait station. 'I'll take this now. And if there's change I'll give it back to you. I won't bring you a check. Does that sound okay?'

He nods, hands me the money, and makes a fast but indirect retreat back to his table.

102

Down in the club bar, the family asks for ketchup, extra Caesar dressing, an Arnold Palmer, and a glass of grigio, but when I get upstairs I can't breeze past the boys in bow ties again. I sidestep Mary Hand dropping salads at her eight and slide to a halt at their table.

The boys look up from their menus at the same time. The father does not look up. But he's familiar. The father is Oscar Kolton.

'How are you this morning?' I say, angling my head to the boys on my right, hoping I can get their drink order before my blush has reached full force.

Waiting on writers is my undoing. Jayne Anne Phillips came in a few weeks ago, and my face flamed up every time I went to the table. Her collection *Black Tickets* is like a prayer book to me. When she and her two friends ordered tea, the cups rattled on their saucers as I set them down. I'll have to get Mary Hand to take over Oscar Kolton's table.

'Fine,' the older boy, the one who gave me the money, says.

'Hot chocolate, hot coffee, hot tea?'

'Hot chocolate? In the summer?' the smaller boy says.

'It's not summer. It's autumn,' his brother says, pronouncing the *n*.

'Sorry,' I say. 'I used to work at this ski resort in New Mexico, and it just comes out like that sometimes: hot chocolate, hot coffee, hot tea.' First comes the blushing, then the babbling. 'I could bring it cold if you like.'

'No chocolate,' Oscar says, still not looking up, thank God. 'Coffee for me. Black.'

'And for you two?'

Silence. Of course they want the chocolate.

'They'll both have orange juice,' Oscar mumbles, flipping over the menu to find it blank and turning it back over with a frown.

Mary Hand gets a six so I can't pass them off on her. I bring my downstairs table their drinks and condiments, then come back up for the OJs and the coffee. They have set their menus in a neat stack at the end of the table. Without menus they have nowhere to look. I place the glasses of juice above the boys' knives and pour the coffee from one of our silver-plated decanters into Oscar's coffee cup. They watch my hands in silence. Even in the chaos and clatter of brunch, I'm aware of the empty chair, the hole where a mother should be.

Oscar reaches for the cup before I've stopped pouring. He takes a long sip and holds it with both hands in front of him. I think of Silas saying Oscar put his hands behind his back while listening to his story and no one knew what that meant.

'Boys,' he says.

'I would please like the eggs with sausage and a biscuit and side of fruit,' the older one says.

'Scrambled, fried, or poached egg?'

He looks at his father.

'Poached is sort of boiled but not in the shell. You won't like it. It's runny.'

'Scrambled please.'

'And for you?'

The younger boy stares at me, having forgotten his lines. His eyes swell, and he ducks his head into the crook of his arm.

I hazard a guess. 'Blueberry pancakes with a side of bacon?'

He nods fiercely.

'Mind reader,' Oscar says, unimpressed. 'I'll have the coddled eggs.' He hands me the menu. 'Only because I wanted to say the word "coddled."' His eyes flash up briefly—the brightest green of all.

I put a rush on their meal. Mary Hand tells me Oscar and his family used to come in for Mother's Day every year. 'I figured I'd never see them again.'

'It's his birthday. The kids are treating.' I hold up the wad of money.

'Cuteness on a stick,' she says in her drawl, punching in her big order.

Marcus comes around the corner. 'You know that's Oscar Kolton, right?'

'Yes, I know.'

When I bring more coffee each of Oscar's hands are in a thumb wrestle. They all pull apart so I can pour.

'Say thank you, Papa,' the younger one says.

'Thank you.'

They resume their thumb wrestling.

I load up the next five-top order and bring it downstairs, clear plates, refill coffees, pass around the dessert menus, welcome a new deuce they've wedged in near the bathroom. Gory, in whites for a croquet tournament in Lennox in the afternoon, stops by Oscar's table. A few people nearby look on.

'Your bennies are up,' Tony tells me as he whips by with five chocolate bombs up his arm.

'You are *not* a waitress if you do not pick up your food,' Clark says when I come into the kitchen. He snaps a rag at me through the window and it catches on some of the hollandaise, which splatters on my cheek and collar. It burns. I wipe it off and my eyes are watering, but I wheel around with my two benedicts before he can see.

'Ugly-ass bitch,' he says as I kick through the door.

It's a question of displeasing everyone a little bit, spreading around the disappointment evenly. When I get downstairs and drop the meals at table 4, table 6 is ready to order dessert. Oscar and the boys' food will be up now, but a man at 6 can't decide between the bourbon pecan pie and the compote.

Clark is waiting for me at the door. His face is slick with grease and bubbled with sweat. 'I break my fucking balls for your rush, and you can't be bothered to come get it.'

'Welcome to brunch. I've got to be eight places all at once, up and down, and I get stiffed if I'm not. Sometimes I have to leave a plate of pancakes under the heat lamp for three minutes. I'd like to see you try it. All you do is stand back there and crack eggs and shit all over people.'

Angus, my only ally in the kitchen when Thomas isn't cooking, lets out a long whistle.

Clark whips around and tells him to shut the fuck up.

'I'm going to get you fired, you little cunt.'

'I'm not scared of a fucking *brunch* chef,' I say and push past him to get my order.

Out on the floor I tell the boys the plates are really hot and not to touch. I put Oscar's eggs down last. They look overcooked. 'More abused than coddled, I'm afraid. The chef today is an untalented prick.'

The boys stare at me.

Oscar's mouth twitches.

'I mean a jerk. He's a jerk. I'm so sorry.' I look at the boys. 'That is an awful word, and I should not have used it. He's a man with a lot of anger, which he tends to dump on me.'

'He probably has a crush on you,' Oscar says.

It's such a clueless, grandfatherly thing to say that I wonder if he's older than he looks. 'Definitely not,' I say. 'He truly loathes me or whatever I represent to him. I actually think he likes her'—I point to Dana—'but she's after him.' I point to Craig at the bar. 'But I think he's pretty asexual.'

The boys stare at me again. I am not used to children. 'Ketchup?'

'On eggs?' the older boy says.

'There's a whole swath of people who like ketchup on their eggs.'

'Really?' He looks to his dad for confirmation.

'True fact,' I say.

'We are not a part of that swath,' Oscar says.

'Nor am I. Bon profit.' I figure Oscar can handle a little Catalan. I'm eager to get away. I can feel the heat where the hollandaise sauce hit my cheek. And their kindness after Clark's vulgarity is making my throat hurt.

I get the rest of my tables squared away while they eat.

'Is that a smile?' Tony says as we wait at the bar for our drinks and I drag an ice cube over the burns on the inside of my right arm.

'Fuck no. Put your fake glasses on, four eyes.'

'You are smiling, and I have never seen you smile.'

'That's bull.'

'Okay, without Harry around. Harry makes you smile.'

'Harry is very funny.'

'Is he? I think he's an arrogant ass.'

Tony has tried to hit on Harry many times with no success.

'That's just his accent.'

'Those kids are staring at you.'

I look over, and they look down.

Craig hands me my screwdrivers.

'You want to split an apple papillote later?' I say.

'Sure.' Tony says.

I've surprised him. It suddenly seems easy to make people happy.

Once he's had his pancakes and bacon, Oscar's younger boy comes alive.

'Do you like mammals or amphibians?' he asks me.

'Mammals.'

'Cards or board games?'

'Both.'

'You have to choose.'

'Cards.'

I know my desserts are up in the kitchen and that two tables downstairs are waiting for their checks.

'Let her get back to work, Jasper.'

Jasper. He looks just like a Jasper should. Little mushed face with thick lips and long lashes and his father's green eyes.

'Blue or red?'

'Blue.'

'Ms. Murphy or Mr. Perez?'

'Ms. Murphy.'

They laugh, Jasper the hardest.

'Tennis or golf?'

'Tennis. But I don't play either.'

'Then how do you know you like it better?'

'Because I hate golf.'

This seems to upset him. 'Even miniature golf?'

'Mini golf is okay.'

'Our dad is really, really good. No one can beat him.'

'I could.' I don't know why I say that. Apart from it being true.

Both boys protest. They make so much noise the tables around them turn. 'You could not!'

They look at their father to defend himself. He shrugs. He isn't grinning exactly, but he's pushed his plate away, and his fingers are laced in front of him. I smile, thinking about telling Muriel. I clear their table and leave.

I return with dessert menus. 'I know there was a no-chocolate rule earlier, so dessert might not fly.'

The boys watch their father.

'Dessert will fly.'

They cheer. I pass out the menus. Behind Oscar's chair, I mime sticking a candle into something and blowing it out. His brother nods discreetly, but Jasper squeals. Oscar turns around and I look away. When he turns back I wink at the boys.

Jasper orders the basil-lavender crème brûlée, his brother chooses the Tahitian coppa, and Oscar goes with the cookie medallions. Cookies are not conducive to candles so I go to the pastry chef, Helene, in her far alcove of the kitchen. It's a different land back here. She plays classical music. Her team wears white caps, not bandanas, and their white aprons are clean save small artistic smears of chocolate and raspberry.

Mary Hand's back there loading herself with desserts. 'Johnny-on-the-spot,' she says and vanishes.

Helene bends over a row of pear compotes, placing a blackberry in the center of each one.

I point to the small machine that's printing out my order. 'Could I somehow get a candle or two on that cookie plate?'

She nods. I wait.

Igor tears the ticket off slowly and places it beside the others. He always looks like a drawing to me, with his tiny upturned nose and long fingers. He moves like a dancer. He must be twenty years younger than Helene, but they've been together since the restaurant opened in the early eighties.

Their small walk-in has a glass door and inside it looks like a jewelry shop with its meringues and feuilletines, caramel tuiles and white chocolate butterflies. Igor pulls out a

crème brûlée, places it on a doilied plate, and torches the top
with a blue flame until the sugar glows and liquefies. Next he
pulls a plate off the shelf and with a big pastry bag squeezes
out a thick spiraled cone of mocha cream in the center. He
slides this plate to Helene at the same time that she slides
John's coppa to him. She arranges three cookies around the
mocha cream and sticks a tall sparkler in the cream while he
drops glazed raspberries on both the sundae and the crème
brûlée. She leans to her right so he can light the tip of the
sparkler with the torch, and they both wipe down the steel
counter as soon as I lift the plates. I leave their Chopin
nocturnes, pass through Zeppelin—'I'm gonna give you
my love,' Clark is screaming at the steaks on the grill—and
emerge into Craig's Sinatra mix in the dining room.

I approach Oscar from behind, so the boys can watch.
John keeps his smile trimmed, but when Jasper sees the sparks
flying in all directions he starts giggling and pounding his feet.

'Oh no,' Oscar says, turning. 'No singing. Please no
singing,' he says, but his boys and I start and the people
beside them and then the two Kroks at table 4 who were
eating with their parents and Tony and Craig and Gory and
pretty much everyone else joins in. Oscar glowers at me,
and I can't tell if his kids are singing or laughing too hard.
Afterward everyone claps and Oscar tries to blow out the
sparkler but has to wait till it blazes down the stick.

'That was a dirty trick,' he says.

'Are you mad, Papa?'

'I'm not mad at either of *you*.'

'Don't be mad, Papa, not at anyone.'

Oscar reaches over and touches John's sleeve. 'Oh sweetie, I'm not mad. I was kidding. This is the best birthday ever.'

Jasper is whacking at the shellac of burnt sugar with a spoon.

'I love doing that,' I tell him. 'It's like ice, even though it's the opposite. Made from heat not cold.'

'Yeah,' he says, lifting out a jagged shard and trying to look at me through it.

I realize I'm just standing there, hovering. 'Can I get you all anything else?' I say, back in my waitress voice. It seems to startle all three of them. They shake their heads.

I stay in the wait station, drying the rack of clean glasses Alejandro brought out, embarrassed that I hovered. I have a problem with that sometimes, getting attached. Other people's families are a weakness of mine.

When Mary Hand's big table leaves I help her clear it. Oscar signals for the check. I print it out but put it in my pocket. It was $87.50. I pull out the wad of cash John gave me. It's mostly ones: $24. Two of the tables in the club bar tipped me in cash so I can cover it easily.

I bring over one of our small check trays with three chocolate mints. 'Your sons paid in advance. Happy birthday.'

'What?' he says, but I'm already walking away.

I watch him haggle with them. The boys are grinning. Jasper's legs are swinging below the table. Oscar stands and John stands and Jasper stays in his chair. His brother pokes him, and he tries to poke back and misses. Oscar signals for John to step away, and he bends down and scoops Jasper up and

112

drapes him on his shoulder as easily as cloth. Oscar turns and looks toward the wait station. I'm over near the far windows, working on roll-ups, and he doesn't turn far enough to see me. Then they're gone.

I clear the table: the martini glass scraped clean, the burnt-down sparkler laid among cookie crumbs, the basil-lavender crème brûlée nearly perfectly intact, minus its sheet of sugar ice. Iván, the brunch busboy, comes and helps me take away everything else, the salt and pepper and sugars and vase of flowers. We pull off the pink top cloth so that only the white one remains. I bring the dishes to Alejandro, and when I come back out Mary Hand says, 'Looks like Marcus's having a little dustup with your fellow.' *A dustup down at the gazebo.* I feel the memory fall through my body like a stone.

Oscar's back in the doorway, pointing at me. Marcus is clearly trying to intervene, but Oscar pats him on the arm and moves past him. I meet him halfway. All the tables are gone now and the room is stripped and Craig has left and no music is playing. I can hear his boys thumping on the stairs below. He's breathing heavily through his nose. I would have thought something awful had happened, except I know it's just about the money.

'Hey,' he says, out of breath. It feels like we're alone in a narrow corridor instead of an enormous dining room. He stands close and plunges his hands deep in pockets, bunching up his shoulders. He looks younger without his kids, nearly boyish. 'So, they pulled a fast one on you, didn't they?'

'They didn't mean to.'

'I'm not so sure. John's pretty good at math.'

'The prices are in tiny font, way over to the side. No dollar signs. He might not have seen or understood.'

He nods reluctantly. 'And you let him get away with it.'

'He was wearing a bow tie.'

He looks at his feet, fighting a grin. He has on beat-up hiking boots with red laces. He lifts his eyes up to me but not his head, and his eyes are even greener now because light from the deck is coming in over my shoulder. 'I suppose I'd rather think of him as unperceptive than unethical. At any rate, I owe you sixty-three fifty, plus tip.'

'I already cashed out.'

He holds out a stack of twenties, fresh from the ATM. 'You have to take it.'

I shake my head. 'Happy birthday.'

'I'm not leaving till you take it.'

I step back. 'Your boys wanted to treat you. I just helped them out a bit. I've got to get back to my side work.'

'Then I'm just going to leave it right here.' He drops the bills on the floor. They fan out. Four twenties.

'I'm not picking that up.' I turn around and walk through the wait station into the kitchen.

After a while Marcus finds me. He's holding a pink envelope with a white iris in the corner.

'Just let the customers pay for their own meals, okay? Even if they look like Kevin Costner.'

Kevin Costner? Oscar Kolton was a lot better looking than Kevin Costner.

He gives me the envelope.

In small, unslanted print it says:

Casey
(interesting name)

I don't open it. I put it in my apron pocket and finish my side work.

Out on the street, daylight surprises me. Somehow between the top floor and the bottom I forgot I worked brunch, not dinner. The Square is quiet. I head to the river on foot. My dinner shift starts in less than an hour. I'm still in my uniform. The sun has come out and burned off most of the rain. I feel the sun on my back, the warmed air on my arms. I walk up the Larz Anderson Bridge, thinking of Faulkner and Quentin Compson, remembering Quentin as I would an old love, with a swollen heart, Quentin who buckled under the weight of Southern sins, who cracked the crystal on the corner of the dresser and twisted the hands off his grandfather's watch his last morning and, later in the afternoon, cleaned his hat with a brush before he left his Harvard dorm room to kill himself.

Halfway across the river I hoist myself on the wide parapet, swing my legs over the edge, and look down in the water for Quentin's body. How does a man in Mississippi in the 1920s create a character who feels more alive to a waitress in 1997, remembered with more tenderness, than most of the boys she's ever known? How do you create a character like that? The concrete is warm. A few people walk by on the sidewalk behind me. A quick shove and I'd go down like Quentin. But I wouldn't die. The drop isn't more than twenty feet, either bank an easy swim. Quentin tied flat irons to his ankles in order to drown.

I open the envelope. Four twenties and a note. I was hoping for a note.

> Casey,
> A lot of creeps have probably asked you to play miniature golf with them. ███████ John and Jasper are not creeps so that's 2 out of 3. They begged me all the way down the stairs to ask you. So I'm asking. 538-9771. I'll call you here at Iris in a few days. ██████ We like King Putt out on Route 12. Lots of mummies and asps.
>
> Oscar K.

I stay on the bridge for the time I have left. I read Oscar's note once more. The bow of a crew shell appears below my feet and lurches out of the bridge in two strong, synchronized pulls. They are women, eight of them, facing backward, faces wrenched to snarls, groaning in rhythm each time they heave with their whole bodies their one oar through the water, which seems from this angle to have the resistance of cement. In the brief pause between groans, as they slide back, the coxswain, a peanut in a baseball cap tucked down in the stern, speaks through a headset: 'Build in two . . . build in one . . . on this one: Go!' And the boat jerks forward and the strokes become fiercer and their sounds disappear, and they become smaller and smaller until they slide under the Weeks Bridge and vanish.

I take out Oscar's letter again. I like the sentence: 'So I'm asking.' I like thinking of him in Marcus's office, crossing out words, not wanting to ask for another piece of the pink Iris stationery, like me writing to Mr. and Mrs. Richard Totman of Weston. It gives me pleasure that a writer of three books would labor even a little over a note to a brunch waitress. He didn't cross out his phone number as heavily as in the other places. I vowed never to hit a golf ball again, but I might have to make an exception for him and those little boys.

On my third birthday my father gave me a set of plastic clubs in a plaid golf bag. There was a cup you had to hit the ball into and my father put it on the rug a few feet away and showed me how to swing and I swung and it went in. My father says I didn't open any of my other presents, that I played with that set till bedtime. My mother says my father forced me to play with that set until bedtime. By the time I was fully conscious, my life outside of school was golf—at four I was playing in local eight and unders, and by six we were traveling to national tournaments. Like many parents, my father wanted to give me what he didn't get, then he wanted me to get what he couldn't reach.

Caleb says he was never resentful of all the time my father spent on me. He says before I came along my father was always dragging him to the driving range. He does a good imitation of our father's face when Caleb once missed the ball seventeen times in a row. It was pure relief when I took his place and excelled. Those were good years, he says. Until my father's friend Stu recommended an all-boys boarding school in Virginia for Caleb, to bring out the man in him. My mother fought the idea, but Caleb left when I was eight.

I used to think it was my golf that made my parents unhappy, that it was the source of their resentment. My mother said he was hijacking my childhood with his own obsession; my father said she was afraid of my success because it didn't fit into her proletariat fantasy of raising revolutionaries.

We were in Florida for the Palm Beach Junior Invitational when my mother packed her things and drove away with Javier. I hadn't played particularly well, but one of my biggest competitors got a stomach flu and the other was spooked by an alligator in the waters of the seventh hole and I'd won. On the plane home my father got me laughing so hard when he held up the safety instructions to his face and imitated the alligator's eyes rising out of the water. My mother had left on a few lights, so we didn't get it at first. It wasn't until we heard the message on our answering machine, the old kind with a miniature cassette tape inside it. My father swiped at her voice and the machine went flying against the wall before she'd finished speaking. The next day I went back to hear the rest but the Play button wouldn't stay down.

Later my mother said it wasn't falling in love with Javier that broke them apart. She said that those last few years with him were the easiest, actually. Javi made her happy, and it infected every part of her life, even her marriage. It was when he started to die that it became impossible. She couldn't share her despair with my father as she had shared her happiness.

There were a few weeks of casseroles and lasagnas in our fridge, men in our living room pouring him drinks. When that ended, he fell apart a little, weeping over the TV dinners I'd heated up. I was in ninth grade then, my first year at the high school where he worked. He taught two math classes and coached, depending on the season, boys' football, basketball, and baseball. The golf with me was after school sports and on weekends. With my mother gone, he added more practice and tournament hours to my schedule, and we started to visit colleges, too, that year, so I could meet with coaches and play a few rounds with the team. Sometimes I could hear him talking to a coach, telling him the whole story of his wife running away with a dying priest, though Javi was just an agnostic folk singer. But it made my father's story better. I feared he was ruining my chances with his sob story, but by the fall of sophomore year, I'd been promised a full ride at Duke.

That year some of his varsity players started coming over to the house at night, seniors and juniors who intimidated me. My father gave them beers and they watched sports on TV and from my room I heard the rise and fall of their cheers and groans. At school I would occasionally go down to my father's office in the basement and do my homework on his couch during a free period, but now they were hanging out there, that posse of them with their deep voices and sardonic jokes. Other times, times I knew he wasn't teaching or coaching, his office door would be locked, which he'd never done before, no sound within. Sometimes at the golf course after school he was absentminded and lethargic, losing count of my strokes or dragging behind when he used to rush ahead, and I wondered if he was getting high with those boys at school.

A few weeks before my mother came back East, I went down to my father's office one afternoon when I wasn't feeling well. I'd gotten out of basketball practice and needed a place to lie down. His door was shut but not locked. It was dim, and I did not turn on the lights. I lay on the couch, sank into the seam. It was too loud to sleep. The girls' locker room was next door—the varsity was going out and the JV and thirds were coming back in—and there was a lot of yelling and splashing and slamming of metal doors. I assumed my father was already in the gym with his team. There were voices nearby, low laughter. After a few minutes I heard the door of the storage closet behind the couch open. Three boys went straight out the office door, already dressed for practice. My father came out last. He cleared his throat, buckled his belt, and left the room. They all moved quickly. They didn't see me. I heard them walk down the hallway and push through the heavy door into the gym. I got up and went into the closet. There were pinpricks of light on the far side. Several holes had been drilled in the wall, small openings, each with an excellent view of the girls.

After my mother returned I never spent another night at my father's house. I showed the athletic director the holes in the wall of the locker room, and that spring my father announced his early retirement. I stopped playing in tournaments, but Duke kept their word and I enrolled there, though I lost the scholarship when I quit the team after the first week. I knew my father wouldn't help out with the tuition if I wasn't playing golf, so I got a job at a barbeque restaurant and took out the first of many loans that have created the compounding debt that trails me now. But I never could go back to golf. Just holding a club made me feel ill.

I n the mail I receive a Cambridge Pilgrim insurance card. It has a big black Pilgrim hat with a white buckle for its logo. I draw a picture of it and send it to Caleb. He lived in Boston for a few years after college and thought it was funny how much mileage local businesses get out of the Pilgrims, those skinflint killjoys. Below the drawing I write: 'Soon I'm going to be as healthy as a Pilgrim! Average lifespan: thirty-four years.'

I'm proud of this card, though, and relieved that I can now afford to get a few things checked out. I have a mole that's changed hue and my period is a lot heavier and more painful than it used to be. I haven't seen a doctor in five years, since grad school when I last had coverage.

They make me see a GP first, to get the referrals.

Everything is pointy. When he looks in my eyes he says my eyeballs are pointy. And when he looks in my ears he says the bend in my ear canal is pointy.

'I feel like a badly drawn cartoon,' I tell Harry afterward.

Next is the dermatologist who has skin the color of quartz, without a freckle or a mole. I don't understand how he has led such a sunless life. This makes me ashamed of my skin, which I burned and blistered religiously in the summers of high school, convinced that a tan would get me a boyfriend in the fall, which it never did. Golf didn't help, either, all that time beneath a strong sun in Georgia or California in sleeveless shirts and no visor. I hated visors.

I thought I could just show him the mole on my arm, but he has me lie on my stomach beneath a series of hot bright lamps. He lifts the blue johnnie to my neck. He does not conceal his disapproval. He huffs and clucks and tsks. He picks at something on my shoulder blade and brings his magnifying cylinder down on it. He pokes at it again and moves on, down my back and legs, picking and scraping all the way. He has me roll over. He uncovers me again. It goes on for a long time, his examination of the front side. He puts his tool on my forehead, temple, chest, arms. He zooms right in on the weird mole and spends a while with it, then moves to my stomach and leg, taking great interest in my calves and even a big toe.

He gives me a lecture about SPFs and how I could never go out in the sun unprotected again. He tells me I should have listened to my mother when I was younger. I don't tell him that my mother taught me everything I knew about frying my skin with baby oil and tinfoil reflection.

He says he needs to biopsy three moles and steps into the hallway to signal to his assistant.

'Today?' I ask when he comes back in.

But he is already laying scalpels on a tray.

I leave the office with three gouges, stitched up with stiff black wire. He'll have the results by Friday, he tells me.

* * *

123

At the gynecologist, lying on the table is painful because two of the gouges are on my back. The doctor was listed on the printout as Fran Hubert, who I assumed would be a woman, but it was a typo. His name is Frank. Unsurprisingly, the Pilgrims don't have many female doctors to choose from.

The doctor inserts the speculum slathered with a cold gel. He has a shiny bald head with big discolored moles that Dr. Dermatologist would not believe.

'So, you're a writer.' He widens the speculum by turning some knob and it feels like a sudden period cramp. He peers in. I feel like a car being jacked up for a tire change. 'What've you published?'

'Nothing really. A short story in a small magazine a few years ago.'

He's not really listening. He unwraps a long Q-tip and inserts it. 'You have a pointy cervix.'

Fucking Pilgrims.

He pulls the Q-tip out and puts it in a plastic tube. 'So, you gonna write the Great American Novel?'

I'm tired of that question. 'You gonna cure ovarian cancer?'

He pulls the speculum out of me, and my insides deflate.

He sits back in his round swivel chair and looks me in the eye for the first time. 'Touché.'

He tells me I'll get the result of the pap in a few days. I forget to mention the heavy menstrual bleeding and the pain.

After dinner setup at Iris, Tony calls in an order to China Dragon, and Harry and I go to get it. They're playing Duran

Duran while we wait at the register and we do a little dancing and he spins me around and I wince and tell him about
the wounds on my shoulder, my back, my leg.

'You poor love,' he says and gives me a gentle hug.

We belt out 'My Name Is Rio' on the way back, and
when we get to the top of the stairs Marcus hands me a note
that says: 'Oscar called.' No number. I've left his note back
at home.

'Did he say he'd call again?'

'No.'

I head into the dining room, and Marcus calls me back.
For some reason I think he's going to tell me something more
about Oscar, what he said or maybe what he's like, tell me
to stay away or go for it. Instead he says, 'Whatever is going
on under there needs to be covered up. It's disgusting. You
are officially on probation for grooming.'

In the wait station Harry has a look and explains that
the Vaseline I have to put on my gouges has made greasy
blotches on the back of my shirt through which you can
see two bloody wounds and their black stitches. The dermatologist told me I could not cover them with Band-Aids,
so we rig up a napkin under my shirt with some staples and
eat our Chinese out on the deck. It's only four thirty and
the sun is high and warm, but you can tell it's weakening,
pulling away from us. We used to have to find shade out
here at this hour.

Thomas opens the French doors. 'Casey, line two.'

Harry trills, and Tony says, 'What?' And Harry says,
'She's got a man chasing her.' And I say, 'No, I don't,' and try

125

to slow down my steps to the door. And Tony says, 'I bet she has a hundred men chasing her.' He's a different guy without Dana around.

I pick up the phone at the bar.

It's Dr. Dermatologist. Two of the three moles are precancerous. The other is a squamous cell carcinoma, and while he's gotten all of it, it would be best to come in for some further scraping just to be sure. This was the kind of skin cancer, he says, that he usually finds on much older people. He repeats that I cannot expose my skin to the sun without protection again. He says, 'I know you are drunk on youth and immortality, but this is how you die.'

I tell Harry, and he gives me another careful hug. And later an old man at Harry's corner deuce complains about his breezy manner and Harry tells him he is just drunk on youth and immortality. The man reports this to Marcus on the way out, and now Harry is on probation, too.

The next day I decide to call Oscar. I work a double and carry his letter with his number around in my apron, but I never get up the nerve during lunch to do it. During my break I go to Bob Slate's for a ream of printer paper—I'd typed the last chapter into the computer that morning and was ready to print out the whole thing—and when I get back Marcus tells me Oscar called.

Harry comes in for the dinner shift and tosses out my coffee and gets Craig to pour me a glass of red wine. 'You drink this, then you call.' But alcohol doesn't have that effect on me. It makes me tired then sad then puking.

While I'm drinking, the phone rings. If you are listening for it, the phone is always ringing at Iris. People call day and night for reservations. Sometimes they're looking for a table for that night. Sometimes it's for a year from now. People are crazy in their planning. How do they know where they will be living next year or if they will even be alive? I'm too superstitious to make plans like that. I've never owned a planner or datebook. I keep everything in my head.

'Marky Marcus at eleven o'clock,' Harry says.

I slide the glass behind the computer.

'Casey. Phone. *Again.*'

I take it on the pastry phone. There's just Helene there, spooning mousse into adorable *pots*.

My heart gallops. The wine hasn't helped.

It's Dr. Gynecologist, who explains that I have severe dysplasia on my cervix and that I have to come in for some scraping of the area. He says his nurse will call in the morning with an appointment time.

I go back to the wait station. 'What's with all the scraping?'

'If you weren't so pointy,' Harry says.

'I feel like a block of cheese.' I pick up the water jug to bring it to the table Fabiana is seating me. 'Health insurance sucks.'

After that I never have a moment to call Oscar until it's way too late to call a man with two small children.

I get home near midnight, exhausted, skin humming. I take off my work clothes, shower, reapply the Vaseline to my mole holes. The black wires make them look like spiders. My phone rings. I'm out of doctors.

'Someone named Harry with a smooth and flirty accent gave me your home number,' he says. 'And he insisted
it wasn't too late to call. And'—he says when I don't say
anything because my throat is burning at what a good friend
Harry is to me—'he seemed to know something about me,
which I took to be a good sign. You there?'

'I'm here,' I say, pulling it together.

'Good. My mother has told me that I mustn't go chum-
ming for women with my children and it's too soon for mini
golf. I'm sure this comes as a huge disappointment.'

I'm surprised that it does.

'So I thought perhaps we might take a grown-up walk
in the arboretum on Saturday. You are a grown-up, right?
I mean, you just look youngish. You're not in high school
or anything.'

'Would college be a deal breaker?'

Silence. 'Yes. Yes it would.'

'I'm thirty-one.'

'Thank God.' He sounds truly relieved.

'How old are you?'

Another pause. 'Forty-five.'

Older than I thought.

'Is that a deal breaker?' he says.

'Depends on the deal.'

O scar is waiting at the gate of the arboretum with an unhappy basset hound. The dog reminds me of a toy I had when I was a kid, a plastic dog on a string whose ears went up and down when I dragged him behind me.

I ride past him to a street sign that I can lock my bike to.

'Is that you?' Oscar says. He doesn't look happy about it.

'It's me.' I unwind the lock slowly. I'm not sure I want to be here.

I feel him standing behind me. 'You have hair,' he says. 'It was sort of up before.'

'Restaurant policy.' I shove the two ends of the coil together and flip around the numbers. 'You have a dog.'

'That's Bob. Bob the dog.'

I don't know what to do once my bike is locked, so I squat down and stroke the head of his dog. It's a little greasy. He presses his head up against my hand like a cat.

'We don't have a great relationship. I'll be honest about that,' he says.

'Wanna go romp around, Bob the dog?'

'Bob does not romp.'

'What does Bob do?'

'He malingers.'

I straighten up and run through the entrance pillars and spin around. 'C'mere, Bob!' Bob turns his head but keeps his body firmly facing the street. I get on my haunches again and pound the paved path. 'C'mon, boy!' The dog clenches his nails more firmly into the sidewalk.

Oscar is studying me. He's making decisions already. I can feel this. Between our call and today he talked himself out of me, and now he is coming back around. I squat there and think about how you get trained early on as a woman to perceive how others are perceiving you, at the great expense of what you yourself are feeling about them. Sometimes you mix the two up in a terrible tangle that's hard to unravel.

Bob bolts toward me. Oscar, holding the other end of the leash, gets yanked along. I let Bob snuffle in my ear. I stand, and we start walking.

'So,' Oscar says.

'So.' I look at him. He's not a tall man, and our gaze is nearly level. I'm not used to that.

'Here we are.' His eyes are even lighter today, with dark rims. 'Walking Bob.'

The dog is on the scent of something now, head sunk between his shoulder blades, nose skimming a quarter inch above the asphalt. Oscar examines me as we walk. He's much looser than he was with the kids or at the signing table. He's looking at me with mirth, as if I'm already saying something funny, as if we have a history of little jokes between us.

'Just so you know, I'm a bit scared of trees,' he says.

There are trees everywhere. It's an arboretum. They all have small brass name tags nailed into them. We're in the

maple grove: Korean maple, fullmoon maple, painted maple.
'Is this some kind of exposure therapy?'

'It's the holes in the trees, mostly. One time when I was a kid I was sitting on the limb of an oak and I see this hole and I peer in and next thing I know I'm on the ground. Just bam. I peer in'—he makes his face like Jasper's—'and then I'm staring straight up at the sky and my mother is screaming from the house. She's not running toward me or anything. She's just screaming.'

'What happened?'

'An owl sank his beak into my forehead.' He stops to show me. There's a deep divot just below his hairline.

'Jesus.'

He smiles when I touch it.

We start walking again.

'Casey what?' he says.

'Peabody.'

'Ah. Very quaint,' he says. 'Very Mayflower. Peabody. It's one of those names that happens at the front of your mouth. Peabody.' He says it fast, exaggerating the popping sounds. 'As opposed to Kolton, which happens all in the back.'

I say both names and laugh. He's right.

He tells me he and his sons have a running list of place names like that, words that pop from your lips. He says some of them: Pepperell, Biddeford, Mattapoisett, Cinnabon.

'Surely you don't let them eat Cinnabons.'

'What do you mean?'

I imitate his growl: 'No chocolate! As you put three packs of sugar in your coffee.'

He laughs. 'Who are you? Where did you come from?'

'You've seen me before. Or I've seen you.'

'Where?'

'At your book party. On Avon Hill.'

'This summer?'

I nod.

'You weren't there.'

'I was.'

'I would have noticed, believe me.'

'I was there. Fancy house. Mansard roof. You were in the dining room, signing books.'

'Did Iris cater that party?'

'I wasn't working. I was with my friend Muriel.'

'Muriel. Muriel Becker?'

I nod.

'She's a friend of yours?'

'Basically my only friend here. Aside from Harry.'

'Harry from the phone?'

'Uh-huh.'

He squints. 'You and Muriel are friends. Yeah, okay, I can see that. She's a good writer.'

'I know.'

He stops walking. 'Are *you* a writer?'

I suspected this might throw him off. 'I'm a waitress.'

'You're a writer.' He's really not pleased by this. He tips his head back. 'First woman who doesn't make my skin crawl and she's a writer.'

'Guess you have a problem with that.'

'I don't date writers.'

'Who says this is a date?'

'This is a date. This is my first date in a very long time. Please don't say it's not a date.'

Bob chooses this moment to put his hind legs though his front legs and produce a soft tan coil of poop at the base of a Japanese lilac. Oscar pulls out a plastic bag from his pocket. He sticks his hand in it, grabs the pile, turns the bag inside out, and knots it twice. He crosses the path to toss it in a trash can and comes back. 'Is that why you're here? Is that why you were all flirty at the restaurant with me?'

'Flirty? With you? With the grumpy dad who can't make eye contact?'

He smirks very slightly.

'I liked your boys, not you. I wouldn't say I was flirting with them, but their concern for you touched me. John was trying so hard to make it a special day.'

He nods. An off-leash dalmatian runs up to Bob's bum and sniffs and prances off. Oscar wipes his nose with the back of his hand. 'You know then, about their mom.'

'I was trying to make a rough day easier.'

'And that's why you said yes to mini golf, because of them?'

'Them, and your note. With all the cross outs.'

'That guy was standing over my shoulder, reading every word. I couldn't think.' He wipes his nose again.

'You're a bit rusty.'

'I know.' He tries to reach out to me with both arms but Bob resists. He lets go of the leash and the dog stops and sits on his haunches, watching us. Oscar rests his forearms on

133

my shoulders as if he's done it many times before. 'You heard the part about not making my skin crawl, right?'

'I've only dated other writers.' I hook my fingers around his upper arms. He's strong, compact. Our hips are aligned. 'It's never worked out.'

'So I'm just the next in line.'

'A *long* line.'

Some kind of hawk drops from the top of a tree toward us and Oscar flinches. The hawk glides up to another high branch.

'You *are* twitchy around trees.'

'Can I please kiss you before they all attack?'

I nod.

He kisses me, pulls back, and kisses me again. No tongue. 'I've never asked a waitress out before.' Another chaste kiss. 'That's not how I operate.' His lips are softer than they look.

'How do you operate?'

'I was married for eleven years. All my skills are obsolete.'

He picks up Bob's leash, and we start walking again. We turn up the Conifer Path, a narrow, empty lane. I ask how she died. He says cancer and tells me that afterward he was angry for three years. He says there was nothing else. No love, no sadness. Just the anger like a big red alarm going off all day for three years. I tell him my mother died in February. I try to think of how to describe it to him, but nothing comes out. He apologizes for not knowing how that feels, to lose a mother. He says that one of the hardest things has been his boys at ages two and five having to go through something he hasn't. 'When my mother dies, they'll be comforting me,' he says.

We go up a hill and down another path and loop back around to the lilacs.

Oscar stops. 'Here is where we had our first fight.' He marks an X with his shoe. He backs up several yards. 'And here'—he marks another X—'is where we made up.' He walks back to me and takes my hand. 'In the spring when all these lilacs bloom it is magnificent. We'll come back then.'

On my machine:

'Hey, Casey. How are you? I just got back into
town. Just a few minutes ago. Uh. I didn't really
plan out a message. I was just hoping to talk to
you. And see you. Go on that date. I'm at the same
place, 867-8021. I hope things are good with you.
I, well. Catch you later.'

I play it again. The rumbling and the little laugh like
a hiccough in the middle of saying he didn't plan out the
message. I play it once more and hit Erase.

I go in the next week for the cauterization. The doctor and nurse show me a drawing of a cervix on a poster on the wall. It looks like a pink cigarette. The lower end is the opening where a baby would come out. They're planning to light that part on fire.

You have no nerve endings on your cervix, they explain, so you don't need to use a local anesthetic. But there is an awful snapping sound, and soon the room is filled with a smell you want to unsmell immediately and can't. This is their job, I think, smelling burnt cervix.

I meet Muriel at Bartley's after.

'It sounded like a bug zapper. And it stank. Like they were burning hair and leather shoes and salmon roe all together.'

Muriel looks down at her burger. 'You have to stop.'

'I did remember to tell him about my periods and the pain and he said I might be a "candidate" for endometriosis. It affects fertility he said. No treatment, no cure. Which means now I can be terrified equally of getting pregnant and not ever getting pregnant.' I eat a fry. I can't eat my burger. 'How's the writing?'

She shook her head. 'I can't get that damn war to end. Every day I sit down and try to end it and I can't.'

'It's a big war. Two fronts. Not a small task.'

'I think I'm nervous about that scene.'

'You mean the lake scene?'

'Yeah.' Muriel got the idea for the lake scene before anything else. All the other ideas grew around it. 'I'm getting all wobbly about it.'

'You just need to write it out and get it over with.'

'I don't know why I feel this way. It's like performance anxiety or something. What if I can't get it up?'

'Your readers will just spoon you and tell you it doesn't matter in the least and that it happens to everyone.'

'It's the whole reason for the book, this scene.'

'No, it's not. Maybe it once was, but it's not anymore. You have to let that go. It isn't a short story with its one perfect culmination. It's messy.'

'Yeah, I know. A novel is a long story with something wrong with it,' she quotes. It's a line that gets passed around and attributed to a variety of writers.

'Just get them down to the lake, and they'll do what they need to do.'

We always sound confident when we're talking about the other person's book.

The small publishing company she works for is sending her to Rome to a conference. For a while she went back and forth about asking Christian to come with her. She says she finally asked him.

'He said no. He told me on our first date he'd always wanted to go to Italy, and then he says no without even thinking about it.'

'Why?' I don't like the idea of Muriel leaving the country. My stomach gets cold and hollow. People die when they go on trips.

'He said Italy was for romance, for pleasure, not for some corporate retreat. I told him there was nothing corporate about it. It's a series of literary roundtables. He said he didn't want to tag along on my work trip. I told him he was being sexist and rigid.'

'He wants it to be special. He travels for work all the time.' Christian is an embedded firmware engineer. I don't know what that means, but he's often away for a part of each week.

'To Detroit and Dallas–Fort Worth.' She waves her hand. 'It's okay. It just makes it clear. I want someone who's supportive and spontaneous, someone who would leap at a chance like that. That's not him, so now I know. How's the rewrite going?'

I've been printing the novel out and going through it, trying to pretend I'm someone else, someone who's just come across it in a bookstore. I make notes all over the manuscript, type the changes into the computer, and print it out again. 'I'm not sure I can really see it anymore.'

'Give it to me.'

'Not yet.'

'Casey, just let me read it.'

I want to. I want her to read it. But she has stacks of manuscripts all over her apartment not just from work but from every writer she knows asking for her opinion, and she's too nice to say no.

'You've got to get another set of eyes on it, Case. I'm going to be insulted if you don't show it to me soon.'

'Okay.'

'When?'

'In a week or two.'

'Date?'

'September twenty-fifth.' It sounds like a long time away.

'Next Saturday. Okay.'

The twenty-fifth is next Saturday?

We walk back to her place. I tell her a few more details about my date with Oscar that I forgot at lunch. The gouge in his forehead and the X-marks-the-spot moment.

'It's freaky,' she says. 'It's like you're talking about a totally different person than the one on Wednesday nights.'

We go into a shop she loves. The owner is tall like Muriel and all the clothes in there look good on tall women. The dresses are over a hundred dollars, the shirts, even the soft T-shirts, are over fifty. I can't afford a pair of socks at a place like this. The only nice clothes I have came from my mother. Muriel, flicking through the hangers on the rack, reminds me of my mother. I haven't seen the similarity before. I don't know how Muriel affords clothing like this or her pretty one-bedroom in Porter Square. I don't know how everyone else is getting by, paying their bills and sleeping through the night.

She doesn't try anything on and when we're back on the street, she says, 'Have you read his books yet?'

'Not yet.'

'How can you not have read them?'

'It will mess with me. It'll sway me one way or the other. It always does.'

'But it's important information.'

'Is it? It's so easy to get the guy and the writing confused.' If Oscar made clay pots I wouldn't care. I could look at his pots and love them or hate them and it would have no bearing on how I felt about him. I wish I could feel as neutral about writing as I do about clay pots.

'Don't you want to at least read the sex scenes?'

'No!'

'He likes to write about sex.'

'Stop.'

'Can I just tell you this one thing about his sex scenes?'

I can tell she's been saving this for a while. 'No. Okay. One thing.'

'He always uses the word "sour."'

'Sour?'

'It's just something I've noticed. Usually pertaining to the woman: sour breath, sour skin. Something is always sour. It's like a tic he has.'

She is laughing hard at the expression on my face.

Oscar meets me after my Friday night shift. His mother is spending the night so he can sneak out of the house when I'm free. She made a carrot cake for dessert, and he brings a big slice. We share it as we walk down Mass. Ave. It's delicious. When we're done and he balls the cellophane in his pocket, he takes my hand. He has a plump, warm hand.

'My mother is very nervous about this. She thinks you're going to break my heart.' He laughs like it's an absurd idea and kisses me. I smile while we're kissing, thinking about telling Muriel later that we both tasted sour because of the lemon in the frosting, and he feels me smile and smiles wider.

I like kissing Oscar. He breaks it up with things that come into his head, a student he had with twelve fingers, Jasper biting him hard on the thigh during John's T-ball game that afternoon. There isn't that feeling you get with some guys, like they're barreling toward one place and one place only and seeing how fast they can get there without complication or too much conversation.

We have beers at the Cellar, and he walks me back to my bike outside Iris where he parked his car. He leans me against the passenger door, his hands on my hips.

'These,' he says. 'These are real baby-making hips.'

I laugh. I'm actually pretty narrow in the hip. I've often wondered how a whole baby would come through.

We kiss for a long time, and I feel him nestle in along the hollow between a baby-making hip and my pelvic bone. It fits nicely there.

'Mmm,' he says. 'Snug.'

I tell Harry about the date at lunch the next day.

'Good heavens,' he says. 'Is that what it's like with writers? The word "snug" and you're mad in love?'

'I'm not mad in love.'

'The man is in his forties with two bloody children.'

Later when we're in the weeds and I'm frantically re-plenishing the tea box for a six-top of librarians, he says, 'Move your baby makers, sweetheart. I need a steak knife.'

And when it's over he tells me there's a cute guy in the hallway who wants to see me.

'See? He's adorable, right?'

'I don't think this is your daddy complex.'

'He looks *a lot* younger than forty-five. And fuck you. It's not a daddy complex.'

I make him check my teeth for poppy seeds and go to the door.

It's not Oscar. It's Silas. The sight of him gives me a jolt. He looks younger, leaner. He's wearing a black leather jacket, an old one, with deep creases and corroded zippers on the pockets.

'Sorry to pull you out of work. I just wanted to make sure you were okay.'

'It's fine.' I wave toward my tables through the door. 'Most of the checks are down. How are you? How was your trip?' I'm trying to calculate how long since he's been back. Two weeks probably. He left me a couple of messages then gave up. I'm done with guys like this, on and off, here then gone. I've learned my lesson.

'Good. Good.' There's a stack of business cards on the hostess stand and he flicks them with his thumb. *Fftht. Fftht.* He looks up. 'I'm sorry I broke our date. I just wanted to tell you that in person. I understand why you'd be mad or—' *Fftht.*

Marcus's door is open, and I know he's listening to every word.

'You don't have to explain.'

'I want to,' he says, more loudly than he meant to. 'Sorry. It's just. Sometimes in the past year or so this feeling would come over me, kind of like a rash, you know? I needed to be in motion. And this time I had the opportunity to really go and I felt like I had to take it even though I really did want to go out with you. Really. A lot. I just wanted to explain that. I thought it would be a better date with you if I'd gotten that feeling out of my system.'

'I get it. I really do. Thanks for telling me.' I try to make it sound final, like that's the end of it and the chance for that date has passed. I try to start moving back into the dining room but my body doesn't budge.

'Any glimpses of the sublime out there?' I hear myself say.

'One or two.' He grins.

144

I forgot about the chip in his tooth.

Shit.

'The sublime always tracks you down eventually.'

He nods. My tables all have probably put down their credit cards by now. He'll go down the stairs soon and out onto the street and this makes my stomach feel hollow, even though it's stuffed with Helene's poppy seed cake.

'So, what do you think?' he says.

'Maybe we should go to the museum.'

'Saturday?'

Fabiana comes out and reclaims her hostess stand. Silas lets go of the little stack of cards.

'Saturday's good. But I work at three.'

'I'll pick you up at ten thirty.'

He goes down the stairs like a boy, fast and all in one motion, one loud rumble. The door at the bottom slams shut.

My tables glare at me when I go back into the dining room. I don't make eye contact and head straight to the wait station.

'Please tell me you did not let that one go,' Harry says.

'I did not.'

'Oh, you are a minx in a stained apron,' he says and hands me the two credit card receipts he ran for me.

E arly Saturday morning I print out my draft for Muriel. I can't bear to look at any of the words as they come out of the machine. I don't know what it says. I don't know what the book is about. I see the name Clara and my stomach sinks. Did I really name a main character *Clara*? After fifty pages my room gets humid and smells like the copy shop I used to work at in college, moist paper and toner and electricity. The pile in the printer's basket grows too high and pages begin to slip off and I take the first part of the book and align the edges and put it facedown on my desk. I do this five times until the printer spits out the last page and cuts off abruptly. I feel like it should break into song. I flip over the stack, and there it is. I put it in an old Kinko's box, write Muriel's name on top, and shove it in my backpack before I start marking up the pages again.

I ride over to her apartment and drop the box on the mail table in the foyer of her building. On my way home I imagine her telling me she didn't get it and then seeing it published a year from now by one of the other tenants in her building—probably the guy who works at the tropical fish store and denied using her fabric softener—and having to sue him with proof of all the pages I have in notebooks and on my computer. Open-and-shut case, my lawyer would say. But I wouldn't be able to pay a lawyer, so I'd have to represent myself. Or I'd call my friend Sylvie in Virginia who was an intellectual property lawyer. She'd studied art history and drama and I saw her in *Three Sisters* and *Arcadia* and both times she completely transformed herself. I didn't recognize her as my friend Sylvie when she was onstage. I think of her in her office in Alexandria, playing the role of a lawyer for so many hours a day. I think of all the people playing roles, getting further and further away from themselves, from what moves them, what stirs them all up inside. And I think of my novel on Muriel's mail table and I hope that tropical fish guy will leave it alone.

When I get back, the room still smells of printing and I have my first wave of fear about it being read. Silas is coming in twenty minutes, so I don't have time to wallow in it. I jump in the shower and when I get out my nose is still red from the chilly ride to Cambridge. I put on too much blush to compensate and find a clean shirt I'm pretty sure I didn't wear to the party where I met Silas. Oscar's party. But he wasn't Oscar then. He was the author signing books I couldn't afford in the other room.

Silas has a lime-green Le Car with a rusted hole that goes clean through the passenger door. On the inside it's sealed with duct tape.

'It's my sister's car. An old boyfriend of hers gored it.'

'With what?'

He goes around to his side and gets in. 'A harpoon. He collected sea weapons. Look, it went all the way through here.' He touches the edge of my seat and I move my leg to reveal a rip in the fabric.

I'm wearing a skirt so my leg is bare and his fingers so close cause a small commotion in my nethersphere.

Bottles and trash in the back roll around as he shifts gears. The car smells like dirty socks and reminds me of Caleb's room growing up. He's wearing the same leather jacket, and it creaks when he moves his arm to the gearshift and back to the steering wheel. I don't know what we'll say to each other. I feel confused by the sock smell and wanting his fingers back near my leg again.

When we speed up, the duct tape starts flapping.

'It was like watching a Viking,' Silas says. It takes me a second, but I realize he's still talking about the hole. 'He had this flaming hair and huge arms. It took a couple of tries.'

'Was your sister in it?'

'No, no. She was out with someone else that night. That was the problem.'

We drive along the fens of the Fenway, thick and green, a low stone bridge over the Muddy River, willows dripping into the water. Boston is bright and bejeweled this morning, and my body feels buoyant, having given Muriel my book. I feel like taking off my shoes and sticking my feet out the window. Even if she eviscerates it, it's movement. Forward motion. I decide not to tell Silas I've finished it. I don't want to sound braggy.

'What've you been up to?'

I scan my life since he left town: Bad moles. Burnt cervix. Oscar. 'I finished my novel.' It's all I got.

'You *finished* it?' He whips around and stares at me until I point to the road.

'It's still a mess.'

'You finished your first novel. You wrote a whole damn novel.' He pounds his palms on the steering wheel and stares at me.

I point to the road again. 'I gave it to Muriel to read.'

'She's a good reader.'

'Yeah. That's what I'm scared of.'

'Man, Casey. That's an accomplishment.' He seems genuinely happy for me. You can't always count on a guy for that.

At the museum he buys us tickets and we fold the metal tabs of our pins over our shirt collars. I haven't been to the MFA since I've been back East.

We go up the wide marble staircase.

'My mother used to bring me here when I was little. She'd let me borrow a hard leather purse from her closet, and I'd wear it the way she wore hers.' I tuck a pretend purse under my arm.

'What did you look like?'

'Puffy pigtails. Big front teeth,' I say. 'And she'd let me buy three postcards in the gift shop, and they'd knock around in the big empty purse on the way to the car.' We reach the top of the stairs. 'I wish I could remember what we said to each other.'

'It's weird, isn't it? My sister and I drove cross country once. She got all these books on tape, big books like *War and*

Peace and stuff. But we started talking and never listened to them. It was kind of a joke we had, that when we ran out of things to say we'd listen. We just kept talking, though. And now I can't remember what we said.'

The air between us crackles, as it does when you speak of your beloved dead. But it's hard to know what to say next.

We wander through Art of the Ancient World, past a Babylonian lion, Etruscan urns, an enameled Nubian bracelet, body parts from Greek statues: a sandaled foot, a muscular male bum with one thigh. It's good to see art, to remember what a natural human impulse it has always been. We move into Art of Europe, the haloes and angels, the sacred birth and bloody murder of one man over and over, a whole continent possessed by one story for centuries.

'There are a lot of holes in the plot,' I say when we stand in front of a Fra Angelico. 'If Jesus was so celebrated when he was born, why are there only stories of him as a baby and a man about to die? Why don't you ever see him as an eight-year-old?'

'Or as a teenager. With acne, rolling his eyes at everything Mary and Joseph say.'

Sometimes I go the opposite way around the room, so we can observe some things separately. Sometimes we lose each other and catch up a room or two later.

We drift over to Art of the Americas and come to a stop at Sargent's *The Daughters of Edward Darley Boit.* Three of the girls look directly at us. The eldest one can't be bothered. She almost looks like she's dozing, her back against the six-foot vase. The next eldest stands erect and uncomfortable beside her, the third off to the left near an unseen window, and the youngest on the floor with a porcelain doll and a skeptical stare.

'Do you think these kids had to pose in those positions day after day?' I say.

'They look unhappy.'

'Yeah, and not just from posing in weird positions. Like they're trying to put a good face on it, but you can tell they're not going to play some really fun game after.'

'Is there one you identify with?'

I study the four girls. 'I suppose I identify with her.' I point to the second daughter, tense, drained of color. 'But I'd like to be her, the one standing in all the light.'

'She's the focus, isn't she? Even though she's all the way over here.'

We lean in at the same time to examine her. She's exquisite, her white pinafore catching every particle of light.

'She knows it's about her, and she's not sure she wants it to be,' I say. Our shoulders aren't touching but the creak of his leather jacket is loud in my ear. I can smell his skin. 'But there's something brewing in her.'

'Look at her left foot. She's about to take a step.'

'If I could write something as good as right there, right where that belt cinches her pinafore.' It's hard to pull my eyes from it. I don't know why it's so moving to me, and I could never explain. There's a madness to beauty when you stumble on it like that.

After *The Daughters of Edward Darley Boit*, I go in the same direction as Silas around the rooms. We stand in front of Van Gogh's *Houses at Auvers* then Matisse's *Vase of Flowers* for a long time without saying anything. After the vivid chaos of the Van Gogh, where nothing is muted, nothing is blended, and the world seems to be separating into fragments before his eyes, Matisse's vase of white flowers beside a window by the sea is serene and buoyant, as if everything can float if you let it.

On the stairs down to the café, Silas says, 'I like coming here. It stirs me up and calms me down in all the right ways.'

He orders coffee and I order tea and we sit on modern plastic chairs in an open atrium. I feel light and elated from the art, and the worry about Muriel reading my novel is gone.

On the way back we're quieter. He's more comfortable with silence than most people. In the pauses I think about confessing that somehow I ended up going on two dates with Oscar Kolton. But it's presuming too much too soon, like he would care. This is the guy who started driving thousands of miles west on the morning of our first date.

When we pull into the driveway I hear the dog barking at the car. Adam is away for the weekend, and I'm responsible for him. 'Do you want to meet Adam's Dog? We could take him for a walk.'

'Adam's Dog.' He laughs. 'I promised my roommate he could have the car about an hour ago. I'd like to, though. Another time.'

'Okay. Thanks.' I get out quickly, before he thinks I'm waiting for something more. But after he's gone I wish I'd been a little slower.

I put my key in the lock. I'm in the mood to call my mother, that happy, shift in the wind mood. I calculate the time in Phoenix. Nearly noon. Perfect. The bolt retracts, and I remember she died.

O scar calls me that afternoon at Iris during setup.
'I've got my mother here on standby,' he says. 'She's willing to give up her auxiliary meeting to help her smitten son.' There's a covered pause. 'She wants me to tell you that it is *not* an *auxiliary* meeting. It's a *film* group. Made up of *very* smart women with PhDs like herself she'll have you know. Tomorrow night. Can you get free?' He lowers his voice to an exaggerated whisper. 'She thinks you're too young for me.' A howl in the background. 'She says she did *not* say that.'

He has a mother, and I do not.

The calendar's on the wall in front of me. Marcus just made the new schedule. I'm off tomorrow night. 'Let me check.'

I cover the phone. I'm alone in the office so no one sees me. I stand there a long time. I can't think. I want to go out with Silas one more time before I see Oscar again. I feel like there's a misshapen ball in my lungs that isn't leaving much room for air.

Marcus swoops in. 'Get off my phone.'

I uncover the receiver. 'Yeah. I'm free.'

On the way back to the kitchen I think about a scene in my book. Dana is telling me to help her set the twelve-top, but I go to the bar instead and write out a new idea on

154

a cocktail napkin and shove it in my apron pocket. I have a whole stash of notes on napkins and dupes in my desk drawer for my next draft.

I can't shake the anxiety that night. Usually I can run it off on the floor. On a busy night there's no time for awareness of the mind or the body. There's just extra vinaigrette to 21 and drinks to the deuce and two tables of entrées up at the same time. There are little jokes with Harry and Victor and Mary Hand as we collide at the computer or the food window. I can always lose myself in the rush. But that night I don't. I stay apart. For the first time the stress of the job does not obliterate my awareness of the stress in my body. It enhances it.

When it's over and we're doing our totals, Harry pats my head. 'What is going on in there?'

I can't explain, so I say, 'I feel like I should tell Oscar about Silas. I mean, he's got kids.'

'You've had a walk and a beer with him. I would be wary of the guy who locks in too soon. It's a sort of premature commitulation.' He laughs at his own joke then gets up to tip out the kitchen. He has a new crush on a surly line cook. I watch him push hopefully through the kitchen door. He can sound wise in love, but he's bad at it, too.

I meet Oscar at a small restaurant called Arancia off Brattle Street. I didn't want him to pick me up and see where I live. He'd want to come in and have a look around.

He's talking to a couple outside on the sidewalk. He breaks away from them when he sees me coming.

He kisses me on the cheek. 'Third date.' He kisses me on the lips. 'I have something for you. Shut your eyes.'

I feel something hard cover my head.

'Perfect fit.'

I reach up. A bike helmet. I take it off. It's silver and sleek and must have cost a lot.

'Thank you. It's lovely.'

He laughs. 'I promise I will buy you something lovelier. But at least now I don't have to worry about you cracking your head open.' He slides his arm through mine, and we walk down the brick steps into the basement restaurant. It's tiny. Eight tables. On the far wall a velvet curtain separates the dining room from the kitchen. The smells are Mediterranean: heated balsamic, shellfish, fig. I'm hungry. I hope he orders two courses. We wait at the door for someone to greet us.

'Who were those people you were talking to?'

'Tom and Phyllis McGrath. They were out for a stroll.' He hesitates. 'She was reading my book. Recognized the mug.'

'That photo looks nothing like you.' I harden my face and squint like a cowboy smoker.

'That's how I look.' He tries to strike the pose.

'You look nothing like you.' There's a woman at a three-top who's watching him. He is good-looking, with those eyes and thick copper whorl of hair. I lower my voice. 'Does that happen a lot, people recognizing you?'

'Not enough,' he laughs. 'Around here occasionally. I mean right here. This block. Maybe the next. Go to Central Square and forget it.'

The hostess emerges through the velvet curtain and shows us to a table. It's round, wood, no cloth, no flowers. Instead of a candle there is a small lamp with an old-fashioned chain. The setup and breakdown here must be so fast.

'So, you've seen the photograph but haven't read the book?' Oscar says.

It catches me off guard. 'I've been planning to get to the library.'

'Oh, the library. That will boost my sales.'

A waiter appears, lifts our glasses away from the table to pour water into them, tells us the specials. He's older than Oscar. He's been doing this kind of work for decades, you can tell. He tells us the rack of lamb comes with yardlongs and a gentleman's relish.

Oscar lifts his head. 'Who's writing this menu, Hugh Hefner?'

I cringe. This is not the kind of career waiter you want to mess with. But the guy cracks up. His laugh is loud and fills the small room. It takes him a while to compose himself. 'No one has said anything all night. It was killing me.'

He leaves us to contemplate the menu. I see him go to the back and tell another waiter what Oscar said. At the table next to us an old man's sweater slides from his chair to the floor and Oscar gets it for him and they have a small exchange about the bottle of wine on the man's table, which was from Australia, where Oscar lived for a year it turns out.

The waiter comes back, and Oscar orders mussels for us to share and the sea bass. I order the grilled shrimp and the tagliatelle. I ask him to fire the shrimp app with the mains.

He nods and leaves and Oscar says, 'Listen to you, speaking the native language.'

I ask him about his boys.

He reaches for my hand and traces a finger along the inside of my wrist. 'You have the softest, most velvety skin.' After a while he says, 'My boys are well. They know I am seeing you tonight. John can still get very frothed up about your mini golf boast.'

He's not much of a drinker, and I like that. We each have a beer then switch to water. The mussels arrive, smelling of vermouth and shallots.

'I saw your friend Muriel Wednesday.'

I've been avoiding the topic of the Wednesday night group. Silas might have been there, and that was strange. And just the word 'Muriel' made my stomach turn over.

'What? Did you two have a falling out?'

'I gave her my novel four days ago.'

'You didn't give it to me.'

'After your freak-out in the arboretum? No, I did not.'

He laughs like he totally forgot about that. 'I was a freak. I'm sorry. Have you heard anything from her?'

'Nothing.' A fresh round of anxiety floods in, the voltage amped up.

He nods, opens a mussel. 'All these writers you've gone out with,' he says. 'Any of them famous?'

I shake my head. 'Just you. In a two-block radius, at least.'

Our entrées arrive. The man at the next table gets up to leave with the rest of his companions and examines Oscar's sea bass, whose head is lolling beyond the edge of the plate.

Oscar tips the fish's eye up toward the man. 'Irises backed and packed with tarnished tinfoil seen through lenses of old scratched isinglass.'

'Bishop,' the man says. 'The great master of disaster.' He's old enough to have been her contemporary.

'Indeed' says Oscar.

'I hope you and your little girl have a lovely evening,' he says and shuffles off to his friends, the women adjusting their silk scarves with gnarled fingers.

Oscar leans toward me. 'Did he just say, "little girl"?'

'I think so.'

'My *little girl*?'

The waiter comes up and asks how everything is.

'Well, my fish is dead,' Oscar says. 'And she is *not* my little girl.'

The waiter laughs. He seems to want to linger as I did at brunch that day. I ask for more Parmesan to get rid of him.

When we've finished, he takes our plates and brings us a chocolate torte and a mango sorbet. 'Compliments of the chef. He's an admirer of your work,' he says to Oscar.

Oscar is pleased but not as surprised or flattered as I would have expected. 'Many thanks,' he says.

The desserts are good. Everything has been good, but nothing comes close to Thomas's scallops or Helene's banana bread pudding.

The check comes, and I don't even pretend to reach for my bag. I don't even have a bag. All I have is my helmet under the seat.

'I'm not ready for you to ride off. Shall we stroll a bit?'

159

We walk up to the Common. Students are smoking on benches, knees up, bare feet. A few others toss a football in the dark. It's still strange not to be one of them, not to be in school on a September night.

Outside the gates of a playground, he points to the place on the monkey bars where John had knocked heads with another kid and to the baby bucket swing Jasper wedged himself into last year and couldn't get out of.

'I could have written three more books for all the time I've put in right here,' he says.

We pass beneath a maple that has already started to drop leaves. They crack beneath our feet and release the smell of fall. I used to have calluses from the monkey bars and the tricks I practiced for hours, showing off for my mother. She and Javi did a good job of pretending it was my skill on the monkey bars they were interested in.

On Chauncy Street I show him the place I had with Nia and Abby and Russell, and two doors down he points to a house that he says he and his wife rented for a year when they were first married. I don't ask when, don't want to know if we lived there at the same time. We pass Harvard's married housing, and he says his parents lived there for his father's senior year and tells a story about his mother nearly burning the place down by setting a dishcloth on fire and how she did the same thing recently in his house.

He stops in front of a house at the end of the block. The lights are on downstairs, blue flashes from a TV in the corner. 'This is us.'

It's a square, perfectly symmetrical colonial, four windows facing the street on the ground floor, four on the second, a pair of dormers on the third. Gray with white trim and black shutters. At the back of the short driveway stands a basketball hoop and backboard on a post with sandbags on top of the black base. Oscar's life.

I look at him looking at it. I can't tell what he's feeling. He turns to me. 'My mother is watching the news. She has a thing for Ted Koppel.'

Upstairs three windows are dark, one a dim green. A night-light, perhaps.

'Do the boys sleep in the same room?'

'When I'm not home. Jasper will slip into John's bed. They both end up in my bed by dawn.'

It's important to him, presenting this to me. I take his hand and he pulls me in and kisses me on the temple and we look through the windows again as if the house and everything inside it belongs to both of us.

I meet Silas at the movie theater on Church Street. We choose seats close to the front. He's wearing a striped wool hat that he keeps on the whole movie, and our bodies never touch. I've never been more aware of not touching someone in my life. Two and a half Merchant Ivory hours of not touching. Afterward we go back to his apartment in North Cambridge. It's three flights of linoleum stairs up. He jiggles the lock, and inside it smells like his car plus tobacco and bacon. I follow him down a hallway, past two closed doors. Behind the second door a guy fake orgasms in falsetto, long and loud.

Silas pounds on the wall. 'You wish, Doug.' He waits for me at the end. 'Sorry about that.'

We go into the kitchen. He pulls two bottles of beer out of the fridge and opens them by hooking the cap beneath a drawer pull. The caps fall into his open hand, and he drops them into the trash. We sit at a sticky little table in the corner. The two chairs are close together, and he doesn't move them apart. There's a newspaper and a pen on the table. Someone has been doing the crossword. He picks up the pen and slides the paper closer, and I hope we don't have to finish the crossword. I don't like them. I don't like any word puzzles or Scrabble or any of the other word games

162

writers are supposed to like. But he flips the paper over to a photo of Ken Starr and gives him long hair that looks like eels, then puts the pen down abruptly.

We talk and tear the labels off our bottles. He asks what Muriel said about my book, and I have to say I haven't heard from her. I think he can tell this makes me miserable, so he tells me that his roommate Doug is in love with a lesbian who sometimes spends the night but nothing happens and that Jim and Joan, his other roommates, have the master bedroom but have to put all of Joan's stuff in the basement anytime Jim's father, a Baptist minister, visits from Savannah.

'What are your parents like?' I ask.

He picks up the pen again. 'Unhappy.' He laughs. 'I tried to say something else, but there's no other word for it. They should have split up a long time ago. I think they were going to.'

'Before your sister died?'

'Yeah. And now they're a hobbled mess.' He draws a sort of hunched Quasimodo figure with two heads, a hump, and a bunch of clubbed feet. He hands me the pen. 'What about your father? Are you close?'

My father isn't second-date material. 'We were once. But he's not a nice man.' I draw my father in profile, the thick *brosse* of white hair sticking straight up, the long straight nose with the tiny tip, the mouth wide open and yelling at me for being a quitter. Silas takes the pen and draws a bubble coming out of my father's mouth and in it he writes: 'I don't want to be an asshole!' I take the pen from him and make a bubble coming out of both Quasimodo heads and write: 'We don't know who we are now.'

163

He laughs through his nose and says, 'That's about right.'

We're sitting so close and our arms are finally touching and I think he might lean over and kiss me, but he doesn't.

On the way out he says he wants to get something, and he opens the door to his bedroom. The bed is unmade, a nubby fleece blanket and a pale-blue bottom sheet. A thin desk covered with papers and an office swivel chair. Stacks of books all around and a manual typewriter in the corner. I stand in the doorway. It smells like him. It's a good smell. I could stand here a long time, but he grabs a book from a pile and shuts the door.

He hands it to me in the stairwell. 'I saw this at Words-Worth.' It's an oversized paperback on Cuban poster art. I flip through it. There are photos from the late fifties to the eighties of posters pasted all over Havana. Political slogans in bright orange swirls, gardens of pop art flowers, a riff on Warhol's soup can advertising a film festival.

'Thank you so much.' I look up. He's halfway down the stairs.

He drives me across the river. The radio is playing Lou Reed. We don't say much. Every time he puts his hand on the gearshift next to my leg my insides lurch a little.

He sings along with Lou about reaping what you sow.

In the driveway he puts the Le Car in neutral. 'That was a good time,' he says.

'It was. Thanks.' This time I give him a few seconds, and just when I turn to open the door I hear him move toward me, but it's too late.

'I'll call you,' he says. The door shuts.

I wave.

Gravel pops and scatters beneath his tires as he backs out.

On my machine Muriel is screaming: I LOVE IT. I LOVE IT SO MUCH.

I'm sitting with Muriel at her table by the window. She's made us tea in cobalt mugs. It's a chilly morning, and heat hisses out of the cast-iron radiator behind me. She's in sweats and a ponytail, glasses instead of contacts. I don't get to see her like this very often. This long table is where she writes. It's impossible not to feel that I could write better with just a little more space and light. I wish my own room of my own wasn't so claustrophobic.

My manuscript is in a pile between us. The first page has two checkmarks in the margin. Beside the stack are four or five pages of her notes.

'I don't know if I ever told you this,' Muriel says, 'but when I read something good my ankles get prickly. It's been happening since I was nine and I read Elizabeth Bowen by mistake when *The Last September* got shelved in the kids' section of our library.'

I'm nervous. I know she said she liked it, but I also know that all those notes are not praise.

'I'm sorry it took me two weeks. I started to think, what if I hate it? I got scared it might turn out like it did with Jack.' Jack is a colleague who stopped speaking to her after she gave him feedback on his memoir. 'Two nights ago

I dug in, and it was such incredible relief. My ankles were going crazy.' She pulls the pile closer and pushes her glasses farther up the bridge of her nose. 'Kay Boyle said once that a good story is both an allegory and a slice of life. Most writers are good at one, not the other. But you are doing both so beautifully here.' She strokes the top page. She starts flipping through the manuscript to show me the parts she loved best. Her checkmarks are everywhere. My body is flooded with sweet relief. My heart slows to enjoy it. She has marked all my favorite parts, the ones that came so easily and the ones I struggled so hard with. She says Clara is so particular, but she's also the embodiment of women undone by the history of men. She goes off on a riff about the male hegemony within Clara's family. She gives me credit for all kinds of things I hadn't been thinking about in any sort of ideological way.

When she begins showing me the spots that need to be cut or expanded, characters who need more attention, I start taking notes. She points out the places where I have described a character's emotion instead of the reaction to the emotion. 'Don't tell us the girl is sad. Tell us she can't feel her fingers. Emotions are physical.' She has put an X through several pages about the Battle of La Plata, which had taken me weeks of research.

'And,' she says, 'you have to write that rape scene.'

'No.'

'You have to.'

'I can't. I don't want to.'

'It shouldn't happen offstage like that.'

I shake my head. 'I tried. It didn't work.'

'Try again. You can't follow her so carefully for most of the book, then just turn away. Is it because of your father?'

'It's not the same. He didn't rape anyone.'

'He got off on watching.'

I nod. My face slowly reddens.

'Use those feelings,' she says. 'Use all of them.'

When I get back to the potting shed I sit with the stack of papers she gave me. I write down some ideas in my notebook, then turn to a fresh page and stare at it for a long time.

You don't realize how much effort you've put into covering things up until you try to dig them out.

The leather couch was cool on my cheek. You feel like a furnace, I remembered my mother saying once when I went to her in the middle of the night and she ran a washcloth under cold water and laid it on my forehead. I missed her then, in a way I didn't let myself miss her anymore. I think I cried a little. It was too loud to sleep, people going in and out of the locker rooms, pushing hard on the metal door to the gym. And those noises—whispers, scuffling—from closer by. I thought they were in my head.

I write it all out in my notebook: the fever, the couch, the boys in their basketball shorts. The sickening sound of my father buckling his belt as he came out last from the closet.

The next morning I read though her notes and flip through all the pages of the manuscript again—Muriel's comments and checkmarks, sometimes four on one page. She understood it. She got it. Even if no one else ever does, Muriel did.

I bake a small banana cake in my toaster oven and drop it off for her before work.

Each morning that week I take Adam's dog to the park as soon as I get up. His name is Oafie, Adam finally told me. The cooler air makes my mind feel sharp and purposeful. In the park, Oafie lumbers around with wiry Fifi and miniature Hugo and I chatter with the owners and none of it derails me. I'm back at my desk by six thirty and know what I have to do. It's nothing like facing the blank page. I have something whole to work with now.

Oscar goes away for readings in the Midwest, and Silas comes by at the end of a dinner shift with baklava and a bottle of wine. We walk to the river.

Third date, I want to say, but I can't with Silas. Our dates are not self-conscious like that. We don't acknowledge that they're happening or say what they mean. It all feels a bit haphazard and weightless, and to call attention to this might let out too much of the air.

He's wearing a thick, Irish knit sweater with holes in the sleeves. He spreads out a blanket, the fleece one from his bed, on the grass. I sit cross-legged on top of it and he lies back, tilted up on his elbows, smiling as I tell him about Muriel's critique and my recent mornings of focus and clarity.

'Muriel is ruthless,' he says. 'It must be really good.'

'It's still a mess. Maybe a more manageable mess now with her notes in the margins helping me through. I always think of that Eliot poem, about the vision and the reality.'

'"Between the idea and the reality/Between the motion and the act/Falls the Shadow,"' he says.

'Listen to your stentorian teacher voice. I do feel like I'm shrinking the Shadow a bit.'

'Eliot would say that was not possible.' He finishes his baklava and wipes his hands on his jeans.

'Well fuck him. I am.' I finish mine and wipe my hands on his jeans, too, lower down, near the knee.

He laughs. He turns on his side toward me.

'How do you teach high school? I don't think I could ever go back there.' The desire to press up against him is on a short loop in my head. His curls are looser now, in the dry fall air. One hangs over an eyebrow.

He starts to answer but there's a sudden clamor downriver. The geese.

We listen to their barking and wailing.

'I love those geese.'

'Should we check them out?'

'Sure,' I say, but really I want to lie down beside him. I just don't have the guts.

We walk in the dark toward the sounds. I tell him about my bike rides home along this path and the night I sang 'Loch Lomond' to the geese. I tell him how I felt my mother right there beside me, or inside me, and he says he knows that feeling. He says he had it a few times when he drove out west.

'Is that where she died, Crested Butte?'

He looks surprised.

'You sent me a postcard from there.'

He nods. 'Yeah. I didn't feel her there. She was long gone.'

'What'd you do?'

'I wrote some bad poetry in a tent, visited a friend in Boulder and my aunt in Duluth, and came back.'

We're walking close and bump against each other. Another person might have just taken his hand and said, Are you *ever* going to kiss me? But I'm not that person. It always takes me by surprise when someone wants to kiss me, even if they've met me at midnight with wine and a blanket. People change their mind. Between the idea and the reality falls the Shadow.

We walk up the footbridge and lean over the wall to watch the commotion. There aren't many geese, seven or eight, but they're keyed up, whacking each other with their wings, lunging at each other's necks.

'What are they fighting over?'

'Maybe they're arguing about when to take off for winter,' he says.

'I don't want them to go.' It strikes me as a terribly sad thing.

'They'll come back.' He nudges me with his arm and leaves it there.

We watch them for a while. Out of the corner of my eye I watch Silas, too, his long body curved over the stone wall. I can feel the heat of him through his sweater, the smell of him coming out at the neck.

He straightens up and pushes off the wall then bends back down and kisses me, as if on a dare. Neither of us pull away. I press against him and he slides his hands around to my back and his fingers trace the knobs on my spine all the way up. I feel him, every bit of him, and it's not nearly enough. We take a few steps and kiss again, harder, longer, against the parapet.

'God, I have been waiting to do this a long time,' he says into my ear. Our bodies are moving against each other at just the right angles, and I can't reply in words.

We hold hands on the way back, but it feels like we're still kissing. My whole body responds to his hand in mine.

He puts my bike in the back of his car and drives me across the river. He says he has to chaperone a ninth-grade field trip to Gettysburg next week, and he'll call me when he gets back.

He parks on my street and we make out some more. No talking. No pecks. The kisses are long and intimate, like we're telling each other everything that needs to be said this way.

When I get out of the car I'm so horny I can barely walk up the driveway.

Usually a man in my life slows my work down, but it turns out two men give me fresh energy for the revision. The emotions get heightened. I give the reader more pleasure. In the margins Muriel has written, 'Linger here' or 'Let us feel this,' and I try to stay and feel the moment and my understanding of it expands. Small unexpected things begin to thrum across the whole book. I feel like a conductor, finally able to hear all the instruments at once. I think back on all the rooms in all the cities and towns where I wrote the pieces of this book, all the doubt and days of failure but also that knot of stubbornness that's still inside me.

I save the rape scene for last. It was supposed to happen on a beach but I change it to a storage room at the bank where she works, and after that it comes out of me in one sitting. I see it, hear it, taste it. It pulses out like a song that's been stuck in the back of my mind. When it's done I'm haunted by what I wrote for a few days, skittish on my bike going home at night.

I stand in line at the post office, two stacks of six boxes at my feet. Inside each box is a copy of the book and a cover letter to an agent. Muriel told me the names of a few of them, and the rest I found in a reference book on contemporary authors

174

at the library. I discreetly kiss my fingers and touch each box. When the line moves I push the boxes forward with my foot. I take a breath, and it becomes so deep I realize I haven't taken one for a while.

The guy behind me is reading the addresses on the top boxes. He's wearing a camel hair overcoat and looks like a Salinger character, the boy who meets Franny at the train station in New Haven. He sees 'Literary Agency' and 'New York, NY.'

'That the Great Amer—'

'Yup. That's exactly what it is,' I say.

Behind the counter a stout woman is working around her breasts, which rest on the counter, in the way of everything she does. She puts my boxes one at a time on the scale. She'll be the last person to touch them before they go out, and I need her to wish them well.

'I've been working on this book for six years,' I say quietly.

'Huh,' she says, punching in numbers.

Her indifference feels like a terrible omen. I don't know how to get her on my side. 'It takes place in Cuba.'

'Huh.'

She drops them in three unceremonious batches into what looks like a big laundry bin behind her.

I pay in cash, mostly ones: $96.44. 'Thank you very much.'

She hands me the long receipt her machine has spat out. 'Let's hope your next six years are a little more exciting, sweetie pie.'

175

I cross the dining room to bring water to a couple at table 6. It's like a dream, the way they transform from sloped strangers, a man with a crackled bald spot and a woman in a gold jacket, into my father and stepmother.

'Look at you,' my father says. He places his napkin back on the table and rises. The old coach, brittle now, the same grimace, as if I've just overshot a hole. We hug loosely.

'Don't get him all wet,' Ann says, because I've got the water jug in my hand.

'I won't.'

He seems smaller, his hug without much muscle.

I bend down to kiss her. She always smells the same, metallic. 'What are you doing here?'

They never leave the Cape in the summer.

'We talked to Caleb last night and he filled us in on you and we thought we'd drive up and say hello,' Ann says.

'I'm working till three, but maybe I can get out early.'

They look at each other. 'We have to get ahead of the traffic,' my father says. 'We're just here for lunch.'

'We wanted to get a glimpse of you. It's been a while.' She pauses. 'And a lot has happened.' It's a risk, alluding to my mother in front of my father.

Ann sent one condolence letter to me and Caleb and signed it for both of them. My father probably doesn't know this.

It has been a long time since I've seen them. Three years, maybe. They look older, like something is gently tugging them to the floor. I wonder if my father knows how much hair is missing at the back of his head.

Behind them Fabiana seats me a four, so I take their drink order and get away.

'It's very fishy,' I tell Harry in the wait station.

He's peering at them. 'She's a shiny little object, isn't she?'

'Why are they here?' I want to call Caleb, but it's long distance and I have too many tables. 'What did he tell them?'

'Maybe he told them the truth. That you miss your mom. That you need some cash.'

I laugh. 'They would never be here if he'd told them either of those things.'

I pour my father a cup of coffee and bring it to him. Ann doesn't drink beverages. She won't even sip her water. She'll order the house salad and nibble on the carrot shavings. My father will order the double sirloin cheeseburger, remove the meat from the bun, and soak each patty and hand-cut fry in ketchup. I know this, but I let them tell me their order anyway.

'Aren't you going to write that down?' he says.

'I got it.'

I feel them watch me with my other tables. At one of them is a Harvard history professor I've waited on before. He's brought his wife and their two granddaughters, and when I set down his enormous sundae he shrinks in his seat and pretends not to be able to reach it with his spoon and I laugh with the little girls. I feel my father's glare. He used to get so jealous of other men: certain golf pros, Tara's father, my favorite high school English teacher.

I ran into him in the Madrid airport a few years ago, that teacher, Mr. Tuck. He introduced me to Faulkner, to Caddy and Benjy and Quentin, in ninth grade. I wrote my first short story for him in tenth. We spent an hour and a half together at an airport bar. He was catching a flight to Portugal to visit his son who was studying there. I was moving to Barcelona. I told him I'd gone to grad school in creative writing because of him, that I was writing a novel. He said he'd stopped reading fiction. It wasn't any good anymore he said. He asked about my father. I didn't know what he knew. I said he was fine, retired, living in Florida, summers on the Cape. After his third beer he wanted me to know it wasn't him who turned my father in. He'd heard about it, the spying, he called it, but he wasn't the rat.

'Can't you talk to us a bit?' Ann says when I bring their food.

'A little.' I look around for Marcus. I'm not going to tell them I'm on probation. 'I've got four other tables. I guess they're okay for now.'

I wait for them to talk if they want to talk. They don't, so I ask how their summer is going.

'Good,' my father says to the center of his rare burger. 'Very good.'

'You'd think they'd give you a more colorful uniform,' Ann says.

'You like being a waitress?' my father says. 'Is that what all those degrees were for?'

'I do like the pink,' Ann says, smoothing out the top tablecloth. 'It's a pretty shade.'

'You think you're making more than Patty Sheehan or Annika Sörenstam? Did you know that the median income for a female professional golfer is over a hundred thousand dollars?'

'Robbie.'

'Five-time Rolex Junior All-American, AJGA Player of the Year, winner of eleven national—'

'I was never going to—'

'Yes, you were,' he says, beginning to stand up before he realizes where he is. 'You don't know anything because you *gave up.*' That narrow face, those yellow-green eyes. He looks just the same now, all the extra years shaved off.

'Robbie,' Ann says more sharply.

'You probably couldn't even par one hole now.'

'Maybe not.'

'You think that's funny? Funny to waste what you had? End up in a place like this?'

Iris wasn't really on his side, with its gold-leaf sconces and French doors and mahogany sideboards.

'Rob,' Ann says again, signaling something more overtly now. But my father is breathing heavily and shoveling chunks of burger into his mouth.

She sighs and takes my hand. 'Pretty ring.'

I look down. My mother's hand. My mother's ring. She strokes the sapphire on my finger. This is what they've come for.

The professor is signaling for the check. I pull my hand out of Ann's.

'They want the ring,' I tell Harry as I run the professor's card through.

'Your mother's ring? That's cheeky.' He's nabbed a duck confit and I get a fork and take a few bites. The tender meat dissolves in my mouth.

I tell Harry about my father and the storage closet and how the athletic director had not wanted to believe me when I told him about the peepholes.

'Oh Casey.' He looked around the corner. 'That slumpy man out there?'

'Ann has no idea. It was all hushed up. They even threw him a little retirement party with cake.'

I bring my father the check. No coffee refill or dessert menus or squares of chocolate.

'Let Ann try it on,' he says.

I shake my head.

'Let your stepmother try on my mother's ring.'

'I haven't taken it off since she died.' I didn't know that was true before I said it. I'm standing just far enough away so neither of them can reach me without a wild lunge.

'How did you get it?'

'She left it to me.'

'Probably all she had in the world to give you, the way she lived. Casey,' he says, trying to sound tender. 'She left us.'

'I know, Dad.'

'Ann came and saved us. She took us in. And when I lost my job—' His voice cracks. 'I've never had much to offer her.'

Ann lifts her purse up on her lap. I look at her hands, big stones on nearly every finger from her ex. She pulls out her checkbook. 'How much?' Her first husband was a Du Pont.

'No.'

'C'mon,' my father says. 'Just tell us your price.'

I tap their bill on the tray. 'Twenty-nine seventy-five. Have a good drive home.'

Instead of just leaving cash on the table they give it to Fabiana on their way out. There's a brief exchange, I can't tell about what, and they're gone.

Fabiana brings me the tip on a tray. Less than 10 percent.

She stabs a piece of the duck with my fork. 'How do you know those people anyway?'

181

I thought once the book was out of my hands the bees would fly off and I could relax. But they are worse. All night I lie in the dark on my futon while they writhe beneath my skin. I try to soothe myself with thoughts of agents reading my manuscript, but my feelings about the novel start to shift. Soon any thought of it scalds me with shame. Six years and *this* is what I have to show for myself? I try to hold the whole thing in my head again and I can't. I think about the first few pages and panic blooms in my chest and spreads like fire to my extremities. I watch the clock run through its numbers until it is light.

During the day I miss working on it. I've lost access to a world where my mother is a little girl reading in a window or twirling in fast circles on the street, her braids raised high off her back. Outside of those pages she is dead. There seems no end to the procession of things that make my mother feel more dead.

The gynecologist has ordered a mammogram. He said my breasts were difficult to examine manually because they were fibrous. It makes me feel like a cereal.

The technician is rough. She shoves and tugs my right boob into place on the glass plate and brings the other plate down with the touch of a button and just when it is as tight and squished as I can bear, she lowers it more. Sometimes she has to lift it back up a bit and cram my flesh in deeper. She should be a potter or a chef. Her hands are strong and certain. She reminds me of the line cooks stuffing potatoes.

When she's doing the final position, she asks me to draw my shoulder back, and when I can't seem to do it to her liking she draws it back herself. 'Good,' she says but keeps her fingers under my armpit. She wiggles them a bit. 'Huh,' she says.

'What?'

She wiggles some more. 'You had this checked?'

'What?'

She takes her fingers out, and I put mine in. 'I don't feel anything.' I wonder if she's one of those people who convinces other people they're sick—Munchausen by proxy. It makes sense that she would be attracted to a medical career.

'Here.' She places my fingers right in the socket and moves them over a hard—there's no other word for it—lump. My fingers spring away from it, denial at the muscular level. I feel the other armpit. I feel and feel. You just want to be symmetrical. A pair of lumps seems far more desirable. Nothing. She feels there, too.

'Mention it to your doctor.'

'Could we take a few images of it right now, just to save time.'

She laughs as if this is a preposterous idea. 'No.'

*　*　*

I call my primary care office about the lump and they ask me when that afternoon I can come in.

I get a different doctor. A woman. She wears gray felt clogs and a barrette on each side of her head. She makes me feel like we're in sixth grade and pretending she's a doctor and I'm a patient with a lump under my arm. She has no quick explanation. She asks if I've switched deodorants, soaps, or perfumes recently. I haven't. She suggests I stop using all products, just in case. And come back in a week.

'I will be very smelly by then,' I say. She says I can wash my hair but only with shampoo I've used before and only leaning way back in the shower, careful not to let the suds get under my arm. And no conditioner. 'Smelly and frizzy,' I say.

After a week, the lump is the same size and sore from how much I've been fingering it. The doctor says that I should continue with the anti-hygiene program. And, she adds, as if it's an afterthought, I should see an oncologist. She puts this on my chart, and when I check out I'm told Donna will call me within forty-eight hours with the date and time of the oncology appointment. She does. My appointment with Dr. Oncologist is seven weeks away. I call his office and beg for something sooner but the receptionist snaps and tells me I'm a lucky young lady to have gotten that date. Someone canceled. They're booking into late spring now.

'Because cancer can wait,' I say. 'Cancer doesn't grow and spread and kill people.'

She hangs up on me. I hope she doesn't delete my name from her calendar.

* * *

I try to write something new. It's bad and I stop after a few
sentences. Even though I didn't feel it at the time, I got into a
rhythm with the old novel. I knew those characters and how
to write them. I heard their voices and I saw their gestures
and anything else feels fake and stiff. I ache for them, people
I also once felt were stiff and fake, but who now seem like
the only people I could ever write about.

'S o,' Oscar says. 'I think you should come to the house for supper Sunday night.'

'Whoa.'

'I know.'

I'm on the kitchen line. Thomas is cranking Nirvana, and I have to plug my other ear.

'You still there?'

'In shock.'

'It's a school night, so we'll eat at six sharp. How do you feel about chicken sticks and cucumber slices?'

'Love them.' My heart is whomping. Chicken sticks and cucumber slices. I didn't realize I'd been waiting for this invitation all along.

I go back to rolling silver in the dining room with Tony and Dana and Harry. We're at one of the round tables, and Craig has mixed up a pitcher of sangria. Angus from the kitchen has joined us, already in street clothes. Fabiana and the new waiter, James, is there, too. He's Scottish, somber, silent as the grave. Harry is smitten.

'That one of your lovas?' Tony says. I made the mistake of telling him about my dilemma one slow night last week.

'Which one?' Harry says.

'Oscar. He wants me to have dinner with his kids.'

'Kids? No.' Craig says. 'Dump that dude.'

'Torn between two lovers,' Dana is singing.

'What're they like?' Angus says. 'We'll help you decide right now.'

'Who says I'm deciding?' I do need to choose, though. I've reached the elimination round. 'So one is my age and quirky and we talk about death a lot. The morning of our first date he left town for three weeks but he came back and I get physically disoriented after kissing him. I'm always surprised when he calls because I assume he's going to bail.' No one said anything, so I go on. 'And the other one is like a herd dog. He calls between dates and leaves me funny messages when I'm at work and doesn't hide how he feels about me. He's older and has two kids and can be pretty adorable.'

They look as stumped as I am.

'The second one's Oscar Kolton, the writer, isn't it?' Craig says. 'I saw him ogling you that day.'

'Just pick the one you like to fuck,' James says, the first words he's ever said to me.

'She hasn't fucked either of them,' Harry says, which isn't his to tell, but I know he can't resist talking to James about fucking.

'Well, there's your problem,' James says.

'There's a big difference between love and sex,' Craig says.

'Pay attention to what they *say*, not what they *do*,' Yasmin says.

Angus laughs. 'Don't pay any attention at all to what we *say*!'

187

'You don't always want what you need,' Dana says.

'It's always a choice between fireworks and coffee in bed,' Fabiana says. 'It always is.'

'You lot are useless,' Harry says. 'I'm with James.' He looks up from folding a napkin, but James is watching Angus drain his sangria.

Craig mixes up another pitcher. 'Imagine you have a roommate who is really hot and awesome,' he says to me. 'Which of your guys wouldn't sleep with her?'

'Imagine you have a kid that spikes a fever of a hundred and five,' Fabiana says. 'Which one won't freak out?'

'Or imagine you have a kid and the kid is possessed and starts spewing blood all over the walls.' Angus says.

'Or you're climbing Everest and your kid is buried in an avalanche on the Kangshung Face,' James says. 'Which one rips off his clothes to make a new baby with you?'

'Listen, Casey Kasem,' Dana says, tossing her last roll-up onto the pile. 'You spend enough time at the racetrack, you know your horse, okay? You always know your horse.'

Sunday night the roads are quiet. I cross Comm. Ave. easily, without the usual wait, and have the BU Bridge to myself. It's dusk and the river is pink and no boats break the stillness. I ride by the Sunoco station where Luke and I said goodbye. The marigolds are gone now. I'm not sure when I stopped noticing them. I feel an unexpected sense of accomplishment as I pedal past. I pass the geese, only a handful, stomping at the edge of the water like swimmers bracing for the cold. Then the footbridge where Silas kissed me. My insides wheel up and over, but he's probably back from Gettysburg by now and hasn't called and I am going to eat chicken fingers and cucumber slices with Oscar and his boys.

All the lights are on at their house. I lean my bike against some stiff bushes near the front steps, and while I'm looking for a bell or a knocker the door opens a crack. A snout appears.

'Hello, Bob.'

Bob barks once. The sound frightens him, and he disappears back in the house yelping.

The door opens a little wider, and Jasper's face hovers over the doorknob.

'Let her in.' John nudges Jasper out of the way.

I step inside. It's not what I expected. I didn't know I had expected anything until it wasn't there. No entryway, no front hall, no doors or doorways. On the outside it's a regular clap-board colonial, but inside all the rooms have been removed. The whole downstairs is one large space, walls painted bright white and a set of stairs that seem suspended by wires cutting a diagonal to the left and revealing an open section of the second floor. The kitchen is in the middle, with an island and bright red stools along its outer edge. Oscar has his back to me, bent over and fiddling with food on a tray in the oven.

'Is Casey in the house?' he says.

'Casey's in the house,' John says.

'She rode a bike,' Jasper says.

'Did she wear her helmet?'

I hold it up for the boys to see.

'Yes!'

'I can take that for you,' John says.

Both boys are wearing button-down shirts and kha-kis. Belts around their small waists. Jasper already has a few smudges on his white sleeve. All three of them have damp hair, cleanly parted.

Oscar straightens up. 'Twelve minutes on each side.' His face is splotched, and his eyes are wild.

'Hi there.' I kiss him on the cheek. He feels stiff and far away. But handsome, in a navy linen shirt and jeans.

I put my backpack on one of the red stools and pull out a bag of chocolate chip cookies I made in my toaster oven, three at a time. I unzip the top. Jasper leans into the smell. John tells him he can't have any until after supper then bends over the bag, too.

Oscar is busying himself in the fridge.

There are pictures taped to its door, drawings in crayon and colored pencil, most of them variations of a curved green line with bits of yellow at one end.

'Is that a snake?'

'No!' Jasper says and slaps his head. 'It's a dragon!'

'A fire-breathing dragon?'

'Yes! A fierce dragon breathing out tons of fire!'

'You're screaming,' John says.

Jasper jumps up and down and whispers, 'Lots and lots of fire.'

The drawings are signed ZAZ at the bottom. 'ZAZ?'

'His nom de crayon,' Oscar says at the sink, with a pretty decent accent.

'What's that?' John says.

Oscar turns on the faucet to rinse the cucumbers and doesn't answer.

'A nom de plume is French for name, "nom," of the pen, "de plume,"' I say. 'Some writers don't want to publish things under their real name, so they use a fake one, a pen name. Your dad said 'nom de crayon' because Jasper used a crayon not a pen. It also works as a double entendre, which is another French word and means 'double meaning' because 'crayon' in French means pencil, and you have a few pencil drawings here, too.' I feel lightheaded after explaining this.

'She's giving me a lot more credit than I deserve, boys. A delightful trait, to be sure.' He glances up at me quickly before he starts peeling the cucumbers. The skin falls off in long fat strips.

'How can I help?'

191

'Just keep educating the heathens.'

'We got new juice boxes,' Jasper says.

'What's a juice box?'

This makes them all laugh. They think I'm joking.

'There's kiwi-strawberry, peach-mango, and grape-something,' John says.

I choose grape-something, and the boys run into a closet and fight over who will bring it to me. It's decided John will take out the straw and push it through the little hole on top, and Jasper will hand it to me.

'You would think Madonna has come over,' Oscar says.

'Don't cry for me, Argentina!' Jasper sing-shouts as John prepares my juice box.

'You're bursting my eardrums. Here.'

Jasper takes the box from John and hands it to me.

'Thank you kindly.'

'You're welcome kindly.' Jasper is still bouncing.

'Do you need to wee?' John asks him.

'No!'

They watch me drink through the tiny straw. It's sweet and chemical flavored. Oscar slices the cucumbers loudly on the cutting board. We drain our juice boxes and make noises sucking up the last drops. Somehow I remember the deck of cards in my backpack.

I pull them out. They startle me. I haven't touched them since the gazebo in Pawtucket.

'You like cards better than board games,' John whispers.

'Crazy Eights!' Jasper says. 'Do you know Crazy Eights?'

'Of course.' My mother taught it to me when I had chicken pox in kindergarten. I made her play for days.

We move to the living room area. The boys start to sit on the couch, but when I drop down on the rug they come join me and we all sit cross-legged, our knees bumping.

'We do have chairs, you know,' Oscar says.

'You have to play cards on the floor.'

It's a good deck. It's old and flexible. The cards belonged to Paco's grandmother. We ended up with them after visiting her in Zaragoza where we played Chinchón. Paco and I used to play gin rummy in bed. I forgot that. Sometimes we'd find cards between the sheets in the morning. They have a woven reed pattern on them. When I pulled them out of my bag in Pawtucket, Luke held them and said, 'Ah, wicker,' and I laughed so hard. I can't say why.

I cut the cards and bend back both halves easily. I release my thumbs, and the cards slot together perfectly, fast and smooth. I slip my fingers underneath the overlapping pile and bend it the other way in a sharply arched bridge, and they whoosh down together beautifully. There is nothing like a good deck of cards.

The boys are staring.

'What?'

'How did you do that?'

'This?' I cut the deck and do it again.

'Yeah.'

'You haven't taught your kids to shuffle?' I call over to Oscar.

'We shuffle.'

'We do it like this.' John splits the deck and tries to wedge one half into the other sideways.

'Stop.' I gently take the deck away from him. 'You must never do that again. That is old-man shuffling, and no one should be doing that under the age of ninety-three.'

'Ageist,' Oscar says, flipping the chicken fingers. 'Twelve minutes.'

'Okay,' I tell them. 'You've each got six minutes to learn.'

I hand the deck to Jasper first, which makes John impatient and Jasper uneasy. He's used to John paving the way, going into the unknown ahead of him. The first few times I put my hands over his and we do it together, then I take mine away. His fingers barely span the length of the deck and the cards scissor sideways and the bridge snaps.

'I can't.'

'Try it again.'

He tries.

'I can't.'

'You can. Again.'

On the fifth try he does it. Splat and whoosh. 'Papa, watch. Watch!'

Oscar comes and stands at the edge of the rug.

After a few more attempts Jasper does it again. And again.

'Wow, Jaz. Look at you,' Oscar says. 'I wish someone had taught me how to do that at age five. I wouldn't be ninety-three now.'

194

I smile, but I don't look up. I've only got a few minutes left to teach John.

He doesn't let me do it with him, but after a few tries he gets it. They pass the deck back and forth, practicing, imprinting it, their small hands more sure each time. John manages a particularly long bridge that flutters down with a beautiful *shushhhhhh*.

They look at each other.

'It's so cool,' Jasper says.

'It's so, *so* cool,' John says.

'Okay. A tavola,' Oscar says.

'Crazy Eights after dinner?' I say.

'After dinner is books and bedtime,' Oscar says. He points to the chair I'm supposed to sit in, opposite him and beside Jasper. 'Five cucumber slices for every chicken stick,' he tells his boys.

We pass around the plates of food. The chicken fingers are golden and greasy. There are two dipping options for the cucumbers, ranch or Italian. It all tastes so good. I get the boys to tell me stories: the day John got on the wrong school bus; the time Jasper took a nap and didn't wake up until the next day; the night they locked the babysitter out of the house.

'Tell the Nurse Ellen story, Papa,' Jasper says.

'That's a bedtime story, not a supper story.'

'Tell it!' John says.

'Tell it!' Jasper says.

He puts his hand on my wrist. 'It's so funny.'

Oscar does not want to tell this story. He looks down at his plate and shakes his head, but the boys persist and he looks at John and says, 'You really want me to?'

John nods.

'When their mother, my wife, Sonya, was in the hospital, there were good nurses, and there were bad nurses.'

'There were happy nurses, and there were sad nurses,' John says.

'There were fat nurses, and there were thin nurses,' Jasper says.

'And then there was Nurse Ellen.'

'Nurse Ellen was mean.'

'She was cruel.'

'She was bitter.'

'She hated everyone.'

'But most of all she hated children,' Oscar says.

'Children aren't allowed in the morning!'

'Children aren't allowed in the afternoon!'

'I had to smuggle them in. On gurneys, in laundry bins, in vacuum cleaner bags, and under the domes on trays of food.'

'Papa would come alone, and Mama would cry, "You didn't bring the boys!"'

'And out we'd pop!'

'When we heard Nurse Ellen, we'd hide under Mama's covers.'

'We had to be so, so quiet.'

'"I smell children!" she'd thunder.'

'And Papa would say, "No, no children today."'

'We tried to win her over,' Oscar says.

'Mama said, "She likes cars."'

'And Papa bought her a book about car racing.'

'Mama said, "She likes outer space."'

'And John gave her his Lego girl astronaut.'

'Mama said, "She likes animals."'

'And Jasper gave her his little dog with the sucked-off ears.'

'But nothing satisflied her.'

'Satisfied.'

'Not flowers.'

'Not chocolates.'

'Not Slinkys or binkies or Twinkies.'

'But then.'

'But then one day Papa brought Mama ice cream.'

'Peppermint ice cream.'

'But it was a day when Mama was very sick.'

'She was too sick to eat.'

'She pointed to Nurse Ellen.'

'And Papa gave her the ice cream.'

'And Nurse Ellen smiled from ear to ear.'

'Like never before or since.'

They go silent all at once, and there is a terrible stillness I don't want to break but know I have to break, a heathen made to speak after their sacred liturgy.

'That's a great story.'

'It's true. It happened,' John says.

Jasper's hand is still on my wrist, tight.

'Dishes to the sink,' Oscar says.

John stands and takes two plates. Jasper lets go and takes the other two. We are left with the water glasses between us. Oscar is resting his chin in his palm. He raises his eyebrows at me. 'And that's the abridged version.'

'I'm so sorry.'

He nods. His eyes are unfocused.

John and Jasper are fighting over the sprayer at the sink. When Oscar notices, he says, 'Up. Go up now.'

They let go and head to the stairs.

'Say goodnight to Casey.'

They say goodnight, and I wish I could give them hugs, but I stay in my seat. 'Sleep tight.'

Halfway up the stairs John says, 'Thanks for teaching us to shuffle.'

'Keep moving,' Oscar says, and they go the rest of the way up. They look down from the balcony and I wave and they wave and Oscar says, 'Face and teeth,' and they are gone.

I bring the glasses to the sink.

'Look at you,' he says.

I'm carrying the four glasses in one hand, the cucumber bowl, chicken sticks platter, and dipping sauce in the other.

'A real pro.'

He opens the dishwasher. A smell comes out of it. I haven't lived anywhere with a dishwasher since high school. I load the dishes and take in the scent of an American home.

'They do this with women. Their teachers, their friends' mothers. Well, you saw it at the restaurant. They sort of throw themselves at them. It breaks my heart because what is it going to look like in ten years with girls their age? All that neediness.'

'They're going to have to fight them off.'

He shakes his head. He rinses the plates and slots them into the machine. I want him to forget about the dishes and pull me to the couch.

He rinses and reassembles the salad spinner and hands it to me. It's a solid expensive salad spinner. I push down on the big red button and the plastic basket inside revs and whizzes like a well-built engine.

'Sorry,' he says, taking it away from me. 'I forgot you don't know where it goes.'

Upstairs there's arguing coming from the bathroom.

'Boys!'

'Ready,' John calls from the balcony. Jasper's head barely clears the railing.

I want to ask him if I can read the boys a book before bed. I wonder what their favorites are.

'Okay,' Oscar says. He wipes his hands on a dishrag. 'Thanks for coming, Casey.'

'I can wait, or maybe I could read—'

He shakes his head. 'Bedtime is still a bit rough.'

'Papa,' Jasper whines.

'Coming.' He starts up the stairs and looks back. And there is Oscar again, Oscar from the arboretum, the little grin as if we already have a past together, hundreds of little jokes, as if me just standing there at his fancy kitchen island is all he wants in the world.

'I'll call you tomorrow.' He lifts his hands briefly in helpless apology.

He climbs the rest of the stairs, puts a hand on each boy's back, and steers them down the hallway and out of sight. The dishwasher starts churning.

I gather my cards from the spot on the rug where I sat with the boys. I can hear bits of their voices above me. I give the cards one last slow shuffle and put them in my knapsack. I put on my coat and my helmet and go out the door. Bob has come out of hiding and watches me from a chair near the window. I wheel my bike to the end of the driveway. I can't see them, but I know what room they're in by the way the light shifts through the windows. I can nearly smell the toothpaste breath, the weight of a tired boy against my shoulder.

Silas calls, and I meet him at a Korean place near MIT. He apologizes for not getting in touch sooner. He came back with a stomach bug the students were passing around on the trip he says and threw up for three days straight. He does look a little wan. He's just shaved, and I can see the blue stubble beneath. Usually his skin is ruddy from afterschool coaching. He orders plain rice and steamed vegetables.

As he's describing the eighteen hours each way in a bus and six nights in a Red Roof Inn policing thirty-seven teenagers with the seventy-eight-year-old librarian, I'm wondering how to tell him about Oscar. I want to know if it matters to him. It seems like the only way to find out his feelings for me. It was easier to imagine doing this when he wasn't in the room, when he wasn't leaning over a table on his elbows, twisting up a chopstick wrapper with fingers that are unexpectedly familiar.

He starts talking about the last Wednesday-night workshop he went to. 'Muriel read this section of her novel, and I swear no one was breathing by the end. Not even Oscar.' Every time he says Oscar's name I feel an unpleasant zap.

'You okay?' he says.

'Yeah. Just a bit tired. How're your vegetables?' I ask.

'Good,' he says, but he hasn't eaten much, either.

After dinner we walk to the T stop. Neither of us suggests anything more to prolong the date. I follow him down the steps and through the turnstiles. I'm headed inbound and he's going out. We stand where our sets of stairs break off to separate tracks. Here? This is where I tell him? This is where we talk? A group of teenagers rush by us, yelling at each other. A train rattles through a tunnel. I want him to kiss me. If I talk about Oscar, he won't kiss me.

'I better get this.' He bats me lightly on the arm. 'See you.' He takes the stairs two at a time and makes it through the doors before they close.

I guess there was no need to say anything after all.

M y first rejection letter arrives.
'We don't feel it's the right fit for us,' it says.

'That agent didn't read it,' Muriel says. 'His assistant or intern read it. That's why it says "we" and not "I."' We're at her apartment. She's made me a lovely sandwich, but I can't eat it. My appetite is dwindling, along with sleep. 'When someone actually reads it, it will be a different story.'

I can't speak, and she gets up and hugs me. 'You are going to sell that fucker. I promise you.'

I need to sell it. I need more money. A guy named Derek Spike from EdFund has gotten my work number and spoken to Marcus about seizing a portion of my wages. Marcus hung up on him. 'Those dicks. They made my sister's life hell. I was smart not to go to college.'

I'm starting to think he was right.

Adam wants to increase my rent. We're standing in the yard beneath the big maple, its last leaves dropping like rain. I ask if I could have until the new year at the old rate.

'What makes you think you'll be able to afford it then?'

'I finished my novel.'

'And?'

'I sent it out to agents and if—'

He knocks his head back and laughs hard.

I call Caleb and rant. 'Your friend lives in a fucking mansion and drives a fucking Mercedes-Benz, but he has to suddenly raise my rent?'

'He has strains of his own, Case.' He and Phil and Adam were in a different orbit, with their houses and their salaries. 'Divorce is a financial apocalypse. Phil says he's lucky it's illegal for us to marry because I would have fleeced him by now. Probably true. Adam says he could get a lot more for that apartment.'

'It's a *room*, not an apartment. A moldy room.' I'm touching the lump under my arm. I can't tell if it's getting bigger. It might be. If it's cancer, I won't have to pay anyone anything. I'll move back in with Caleb and Phil, ruin their lives for a year or two, and die.

'Still. It's a tight market in Boston.' When I don't respond, he says, 'You there?'

'Just stroking my lump.'

'Casey. Phil says it's most likely nothing.'

Caleb must have called Adam, because he meets me at the door the next morning when I come in for the dog.

'Could we talk?' he says and points to the kitchen table. We sit. Oafie walks in circles around us, waiting for me to get free. I'm thinking he's reconsidered the rent hike. Instead he tells me he's decided to divide his property and sell the garage and the yard to the far side of it. He's evicting me.

'When?'

'We're going to list it in three weeks. You don't have to clean or anything. Whoever buys it will tear it down. It's the land they'll be looking at.'

S ilas leaves me a message, then another, and I don't call back. I've made my choice. I'm done with the seesaw, the hot and cold, the guys who don't know or can't tell you what they want. I'm done with kissing that melts your bones followed by ten days of silence followed by a fucking pat on the arm at the T stop.

Oscar's boys have a day off from school, and he invites me over for lunch. It smells delicious. He's making grilled cheese sandwiches. The boys are drawing at the table.

I've spent the last few days reading Oscar's books: his first novel, a collection of short stories, and *Thunder Road,* which is the story of a boy in the late fifties, losing his mother to cancer in the course of five days. It's told from a many-years-hence perspective, when the boy is grown and has sons of his own. The sentences are pristine and careful. The arc of the story is clear and controlled, with a swell of emotion at the end that he's withheld and we've been waiting for. There's a sadness that surprises me, not in the plot, which of course is about loss, but a sadness within the prose separate from content that I find in all his work—in his first novel, which was billed as comic, and in all the short stories. It's a sense of despair about writing itself, a sort of throwing up of hands, as if to say I'll put this down on the page but it's not what I really mean because what I really mean cannot be put into words. It creates a sort of drag on the narrative. I looked up some reviews on microfiche to see if anyone else has commented on it. They have not. The early reviews I read were all positive, young writer with great promise and a bold future sort of thing. And for *Thunder Road* they were glowing and grateful. At long last. Silent for nine years. The novel we've been waiting for.

'I read *Thunder Road*.'

'Really?' He flips the sandwiches and puts down the spatula. 'Heavens.' He touches his wrist. 'My pulse is starting to race.'

I'm not sure if he's serious. Does he care what I think, or is he just pretending?

'I loved it.'

'Honestly?' He does seem in earnest.

'Yes, yes.' I tell him all the scenes I admired and why, the small moments and gestures. He seems eager for this approval, and I exaggerate my initial responses. I don't mention I read the earlier books as well, because I'm not sure I can keep up this level of enthusiasm that long.

He calls the boys and they come to the stove with plates and when he slides a sandwich onto John's plate he says, 'She liked my book.' And when he slides one onto Jasper's plate he says, 'She liked my book.' And when John asks if we can play cards at the table, he says, 'Why not,' and we eat and play and afterward at the sink when the boys are zooming their plastic planes around the woodstove, he pulls me close and tells me he loves me. I kiss him and our lips are slippery from the grilled cheese and the boys' planes have stopped flying.

I tell Oscar about Adam selling the garage. We're at the boys' swim lesson in East Cambridge, watching them by the indoor pool on lawn chairs. The air is humid, rank with a chlorine and soggy human smell. My jeans are stuck to my legs.

'Come live with us,' he says.

The boys' thin arms are thrashing toward the deep end. They're learning the crawl. It's hard to breathe in the wet air. 'I wasn't—'

'I know you weren't. But why not?'

He doesn't know how I live, how far I need to run, how much I owe, how little I sleep, or that I've now gotten rejection letters from three agents. I haven't told him about the lump under my arm. He calls me his waif, his down-on-her-luck waitress, but he takes it all lightly. In fact, Holly Golightly is one of his names for me. If we lived together I would expose myself as the blighted Jean Rhys character I really am.

The next Saturday he and the boys pick me up to go apple picking. They know an orchard out in Sherborn where you get cider doughnuts afterward. I'm excited about it all week. We never did those kinds of things in my family. There were never outings. Oscar and his boys love an outing.

I prepared them for the size of my place, but they are still surprised when they come in.

'It's like Thumbelina's house,' Jasper says.

'It's smaller, and Casey is a regular-size girl,' John says.

They jump on the futon, which is disappointingly un-bouncy, examine my nibs and ink bottles on the window sill, and stick their heads in and out of the bathroom.

I think Oscar for once has no words at all.

'The apples await,' he says finally.

We head out to the car.

'Back on your thrones,' Oscar says and the boys strap themselves into their big car seats in back.

'We think you should come live with us,' John says.

'Our beds are better.' Jasper says, kicking the back of my seat.

'Wow,' I say. Oscar is smiling but looking at the road. 'Wow.' I turn to the boys behind me. They're waiting for my answer. 'That is such a kind offer.'

'It would be free. We wouldn't charge you a penny,' John says.

'I will have to think that over very carefully. Thank you.'

At the orchard we get a green cart and bags for our ap-ples. The boys get in the cart and Oscar zigzags them down the paths between the rows of apple trees and when the cart goes up on two wheels they shriek. We follow signs for the apples with the weirdest names—Crow Egg and Winter Banana—and we lift the boys up to reach the higher branches. Our cart fills with bags full of apples. We sing 'This Old Man' and 'She'll Be Comin' Round the Mountain,' which they have all sorts of newfangled verses for. Every fifteen minutes, either John or Jasper asks if I've thought carefully enough yet.

The boys play on a swing set while we stand in line for the doughnuts.

'I'm sorry,' he says. 'I had to run it by them.'

'It's so soon.'

'You moved to *Spain* with Paco.'

'I met Paco two and a half years before I moved in with him. This is just a few weeks.'

'A few weeks? I met you in July, Casey.'

'It didn't get serious for a while.' I think I was measuring from my last date with Silas.

'It was always serious with me.'

'With Paco it was just Paco. There were not two vulnerable little boys. What if it doesn't work out? I don't want them ever to be hurt again by anyone.'

'Well that's a bit unrealistic.' He nuzzles his chin in the curve between my neck and shoulder. 'Besides, we're going to work out.'

They drop me off at Iris for my dinner shift.

'Think about it.' Jasper taps his head as they pull away. 'Think!'

I wait for the idea to calm me down, but it doesn't. Oscar asking me to move in doesn't seem like a solution to Adam selling the garage. It seems like another problem. And the problems are mounting. Thomas announces he's opening his own restaurant in the Berkshires. Clark the brunch chef is to replace him as head chef.

'But he's ooful,' Harry says to Thomas. 'He's supremely untalented. And he's a petty, miserable troglodyte.'

'It's Gory's decision,' Thomas says. 'I suggested others.'

On his last night I'm able to say my own goodbye to him in the walk-in. I'm getting a ramekin of butter florets, and he's sitting on the crate I usually sit on.

'Casey Kasem,' he says, but kindly. We've always had an understanding. I'm not sure what we understand exactly. We've never spoken about anything but apps and entrées. But it's there. At least for me.

'I wish you weren't leaving.'

He nods. 'Thanks. It's been a good run here.'

'Good luck with your restaurant.'

'Good luck with your book.' He smiles at my expression. 'Harry mentioned it.'

'Thanks.'

212

At the end of the shift, his wife comes in and helps him take out the last of his stuff. She's pregnant and carrying the baby way out in front. She balances a fat cookbook on top of the bump. 'Look, Ma! No hands!' she says, and Thomas rushes over and grabs the cookbook.

'You'll crush her.'

'Feel this,' she says, drumming on her belly. 'She's encased in steel.'

I didn't know they were having a girl.

The next night Clark takes over. He brings some of his brunch guys with him and tells Angus and two other line cooks to come back at lunch. He appropriates one of Helene's pastry counters for salads. He tells Dana to stop scowling, Tony to look him in the eye when he's talking, and me to wear more makeup or something. 'You look like a vampire. And not the sexy kind,' he says.

When service begins he slaps my hand as I reach in the window for my first entrées.

'Use a napkin.'

'It's not hot.'

'Use a napkin. Every time. Customers do not want to see your filthy fingers on their plate.'

Once Clark starts working nights, more bees swarm into my work life. I start getting my customers confused, my orders mixed up. I have to take long breaks on the fire escape. My whole body feels like it's a big iron bell that someone has struck, and it won't stop ringing. It's like not being able to catch my breath except that I can't catch any part of me. Muriel tells me to take long slow breaths and scan my body from head to toe when this happens, but I end up gasping for air. Out on the fire escape I do some clenching. It's the only thing that helps. I clench my fists or press my knees together or squeeze my stomach muscles all at once. Sometimes I start with my face and work down my whole body, tightening each muscle one by one for as long as I can stand it, then letting go and moving on to the next. It's enough to get me back into the dining room. After a few nights of this Marcus figures out where I'm going and finds me there midclench and drags me back. Sometimes, standing over a six-top and reciting the specials, I feel like I'm breaking up in tiny fragments, and I don't understand how phrases like 'with a cranberry cognac glaze' are still coming out of my mouth or why my customers watching me don't signal to someone that I need help. There's some thin covering over me that hides it all. If someone saw inside and called an ambulance, I would go off willingly. It's my biggest fantasy at these terrifying moments, two EMTs in the doorway with a stretcher for me to lie down on.

The next Saturday night is particularly bad. When it's over I tip out and settle up and leave as soon as I can. I don't even say goodbye to Harry. My body is ringing. I can't feel my fingers. The only way I know I'm still breathing is that I'm still moving. Outside the cold feels good. I want colder. I want ice and snow, something to numb the panic. Two

Harvard boys in tuxes come out of the building across the street and go into another. A group of old people, crumpled and slow moving, get into a Volvo near my bike. I hate old people. I hate anyone older than my mother, who didn't get to become old. At the top of the street there is a guy walking on Mass. Ave. toward Central Square, loping, hands in his pockets. It isn't him. It isn't Silas, but the slope from neck to base of the spine is similar. Something awful rises up in me, and I have to get out. I have to get out. I have to get out of this body right now.

I crouch down on the pavement and raw terror overtakes me. I don't know if I'm making sounds. I'm like that boy in second grade who had an epileptic fit on the classroom floor, shuddering like a machine, only it's all inside my head, everything in my mind juddering like a hydraulic drill that I cannot stop. There seems to be no way to survive it or to make it end.

I don't know how long it lasts. Time frays. When the worst of it has passed I'm still crouched on the ground, my forehead pressed to my knee. I raise my head and see my backpack, house key, and wad of cash tips spread out all around me on the pavement. I stand up, worried that someone from Iris will come out and find me crumpled there. It takes me a while to unlock my bike. My body is still trembling, just like Toby Cadamonte's after his seizure.

I pedal slowly home, spent, but when I lie down on the futon after a warm shower and some muscle squeezing I feel like my body has been plugged into an outlet. More slow breathing. More clenching.

I try to pray. I kiss my mother's ring, and I pray for her, for her soul and for peace in her soul. I pray for my father and Ann and Caleb and Phil and Muriel and Harry. I pray for the earth and everyone on it. I pray we can all come together and live without fear. And at the end I pray for sleep. I beg to have back the ability to fall asleep. I was once so good at it. I pray hard and yet I'm aware that I have no sense of what or whom I am praying to. I went to church until my mother went to Phoenix, but I never believed the stories in church any more or less than I believed in Pinocchio or the Three Little Pigs.

The panic feels loud as hell in my head, like being next to a speaker at a concert. I turn back on the light and try to read. The words remain words. I can't hear them. I can't lose myself in them. A friend in college once said that she didn't understand how people read for enjoyment. She couldn't see or feel anything beyond the words. They never transformed into anything else but the sound of her internal voice reciting sentences. She concluded she had no imagination whatsoever. I wonder if I'm losing my imagination. This fresh fear is ice-cold. Never to be able to read or write again. But really, what does it matter? Two more rejection letters came this week.

I spend the night that way, passing through layers of anxiety, humiliation, and despair. Somewhere close to dawn I lose some consciousness. It isn't sleep exactly, but I have to think of it as sleep because it's all I ever get anymore.

When the sun comes up, I surrender and go out running. It has to be a long one, because Oscar and the boys are taking me to play miniature golf. John never forgot my boast that I could beat his father, and today is the day I have to live up to it.

It's cold, the coldest morning yet. There's already traffic on Beacon, and I have to wait for the light. The river is flat steel, the sun not high enough to hit it yet. I'm still running in shorts because I don't have sweats, and after a few miles I lose feeling in my thighs. I run to the Watertown Bridge and come back on the Cambridge side. I pass the tall gray hospital with its stacked rows of windows. On the lower floors you can see flowers on some of the sills. Bless them, my heart seems to say. Bless them all. And my throat closes from the thought of people dying in those rooms and their loved ones losing them, and I have to stop running to suck in enough air.

When I get back, a man and a woman are peering into my windows.

'Can I help you?'

They whip around. The man sticks out his hand. 'Chad Belamy. Belamy Realty. You must be the writer.'

The writer. Adam is using me to add some clout to his garage.

'Jean Hunt.' She's my age, but her hair is shellacked in place, and she wears a gray suit, stockings, and pumps, all on a Sunday morning.

She asks about the neighborhood. From her tone and the way she phrases her questions I know she thinks I'm younger than she is. I tell her it seems like a mix of families and empty nesters.

'And you pay to live in there?' she says.

217

'It's a very desirable location,' Chad Belamy says, urging me with his eyes to agree.

'It's not as bad as it looks from the outside. You're welcome to come in.'

She and Chad share a look. 'No need,' she says. 'I'd start from scratch.' She looks at the yard on the other side. 'It's a smaller lot than I'd expected. But it might be all I can afford.'

Adam has listed the property for $375,000. And then she'll have to build a house on it. All she can afford.

She asks me what kind of writing I do, but I say I have to shower before a friend comes over and excuse myself.

That conversation eats away at the protective coating the run gave me, and I'm feeling pretty jagged when I get in Oscar's car.

Jasper's crying. I ask what's wrong and he shows me his hand, his tiny smooth hand with a fresh bloody scrape across it.

'Oh my God. What happened?'

Oscar bounces a flat hand covertly near the steering wheel, trying to signal that I should lower my voice.

'Oscar, he has this *gash* across his hand.'

The hand bounces more emphatically.

John starts shrieking.

'What's going on?'

'He hit me first. He hit me in the eye!' John screams.

His face is so red it's hard to tell, but I think I see a purplish bruise to the side of his left eye.

I turn to Jasper. 'Did you do that?'

Jasper wails a long incomprehensible sentence.

218

'Casey, please turn around,' Oscar says. 'You're just inciting them.'

'Inciting? They're clobbering each other back there. You need to pull over.'

He laughs. 'If I pulled over every time they beat on each other we'd never get anywhere.'

'Oscar, he's bleeding.'

'I mean it,' he says sharply. 'They'll be fine.'

I don't like his tone of voice, but after a few miles they both stop crying. They are laughing about a dog in a pink coat and booties Oscar points out.

Then I start to smell something revolting.

'God, what is that?' I try to put down the window but the child locks are on.

There's giggling from the back seat. Oscar smiles into the rearview. I wheel around.

'It's him,' John says, pointing to his brother. 'It's him.'

Jasper gives me a big smile. Then the smell gets even worse.

'That is so gross. It's like poop mixed with rotting seagull.'

They all laugh. I'm not trying to be funny.

'Please let me put down a window.' I'm trying so hard not to swear in front of them.

'Someone left her funny bone at home today,' Oscar says.

'Someone forgot to take her giggle medicine,' John says.

Oscar unlocks my window. I lower it and stick my head out as far as it will go.

* * *

The clubhouse at King Putt in Saugus is in the shape of a pyramid and the snack bar is a sarcophagus. I decided long ago that if we ever did play mini golf, I'd let Oscar win. I thought I should preserve John's faith in his father's invincibility a little longer. But once I get a club in my hand I know I'm not going to go the noble route. I'm in the mood for some glory today.

I fake lightness. For the first two holes I feign unfamiliarity. I'm not completely pretending. I've played miniature golf three times in my life. I'm sussing him out, though. I know he's coordinated. I've seen him kick a soccer ball and crack my wiffleball curve into the neighbors' trees. And I've deceived him. I haven't told him about my years of golf because I knew it would make him curious. It always makes the athletes curious. They think they can beat me, and it ends badly every time. Then they either sulk or try to convince me to start playing again.

The boys hit first, John taking whole minutes to line up his shot and Jasper knocking the ball without thought, surprised when it flies out onto the parking lot.

I'm not very good at the start. The anxiety is at a steady buzz and the putter head is made of red plastic and the carpet is a mangled mess. But I get the hang of it. On the third hole I can it through Cleopatra's Cave.

The three of them shout my name, gleeful. A stroke of lightning. I keep doing it. I can't help it. Something takes over. I play the break of the scarab of the fourth hole and put it straight into the mouth of the asp of the fifth. So many years since I've held any kind of club. So many years since I've felt naturally good at something, good in an empirical, undeniable way that is not reliant on anyone's opinion.

John is holding the scorecard. 'She's beating you, Papa.'

'I know it,' Oscar chuckles.

On the seventh hole, when both boys hit their balls into the Nile and run ahead to the shore where they will get them back, he says, 'What's going on?'

I shrug and take my next shot.

He shakes his head. 'Look at you. The way you move. The way you curl over the ball.'

The bees are gone. Muscle memory has taken over, brought my body back to a time when it did not know panic, even under great pressure. Holding this cheap club has calmed me. I give him my first real smile of the day.

'I played when I was a kid, and I was good. My father started calling me Casey, from that old poem "Casey at the Bat." Do you know it?'

He shakes his head.

'It's just a cheesy poem he loved when he was a kid about a baseball player. Casey's the best hitter on the Mudville team. And they're down four-two and it's the last inning and they have two outs but two crappy players actually get on base and then Casey gets to bat and the crowd goes wild. Strike one. Strike two. And then another swing. "And somewhere men are laughing, and little children shout," I recite in my father's baritone. "But there is no joy in Mudville; mighty Casey has struck out."'

221

Oscar is delighted. 'Mighty Casey.'

'That's me. Named for a guy who struck out when it mattered most.'

'You secretive little prodigy.' He nudges my shoulder. 'I've got a friend up in Vermont who belongs to the Woodstock club.'

'No thanks.'

'It's the best course in New England.'

'I know it well. No thanks.'

'Why not? Look at you.' He keeps saying that. *Look at you.* 'You love it.'

I walk ahead to catch up with the boys.

'I'm just saying that if you have that kind of talent you should use it from time to time.'

I walk faster.

When we're done, John tallies up our scores. I've beaten Oscar by nine strokes. We bring in our scorecard and the manager writes me up on the chalkboard. First place for the month. 'I don't think anyone's going to top that anytime soon.' I can tell he doesn't believe it.

On the way home, the boys are sad I've beaten their father. They take it hard. Oscar tries to cheer all three of us up, but it doesn't work. I have them drop me off in the Square. After the car is gone I sit down on a bench outside of Grendel's. My head is ringing again. I can't follow a thought. I feel like crying, but nothing comes. I sit and do my clenching, every muscle I can, over and over.

* * *

I have an hour till work, so I wander around WordsWorth. *Darkness Visible* is on the remainder table, and I pick it up. I've never read it before. 'A Memoir of Madness,' Styron calls it. Caleb is always giving it to his depressed friends. I start reading the first chapter. Styron has flown to Paris to receive a prize. He is certain he will not overcome the disorder in his mind. He has lost the ability to sleep, is riddled with fear and a sense of dislocation. The writing has that stark lucidity of someone trying to tell you the truest thing they know. The pages are small and I turn them one after the other and my insides burn in terrifying recognition. Paris is only the first chapter, only the beginning of his descent. I shut the book, wipe my face, and leave the store.

*W*hile we admire the scope of

We are grateful for the look at

Your project did not strike a chord

This is not quite right for

Unfortunately, at this time we aren't

Thank you for your submission but

We appreciate you thinking of us

We do not feel passionate enough

A fter eleven rejection letters comes a message on my phone from someone called Jennifer Lin. She says she's Ellen Nelson's assistant and leaves a number. Ellen Nelson is the agent of two of my favorite writers.

I call back the next morning before work.

'I read *Love and the Revolution* over the weekend. I loved it.'

'Thank you.'

'No, I really loved it. I think it's extraordinary, Camila.'

Camila. I forgot I'd put my real name on the manuscript.

'Thank you so much.' But what does Ellen Nelson think? I'm impatient to know where we're going. And I can't be late for work.

'So Ellie isn't taking on new authors right now. I'd like to do this one myself. I'd like to represent you. I'm sure you've had a lot of interest, and I'll just say up front that this would be my first book. I've been working for the Nelson Agency for three years and I've been waiting for the novel that would lift me a mile high and it's yours.'

I have no idea what to ask, what to say. Why haven't I prepared for this?

'Have you already made a decision? Am I too late?'

'No, I haven't. Not yet.'

'Phew,' she laughs. 'My palms are sweaty right now. Makes me wonder how people ever propose to each other. I have no track record,' Jennifer goes on. 'And I will completely understand if you are interested in a more trodden path. But you would be my only client.' She laughs again. 'I would give you all my attention and focus, which, if you talk to someone in my family, can be very intense. I work very hard. Ellie said she would be happy to give you a full and lengthy evaluation of me. Shall I put her on?'

There's a click and another voice is talking, as if I've been patched in to a conversation late. 'You might have someone lined up with big name authors and a fancy address, but I'm telling you, you want Jennifer steering your ship. No one else.' She takes what sounds like three fast intakes of a cigarette and blows it out all over the receiver. 'First of all, she hates everything. Everything. I had three debut bestsellers last year. She *hated* all three. Told me not to touch them. Your book—I haven't read it yet—but your book must be something outstanding because this girl passes on everything. Second, she's ambitious. She'll work her fanny off for you. She'll tell you exactly what she's doing and why she's doing it. You probably have other options.' She waits for me to confirm this, and when I say nothing she says, 'You're coy. Okay. I get it. However, I know this business, and I am giving you grade-A advice.'

I thank her and am relieved when she passes me back to Jennifer. Jennifer starts talking about the manuscript. I can barely take it in, her enthusiasm, her close reading, her kindness. Each time she brings up a scene I remember where I was when I wrote it—in the yellow kitchen in Albuquerque, in the bar below Paco's mother's apartment. She talks about the clever break in the narrative, the abrupt end of Clara's childhood and, when it resumes, the subtle but clear shift in voice. That happened in Caleb and Phil's guest room in Bend, in the weeks after my mother's death and I couldn't write at all, and when I started up again it had to be from a different place. Clara's young voice was gone. She talks and all I see is what she cannot, these years of my life woven into the pages.

'There are just a few things I wonder about,' she says and lists a few elements of the book that she feels needs some attention. They make sense. She has identified things I didn't even know were there and things I'd skirted past. She talks for a long time, and I'm looking at the clock and thinking about asking her if I can call her back after work, but I don't want to interrupt her. I want to know where she's going with all this. Will she represent me, and how exactly does that work?

She asks if I'd like to do a revision and send it back to her. She asks if I could do that in a month. 'We'd want to get it to editors before the holidays. You can't sell anything over the holidays.'

I agree to write a revision, and we hang up. It's 11:34. The restaurant has just opened for lunch. I bolt out the door.

Marcus is so mad he almost sends me home, but a party of eight reporters from the *Globe* comes in without a reservation and no one else can take them. He tells me I'm now on double probation. He says I have one slim straw left. I don't care. I have a fucking agent.

227

I find Harry in the kitchen picking up his turkey clubs. I tell him about Jennifer and he puts the clubs back down and hugs me hard. He whoops loudly and Tony tells him to shut his mouth. He doesn't. He keeps yelping. I tell him what she said and how I have to do a revision, that she has all kinds of ideas.

'Like what?'

I look at him. I can't remember anything Jennifer said except for something about a transition in chapter 5.

'Something about chapter five,' I say.

'You took notes, right?'

'My heart was pounding and I was late for work and I didn't know where we were going.'

He rubs my back. 'You can call her back later.'

'Yeah,' I say, but I know I won't.

I think when I get home and sit at my desk with the telephone pressed to my ear that I'll remember what Jennifer said, but I don't. It all made so much sense to me at the time. I remember the feeling I had, the thrill of it, but I don't remember many of the words. We talked about the theme of possession, I think, that runs through the book, but I don't know what she said. I remember nothing she wanted me to work on except the party scene in chapter 5. She thought it needed a few lines of transition from the scene before it. I think she said it could be a few pages longer, too.

I call Muriel. She's packing for her conference in Rome. I barely get it out. She tells me to write down every word of the conversation I can remember no matter how disjointed.

I do and call her back. She listens then speaks at length about the idea of possession in the novel and how the whole history of Cuba is enacted on Clara's body. She tosses out a few more suggestions that had occurred to her since she read it. I don't know if Jennifer said anything like this, but they are smart insights, and I write them all down.

I tell her to have a safe trip. I say this three or four times before we hang up.

Oscar says agents are full of it, and it doesn't matter that I've forgotten what Jennifer said. 'It was clearly unmemorable.'

We're driving to Wellesley for his reading there. I'm wearing a skirt and a long strand of my mother's beads. 'It wasn't. She's smart and sharp, and I really liked her ideas.'

'But not enough to remember them.'

'I was late for work and hadn't slept well and my brain is foggy these days.'

'Listen to you, sounding like a menopausal old lady.'

We get to the bookstore a half hour before the reading. Oscar tells the girl at the register his name, and she doesn't recognize it and doesn't know about the reading. She points us to a woman in back, who flushes when she sees Oscar. She says it's an honor to have him, and she takes us to an alcove where there are rows of seats for his reading and a table with stacks of his three books on it. Two people are sitting in the back row already, knitting. The bookstore owner says that the writer Vera Wilde is coming to the reading and to dinner afterward.

'I hope that's all right,' she says.

'It will be good to see her.'

'Oh phew. She said you were old friends. We hosted her at the church last week.' She shows us to a room in back full of boxes of books and a desk covered in paperwork. There are two plastic molded chairs in the middle. 'You can put your stuff in here and just relax until seven. Can I get you a glass of water?'

'No. I think we'll have a walk,' Oscar says and heads to the door.

I thank the woman and catch up with him on the street.

He points back to the bookstore. 'Did you see that pathetic Xerox they taped to the door? Vera Wilde fills the church. I get six chairs and a music stand they nicked from high school band practice. Fuck.'

'There were at least twenty chairs. Maybe thirty.'

'I am forty-seven years old. I was supposed to be reading in auditoriums by now. Did you see the cover of the *Book Review* last week? That was my student. My *students* are blowing by me. I'm not doing this. I always think it will be okay, but it's not okay.'

'I thought you were forty-five.'

'I know I have a better book inside me. I have something big inside me. I just. Ever since. Fuck.' It almost seems like he's going to punch the bricks of the gift shop beside us. Instead he lays his palms on the wall and lets out some jagged breaths.

Nearly every guy I've dated believed they should already be famous, believed that greatness was their destiny and they were already behind schedule. An early moment of intimacy often involved a confession of this sort: a childhood

231

vision, teacher's prophesy, a genius IQ. At first, with my boyfriend in college, I believed it, too. Later, I thought I was just choosing delusional men. Now I understand it's how boys are raised to think, how they are lured into adulthood. I've met ambitious women, driven women, but no woman has ever told me that greatness was her destiny.

My father had this kind of drama in him, sudden surges of despair about his life and wasted chances and breaks he never got. It took me a while to understand that my wins on the golf course, no matter how hard he strived for them, only made him feel worse. I figured that an actually successful man like Oscar would have outgrown all that crap.

He straightens up and looks around for me. I've moved a few yards up the street.

'Every now and then I have a small pity party.' He wipes his face with his hands. 'It's over now.' He swings an arm around me and we walk back toward the store.

They don't have enough chairs in the end. The owner's son is sent down to the basement for more but there are still people who have to stand against the shelves. I sit in the middle of the fourth row, next to a student who takes notes. The owner prepared a long and heartfelt introduction, about where she was when she read his first book and how overcome she was. She quotes passages from reviews, and she lists his awards and fellowships. She tells us a major motion picture is in the works for *Thunder Road*, which I didn't know.

Oscar stands up and thanks her—Annie, he calls her now—and praises her 'renowned collection' and thanks her for the hyperbole. He thanks everyone for coming out on such a beautiful evening. He takes long pauses between his sentences, giving the audience the sense that he is bashful, that appearing in public is difficult for him, that he never expected to have to do this. When he reads, he puts the book on the metal stand and his hands deep in his pockets. He raises his shoulders and tips his head down so that his eyes come at us at a sheepish glance, almost as if he feels the words aren't good enough to be read aloud. It's a pretty adorable performance, if you hadn't heard him moaning about not reading at the church.

In the middle of the reading, my heart starts beating way too fast. My hands and feet feel swollen, like my pulse is inflating them. There are three people to my left and four to my right and we are packed in so tight my knees are pressed against the back of the chair in front of me. Getting out will create an upheaval. And all I can think of is getting out. I'm like a bag of panic held in by a thin sac of skin. I clench and unclench discreetly in my metal chair that has come up from the basement.

When he's done, people smash their hands together, and it sounds like an audience of hundreds. He steps away from the music stand and sits at the signing table. A line quickly forms, and people begin gushing one by one. He moves them along quickly, as he did on Avon Hill when he was a stranger to me.

I drift over to the wall of fiction. Annie does have a good collection. Many of my favorites are there: *The Evening of the Holiday, Beloved, Independent People, Troubles, Housekeeping, Woodcutters.* In college, my litmus test for a bookstore was Hamsun's *Hunger*. It's there, too. They calm me, all these names on spines. I feel such tenderness toward them. I brush my fingers across the row of Woolf novels. I don't own many books anymore. I shipped my books to Spain but I couldn't afford to send them back. They're still at Paco's. I doubt I'll see them again.

There's a woman hanging back from the table, watching Oscar with a small smile. When the last person in line moves away, her smile grows and changes her whole face.

'Vera!' Oscar stands up and comes around the table and hugs her tight and they're laughing. She points to something on the cover of his book and they laugh harder. She's around his age, in black jeans and pale leather boots, the posture of a dance teacher.

We walk to a bistro down the street. Oscar slips his arm through mine and slows us down a few steps behind Annie and Vera.

'So,' he says.

'You were great. You're a pro. You had them eating out of your hand.'

'I want to have *you* eating out of my hand.'

'I was.'

'What's wrong? Are you nervous?'

The boys are sleeping at Oscar's parents' house. The plan is for me to stay overnight at his house.

'I don't really sleep.'

'Good. I have no plans to sleep, either.'

'No,' I say, but Vera is holding the door of the bistro open for us, and I can't explain.

We are put at a small round table, Oscar on my left and Vera on my right. Annie is across from me, but I don't exist to her. She swivels back and forth from Oscar to Vera, pounding them with questions.

After a few rounds, Vera turns to me. 'What are you interested in?'

I look at her blankly, and she laughs. 'I'm just trying to subvert the where-do-you-live-what-do-you-do line of inquiry.'

'Well, that's refreshing. I am interested in—' Feeling normal. Not having cancer. Getting out of debt. 'Books, I guess.'

'What do you read?'

'I love Shirley Hazzard and—'

'I love her.' She glares at me.

'She's my personal god.'

'I never meet people who have read her.'

'They actually had *The Evening of the Holiday* back there at the store.'

'My favorite.'

'Mine, too. The glove.'

'The glove!' She puts her hand on my arm.

We compare other writer loves, exchanging names and bouncing in agreement and writing down the few that don't overlap.

When she asks me if I write, I nod apologetically. Another wannabe. She must be surrounded by them. But she seems pleased. She asks me what I'm working on and I tell her and she asks all sorts of questions about it and I wind up telling her about my mother and Cuba and the long list of questions I was keeping at the back of my notebook to ask her when she got back from Chile and how she died instead. She puts her hand back on my arm and says she's so sorry and she means it. She's one of the ones who knows. She says her mother died six years ago, also suddenly, also with no goodbye. 'For years the only sentence I could write that meant anything to me was: "She slipped on the ice and died." I don't know how you finished that novel. Have you read it, Oscar?'

'Read what?'

'Casey's book?'

'She won't let me near it.'

Probably true. Though he's never asked.

Our food comes, and Oscar asks Vera about New York and the friends they have in common and the editor they once shared until the editor tried to write his own book and had a full psychotic break.

Vera leaves before dessert. She's driven more than an hour to Oscar's reading and has to fly to London tomorrow for another leg of her tour.

'I loved her,' I tell Oscar on the way home.

'You two really hit it off.'

'She likes you.'

'We've known each other a long time.'

'She likes you likes you.'

He chuckles and does not deny it.

'Have you guys ever—'

'No,' he smiles. 'Not really.' He feels me looking at him. 'There was some kissing. Years ago. In our twenties.' I picture him giving her his little pecks on a couch in the seventies. 'She was too serious for me.'

'Serious? What are you talking about? You two laughed for five minutes straight when you saw each other.'

'No, she laughs, she's fun, but you heard her. Like when she brought up that article on Edmund Wilson. She's pretentious.'

'She was curious what you thought about it.'

'But the words she uses.'

'You think she's trying to impress people?'

'No, I think she probably thinks that way.'

'So, she's being authentic. You have a problem with her authenticity?'

'Look, she's a good woman.'

'A good woman?'

'She's rigid. Fixed in her ways. She's like a confirmed old bachelor.'

'She seemed loose and vibrant and happy to me. Why wouldn't you want that?'

'Are we really fighting about why I'm not with someone else?'

'She's your age, she's beautiful, and she's into you.'

'It's just that je ne sais quoi.'

But I know the quoi. She is reading in churches and auditoriums. She's going to London tomorrow for a European leg of her book tour.

The house is dark. I've never been here when no one's home. Oscar flips on the lights, and it all feels different, like they've painted the walls a cooler color. Even Bob has been taken away.

Oscar takes a glass from a shelf and fills it with water. 'Want one?'

'No thanks.'

'Look,' he says. 'You made it on the fridge.'

I go over to him. It's a new drawing by ZAZ. A few black lines, a green squiggle, and a small brown tornado. Oscar points to the tornado. 'That's your hair. And that's your body over here. And that is either a golf club or an asp. I'm not sure.'

'Wow. This is a great honor.'

He puts down his water and kisses me. 'Thanks for coming tonight.' He kisses me again. 'You made it so much nicer.' Kiss. 'Those things really knock it out of me.' He rests his head on my shoulder heavily. 'I'm beat. Let's go up.' He picks up his glass and moves to the stairs.

I stall, pretending to look at the drawing a little longer.

'Can you hit the lights?' he says, halfway up.

His bedroom is big, with a king-size bed. You can see that his wife initially designed the room, with a pretty painted mirror and white bureaus, but you can also see where time has crept in. There's a cheap laminate desk in the corner with piles of paper and a cardboard box for dirty laundry.

He comes out of the bathroom in a T-shirt and boxer shorts. 'Come here.' His mouth is minty.

I'm used to boys. I'm used to their colt-like energy. I'm used to making out on sofas and peeling off our clothing bit by bit. I'm not used to a guy brushing his teeth before fooling around. I'm in my head, and my head is racing. I take off my skirt and sweater and get into bed with him. He slides an arm under me and pulls me against him. I thought maybe sleeping in someone else's bed might be better, but it's worse. I can feel the panic mounting.

His arm glides down my back, over my bum, and back up. 'Mmm,' he says. Our bodies are lying down alongside each other for the first time and it doesn't feel as good as it does when we are standing up with more clothes on.

I don't know what I want. It's nothing like lying next to Luke or kissing Silas in his car. Fireworks or coffee in bed, I hear Fabiana saying.

'Are you nervous?' he says, grinning and kissing me. 'We can take it slowly. This is nice just like this. This is what I want. And it's been so long since I've wanted anything.'

His tongue is cold. He moves to one of my breasts. My mind is full of people in chairs at the bookstore and Vera Wilde leaning against the restaurant table. He slides his fingers into my underwear but they don't go in the right places and he has a couple of sharp fingernails. I imagine him bringing Vera Wilde home and going down on her on the living room rug. It helps. I shift away from his fingers and press my butt against him and we find a rhythm and he is breathing hard at my neck and we move faster and he tenses and stops breathing and I feel the pulse against me through our underwear and when it's over he says he feels like a teenager and laughs loudly in my ear.

He puts on a fresh pair of boxers and pulls me close. '"But O that I were young again/And held her in my arms,"' he says in my ear. Three minutes later he's asleep. I try to follow him there, try to imitate his long sleep breaths and trick my body into it, but I'm awake. I lie there a long time. After an hour or more I get up and go downstairs.

There are a few extra chairs pulled up around the coffee table from the workshop the night before. It's clear where Oscar sits, in the walnut chair with the leather seat, pulled back from the others, a bit higher. I take the seat I would sit in if I were in the workshop, in the middle of the couch, protected by people on both sides.

I should have wanted to be him, not sleep with him. I don't seem to want to do that either, though.

My body won't stay seated so I walk around, past the front door, the closet, the bathroom, the TV nook, the fridge, the island, back around to the living area. There's very little clutter. No photos. A bookshelf neatly organized by author. One copy of each of his own. I open the closet: parkas, boots, tennis rackets, a wiffleball bat. In the kitchen is another closet: broom, mop, bucket, slender vacuum cleaner, and a recycling bin. There, on top of a stack of papers, is a story called 'Star of Ashtabula.' It's been typed on a manual typewriter so it has a faded, irregular look to it. Silas's name and address are in the top left corner. I shut the door. I go sit on a chair near the window. I shuffle a deck of cards near the TV. I go back to the closet with the recycling bin.

It's a clean copy. Oscar hasn't made a mark. I bring it to the couch. Star is a woman trying to save an old tree from being chopped down in the town center. She goes door-to-door to a series of oddball neighbors, and when the men with a backhoe come there is a protest with all the people she has mustered, awkwardly holding hands around the big tree. It turns out Star's ex-husband proposed to her under the tree, extemporaneously, with few words and no ring. She hadn't liked the proposal at the time and made him do it again properly a week later by the lake with a diamond and a dozen roses, but it is the first proposal beneath the strong branches of that tree that she remembers and that moves her, years after they have divorced, at unexpected moments of the day.

I wonder how the discussion of the story went. Muriel is in Italy, so I have no mole. I wonder where Silas sat. I can imagine how people might talk about it, how it lacks narrative tension, how there are unnecessary adverbs in the tag lines, like 'she said pleadingly,' how we don't find out if she saves the tree. It seems like it was written in a rush of feeling, as if the writer were determined to follow the emotion no matter how rough-hewn the prose. There is something raw and uneven about it that people would try to fix.

I get up and put it back on the pile. I look at the pictures in magazines on the couch. An hour later I return to the recycling bin and shove the story into my bag, deep down to the bottom. It's the only thing I've been able to read in weeks. I should save it for that reason alone.

After a few more hours I go upstairs and slip back into bed and wait for morning.

When I walk the dog I'm aware now of the size of the three oak trees on the far side of the park. Their limbs are enormous, ribbed with muscles and veins, as alive as we are.

At Iris, a woman takes a bite of her BLT and sends it back. She says she doesn't like the spicy mayonnaise. The kitchen makes another, with a milder aioli. I bring it out to her, and a few minutes later she asks me to bring some of the spicy mayonnaise back.

'I thought I didn't like it, but I did,' she says.

Muriel returns from Rome and meets me for coffee before work. She laughs at how hard I hug her. She tells me that on the second day of her conference she came out of the hotel and saw Christian across the street under a jacaranda. I told you I'd only go to Italy for romance, he said and asked her if she would marry him.

Star would have liked that proposal.

I pore over the *Globe* classifieds for an apartment. I call about the smallest, cheapest ones, and they are already taken. Finally, I find one I can go and see. It's in Cambridge. Inman Square. A basement studio in a yellow Victorian. The landlord is surprised by how captivated I am by it. I stand at the stove for a long time. A real gas stove. I turn on and off each gas burner. And the fridge is enormous. He laughs at my awe and says it's standard size. The wall-to-wall carpet smells a bit, but nothing like my potting shed. Off the back, through sliding glass doors, is a private patio encircled by flower beds and a crab apple tree. It's more than I can bear.

Probably because I'm so taken with his worst apartment, he asks if I want to see the two-bedroom he's renovating upstairs. I follow him up three flights. As he unlocks the door he says he's planning to renovate all four units. The basement will be last, he says, but he'll get to it. He swings the door open. It's all light and shiny wood floors. The kitchen gleams with new appliances. A bay window with a wide built-in seat looks down on the neighborhood. Big arms of a maple tree stretch out at eye level as if protecting the house. Beyond it you can see out across the tops of all the other trees and gray roofs. Something in my chest eases and aches at the same time.

'They're still working on the bathroom.' He looks at his watch. 'Of course they haven't shown up yet.'

He shows me a big bedroom with the same polished floors and the attached bathroom where the floors are still plywood and the vanity is in a box. In the corner is a modern tub below a skylight. We go through to the second bedroom. There is a wall of bookshelves and a space between two long windows where a desk would go.

I go back to the window seat in the living area. I know he'll make me leave soon.

'What do you do?' he asks.

I shake my head. 'I don't even make enough for the basement.'

'I wasn't asking for that. Just curious.'

I need him to know how pathetic I am. 'I'm a writer.'

'A writer. That's cool. Tough, making a living in the arts.' He turns toward the door, jangling the keys. 'But worth a shot, right?'

Finally, I get fired from Iris. It's the night before the Harvard-Yale game. We have 192 on the books and a line of walk-ins down the stairs. We open a half hour early. Harry, Dana, James, and I are upstairs. Tony and Victor are down. An hour in, Fabiana tells me Tony is swamped and I need to take a four down in the club bar. She's already punched in the drink order with my number and when it's ready I bring the drinks down and take their order. On my way to the computer upstairs, I see my two sixes have been seated.

I approach the closest one, and the man at the head of the table grips my waist. 'Listen, sweetness.' He squeezes. 'Men of a certain age need cocktails of a certain proof within a certain amount of time.'

The three men give me very specific drink orders with the importance of doctors giving pre-op instruction. The women order glasses of house white. The man lets go of my waist.

The six beside them is a family that is ready to order everything and put a rush on it because they have to get to their daughter's performance. She's a flautist. At Harvard. The two younger daughters, not yet in college, roll their eyes. The mother sees them. 'There are a lot of schools in this area,' she says. 'I just wanted to clarify.'

I'm interrupted three more times before I can get to the computer: another Coke, a cleaner fork, Worcestershire sauce. I punch in the drinks and the rush order and hear the kitchen calling my name for entrées on my deuce, two Radcliffe ladies who tell me they are celebrating fifty years of their Boston marriage.

In the kitchen, Clark is sucking down the beers and the swordfish steaks come back overcooked and the chicken bloody and he's lashing out at every waiter who pushes through the door. By eight he's lit into management, calling Marcus a cunt and Gory a sexless cow, and he's scalded his right hand on the handle of pan that had been under a broiler. He's like a bull at the end of a fight. Everything is flashing red. I stay far away.

And something's wrong with the Kroks. They're early and they're not in their usual tuxes and they do things in reverse, start in the middle of the room and fan around it, singing a few songs I've never heard before, their voices loud and sloppy. But the diners don't know the difference. They eat it up. At the end of their last song the singers take blue Yale caps out of their pockets and fix them on their heads. 'Thank you,' they shout. 'We're the Whiffenpoofs!' The crowd loves the caper. They boo and clap at the same time. The Whiffenpoofs blow kisses. In the doorway are the stunned Kroks in tuxes, the wind finally out of their annoying sails.

I'm dropping desserts at the first six-top—the second has already left for the concert—when Clark comes tearing out into the dining room, hand packed with ice and bandaged with rags and duct tape. He grabs my arm and a small cylinder of hazelnut mousse goes flying to the carpet.

'Marcus says there's a five in the club bar that's been here two hours. I have no dupe.'

At first my table thinks it's another Yale prank and watch with amusement. When they understand his blood and rage are real, they bend their heads toward their plates. The man at the head reaches out for my hip again. 'That's no way to speak to this sweet young lady.'

I sidestep his grab, and I shove Clark's arm off me. It smashes into his other, bandaged hand. He howls.

'Get your fucking hands off me.' My voice is very loud, much louder than I expect, louder than any Krok or Whiffenpoof. I move quickly through the silent dining room out to the fire escape.

My throat has seized up, and I'm sipping small bits of air. I have a lot of crying in me, but not a tear comes out. I'm just trying to breathe. It's starting again, that need to somehow get out of my body. My heart is hammering so fast it feels like one long beat on the verge of bursting. Death, or something bigger and much less peaceful, feels so close, just over my shoulder.

'Casey.'

It's Marcus.

'I know. I'm leaving,' I manage.

'Good,' he says and goes back in.

I change in the bathroom and leave my filthy uniform on the floor of the stall. In the other stall are two little girls. I can see their white tights and black patent leather shoes. I wash my hands and do not look in the mirror, do not want to see who is in there. The girls are whispering, waiting for me to leave before they come out. I shut the door loudly when I go, so they know the coast is clear.

I go down the narrow stairs then the wider fancy stairs. The presidents watch me go. My chest feels like an old swollen piece of fruit about to split open with wet rot. I hear the little girls' small voices. I want little girls. I haven't gone back for the follow-up appointment Dr. Gynecologist suggested. Now I won't have health insurance anymore. I don't want to be infertile. I also don't want to be pregnant. Fitzgerald said that the sign of genius is being able to hold two contradictory ideas in your head at the same time. But what if you hold two contradictory fears? Are you still some kind of a genius?

I unplug the phone when I get home so Oscar can't call me and Harry can't call me and Muriel can't call me after Harry calls her. I can't stay inside. I can't stay still. But I'm scared to leave. I don't want to walk down the driveway and out to the street. I'm scared I won't come back. I'm scared I'll burst or dissolve or veer straight into traffic. I'm scared of men at this time of night when I'm on foot, not on my bike. I'm scared of men in cars and men in doorways, men in groups and men alone. They are menacing. Men-acing. Men-dacious. Men-tal. I'm outside now. I'm circling the big tree. You hate men, Paco said once. Do I? I don't like working for them. Marcus and Gory. Gabriel at Salvatore's was an exception. My French teacher in eighth grade rubbed my neck during a makeup test, swaying hard against the back of my plastic chair. I actually thought he had an itch. And when I asked Mr. Tuck at the airport in Madrid why he hadn't told someone about my father he said, I liked your dad but you know what happens to the messenger. I hate male cowardice and the way they always have each other's backs. They have no control. They justify everything their dicks make them do. And they get away with it. Nearly every time. My father peered through a hole at girls, possibly at me, in our locker room. And when he got caught, he got a party and a cake.

I circle the yard. It's noisy. The ground is covered with dry leaves. The tree is nearly bare. Adam doesn't rake. He doesn't garden. The raised beds are thick with dying weeds. My mother was in her yard every weekend. It was the only time I ever saw her in jeans. High-waisted ones, showing off her bum. She had a nice bum. It was high and pert, even into her fifties. I didn't get that bum. All her neighbors had crushes on her, but she was done with men. They'd come by with cuttings and compost in the spring, bulbs in the fall. They'd linger, ask about her goliath tomatoes or her trumpet vines. 'I think my husband was half in love with her,' more than a few women told me at her funeral. But they were not threatened. They loved her, too. They told me stories about how she cared for them during a hip replacement, a car accident, a son's suicide. How she slept on their couches and cooked meals and ran errands. How she fought the town on pesticides on school property and wrote letters to the editor about gay rights and racial justice. I kick through the leaves. Someone reminded me of her recently. I feel the memory, just out of reach, sweet, as if memory has flavors, a woman about her age. I can't remember. My mother was a real person. I am not a real person. She had convictions and took action. She had purpose and belief. She helped others. I help no one. She helped found that donation organization. I couldn't even write one thank-you letter for a refrigerator. All I want is to write fiction. I am a drain on the system, dragging around my debts and dreams. It's all I've wanted. And now I'm not even able to do that. I haven't been able to go near my book since I spoke to Jennifer Lin.

The crunching of leaves wakes up the dog, and he barks from the mudroom window. I crouch beside the tree trunk and stay still though everything inside me is churning. The ground beneath the leaves is warm, but the air is cold. Something flashes in front of me. It's my breath. I can see my breath. It's been a long time since I've lived in a place where I can see my breath. I am a child buttoned up in a wool coat and white mittens, driving with my mother, sliding on the blue leather of the passenger seat, toes like ice cubes, waiting for the heat to kick in on the way to school or church or the grocery store. Oafie stops barking to listen to the silence. He pushes off from the sill and goes back to bed.

I can't go inside until I slow down. My heart and mind feel like they are in a race to the death. I watch my breath. I squeeze my muscles one by one. It's Star of Ashtabula who reminds me of my mother.

I go inside and lie on my futon and wait to explode.

'It's a bit late to be playing hard to get, don't you think?' Oscar says.

'I got fired.'

'Fantastic!'

'Not for me.'

'You can do better than that job.'

'Like what?'

'Anything. Work in an office. Something with normal hours.'

'But I want the normal hours for writing.'

'I have a little job for you.'

'What?'

'It's your fault. They like you too much.'

'What are you talking about?'

'So I have to go to Provo next weekend and I thought my mother had it on her calendar but she didn't and she's going to Lennox on some girls' weekend. And she won't cancel. I tried to tell her she was no longer a girl by the most generous standards and most of her friends are so butch they should call it a men's weekend and she did not think that was funny and hung up on me, and when I tried to call Brenda, you know, down the street, the boys started whining about how all she cooks is shepherd's pie and she sticks toilet paper up her nose and it comes out bloody and they asked for you. They asked me to ask you to come stay for the weekend. I told them you were working and it was impossible, but now maybe it's not.'

'How much do you pay Brenda?'

He laughs until he realizes I'm serious. 'Two hundred a day.'

'Okay. I'll do it.'

Oscar leaves me a check and a note on his fridge.

> This is just to say
> You can eat all the plums
> And all the grapes
> And the bananas.
> But don't eat all the kiwis
> Or Jasper will weep.
> And don't leave Sunday
> Or ever.

I walk down the street to the bus stop. All the other women there are nannies. John comes off the bus quickly, but Jasper moves slowly. The girl behind him looks ready to give him a shove. They're shy on the way home. I ask them about school, and I get one-word answers. Jasper asks three times when Papa is coming home.

'What *time* Sunday night at seven?' he says, blinking heavily.

John laughs. 'Here come the waterworks.'

Everyone needs heavy snacks. I bring out all the fruit and set two kiwis cut in half with a spoon in front of Jasper. Oscar prepared plastic containers of cheese, celery, and carrots for this time of day, but I see bacon in a drawer in the fridge and remember what I used to make after school. I cook up the bacon, slather some saltines with mayonnaise and pile each one with chopped onion, bacon, and cheddar and put them under the broiler. They come out perfectly. We devour them. I'm back in sixth grade, eating them. I make more. We devour them, too.

'Papa says mayonnaise clogs up your arteries,' Jasper says.

'And bacon,' John says. 'And cheese.'

'We're young. We don't have to worry about that yet.' Do parents these days really make kids worry about their *arteries*?

'Papa is so old!' John says.

'Well, he's not old, but he's not the perfect machines that we are.' I pop another cholesterol bomb in my mouth.

'He's not going to die though,' Jasper says. 'He promised.'

'He can't promise. No one knows when they're going to die,' John says.

'He promised. And a promise is a promise.'

'But—'

'How about I teach you a game called Spit?' I say.

Oscar said that they had to take a bath each night. I'm not sure what to do. I can't leave a five-year-old and a seven-year-old in a bathtub alone, but I doubt they'll be comfortable with me in the room. I dread it and extend dinner and cards and a game of Sorry! out as far as I can to avoid bedtime. But

John looks at the clock and says it's bath time. And Jasper says, 'I call the surfboard!' and runs toward the stairs and John chases him and by the time I get up there the water is running and both boys are naked at the toilet, sword fighting with their streams of pee. I duck out, but John calls me back and asks me to get the bath toys down, pointing to a high shelf with his free hand.

I sit on the floor next to the tub and man the submarine. Jasper has the spy on the surfboard and John has the Special Op parachuter. We play till the pads of our fingers are blue and shriveled.

When I say it's time to get out, Jasper says he needs a shampoo.

'Papa just washed it last night.'

'It got dirty again.'

John shakes his head. 'He always wants a shampoo.'

Jasper hands me the baby shampoo. Nothing about it has changed. The golden color. The red teardrop that says 'no more tears.' The smell. Unlike so much, it is exactly the same as when my mother used it on me. They dunk their heads wet, and I lather them up. I shape Jasper's foamy hair into dog ears, flat and flopped over, and John's longer hair into straight-up antennae. They giggle at each other, and I allow them to stand up carefully, one at a time, to look at themselves in the mirror above the sink. I hold on to their waists as my mother held on to mine. They come slowly back down, and I make new shapes. I breathe in the smell.

After I get them out and dry them off, they put on their pj's. John's are plain navy with white cuffs that don't reach his wrists or ankles, and Jasper's are faded red-and-green plaid, hand-me-downs from John. They show me their rooms.

'John's is bigger, but mine is cozier,' Jasper says, leading the way.

'That's what we tell him when he complains.'

'Mine is big in con set. See?'

'Concept,' John says.

'It's the whole universe.' He spreads his arms out. It's definitely a space-themed room, with the planets from our solar system hanging in one corner and the sun in another, a poster of *Apollo 17*, and a glow-in-the-dark night sky on the ceiling. There's a twin bed in the corner, and the rest of the floor is covered with an enormous Lego space station.

'How do you get from the door into bed?'

'I tiptoe, like this.' And he picks his way, nearly en pointe, across without disturbing one thing.

John's room is neat and spare.

'I don't like things on the wall. They can catch fire.'

Anything can catch fire. Being around kids means thinking a whole lot of things you can't say.

He sees my eye land on a shelf of framed photographs. We move toward them together.

There she is. Sonya. Pixie cut, round brown eyes, Jasper's mischievous smile. I realize I had an image of her as willowy and bohemian and dreamy looking, but she is compact and purposeful. No nonsense my mother would say. Beside her—at the top of a mountain, on their leather sofa, at the alter—Oscar looks tall. She seems active and zestful, the way people who die young always do, as if they were given an extra dose of energy and passion for life, as if they knew they had less time to spend it. Or maybe it's just the way we see their photos afterward, when any life we still find in them feels exaggerated.

'That's our mom.'

'She looks really kind.'

'She was.'

I don't know how these small bodies have sustained the loss of her, how they make it through to the end of each day.

'I lost my mom, too. Last winter.'

'Was she old?'

'No. She was fifty-eight. But she wasn't as young as yours.'

'She was thirty-seven.'

'We saw her. When she was dead,' Jasper says. 'She looked like a piece of driftwood.'

'Papa told you to stop saying that.'

'Well she did,' Jasper says. 'John has a journal!' He bolts across the room, claws around under the bed, and brings back a fat notebook.

'No.' John grabs it from him.

'Just the funny page.' Jasper finds a page close to the beginning with big words in black magic marker: I HAIT POPA over and over. And at the bottom: JASPR IS A POOPSY POO.

We all laugh.

'What did you mean?'

'I don't know. I don't remember.' He is still laughing hard. He takes the book from Jasper and starts flipping
through the pages.

'Have you been keeping that a long time?'

'Since I was four.'

He's probably written a hundred pages. The writing
starts off big and wild, mostly in thick pens, and then gets
smaller and thinner. The most recent entries are meticulous
and tiny.

'You're a writer like your dad.'

He shakes his head. 'I just like to record things. So I
don't forget.'

I feel the photographs beside us, a family frozen in
motion.

Below the photos are books. We look through them,
and Jasper pulls out his favorites, which we narrow down
from a huge stack to a smaller stack. John just wants *Robinson
Crusoe*, which they are nearly halfway through.

'Can we read in Papa's bed? There's more room.'

But when we get settled there, they press up so close
on either side of me that we didn't need the extra space. The
smell of the baby shampoo comes up from their hair and my
fingers as I turn the pages.

After the books, they are tired and go to their own beds.
I ask if anyone would like me to sing a song, and they say
no, but as I'm leaving Jasper's room he says he's changed his
mind. I sing 'Edelweiss' and 'Blowin' in the Wind,' and then
John calls across the hallway saying he changed his mind,

too. I tell him about the Kroks and sing him 'Blue Angel' and 'Loch Lomond.'

I go back to Oscar's bed. He hasn't changed the sheets and the pillows smell like him, his skin and his shaving cream. I think about his wife and her bright face. If my lump turns out to be deadly cancer, I don't think anyone will look at photos of me later and think I had an extra dose of anything. I fall asleep around four and Jasper comes in before five. He knocks his body against the bed until I wake up, and he stands there until I pull back the covers for him to crawl in. He's wide awake. He tells me about a boy named Edwin in his class.

'He's a hitting and punching guy,' he says.

'And what do you do?'

'I karate chop him. In my magination. In true life I go to the other side of the room.'

'That seems like a good strategy.'

We talk about popsicles and our favorite flavors and all the places he's swum in his life and a rock John jumped off of somewhere in a place that began with an *m* where there were kittens under a porch. He's taken my hand and holds it like a map, with two hands in front of his face, spreading out the fingers then pushing them together.

'I don't remember my mama,' he says.

'You were only two, right?' I can't bear to say *when she died*.

'Uh-huh. I don't know if she was like you or completely different. If she was like Aunt Sue or completely different. Who was she *like*?'

'She was probably like you.'

'Me?'

'She was probably curious and smart and silly in the best way.'

He brings my fingers up to his mouth and bounces them absently against his lips.

'When my mother died, I sort of felt her inside me sometimes,' I say. 'Like I'd swallowed her.'

He laughs. 'Swallowed her.'

'I still have moments when I feel that, when it feels like she's inside me, and there's no difference between us or that the difference doesn't matter.'

He's listening, bouncing my fingers still. He doesn't say anything.

'I think it is all that love. All that love has to go somewhere.'

He gnaws a little on my pinky. He nods slowly. 'I think she loved me,' he whispers to my knuckles.

'She did,' I say. 'And still does. Very, very much. And that love will always, always be inside you.'

Time is mercurial when you're with children. A whole morning making pancakes and playing freeze tag goes by in a minute, whereas waiting for Jasper to tie his shoes or catch up on his bike is endless. They bring me to their favorite playgrounds: the one with the tunnel slide, the one with high swings, the one with the rock-climbing wall. We eat quesadillas at the taqueria on Bow Street and banana cupcakes at the café next door. On the way home we pick up *Mrs. Doubtfire* at Blockbuster, and I make mac and cheese without a vegetable side and we eat it on the couch, which

Oscar doesn't allow. Jasper crawls into my bed at three that morning and falls asleep quickly this time and I don't think I will but his breathing and his small hot feet against my shins lull me back. On Sunday it's the aquarium, the grocery store, baking cookies, and playing cards. For dinner they help me make a lasagna for Oscar's return. His flight lands at 6:14. We pull the lasagna out at quarter past and stare at it, the cheese still bubbling at the sides. We're hungry. We play ping-pong in the garage to distract ourselves, but the boys fight about who will play on my side so I cut that short and suggest I read them another chapter of *Robinson Crusoe*. They settle in on either side of me again. Maybe it's not too soon. Maybe this is where I belong. I think this might be where I belong.

We're right at the part where Crusoe finds a human footprint on his island when Oscar opens the door. I'm relieved. I didn't want to have to explain the cannibals to them. The boys spring from the couch and run to him.

'You weren't in the driveway!' He lifts them up easily, one on each hip.

'We didn't see the lights,' John says.

'I flashed them.'

Oscar told me once that the only good thing about these trips is flashing his headlights as he pulls in and watching the boys run past the windows and out the door to the driveway, their little bodies bright and glowing against the asphalt. But I have forgotten that. He sees *Robinson Crusoe* in my hand. 'You've been reading it without me?'

'We can read it over,' John says. 'We didn't understand it all. We can start where we left off on Thursday.'

260

Oscar puts them down and takes off his coat and hangs it in the closet. He rests a palm on each of their heads. 'What else did I miss?'

They shout out our activities and he nods, bent down toward them. He hasn't looked at me yet.

'How'd it go?' I say when I can't bear it any longer.

He doesn't look up. 'Good.'

'We made lasagna, Papa! A real lasagna.'

The boys drag him to the counter to look.

We set the table with plates John had chosen from a high shelf. Jasper drew designs on the paper napkins. We didn't have flowers so we made a Lego centerpiece.

'Can we eat now?' John asks me.

'Sure,' Oscar says.

I sit with them. My body is going haywire. I perch at the edge of my chair. I keep rehearsing words, explanations of why I have to leave, but I don't say them out loud.

Maybe he met someone in Provo. Maybe he just got some clarity. Maybe the whole weekend, while I was falling in love with his kids, falling in love with this whole life, he was changing his mind.

The boys recount, blow by blow, our two days together. He listens, bent over the lasagna, nodding. None of it pleases him. That's clear. And they are working so hard to please him, working so hard to be interesting and amusing, to say something he will like. Muriel has said that sometimes she gets to the workshop and he's just absent. But this is more than absence. This is willful, strategic withdrawal. It seems cruel to inflict it on children.

261

I get through the meal. I clear the plates. I stand at the sink, my back to the table. I know I should stay, help with the dishes, wait for the boys to go to bed, and talk to him. But I can't. I have to leave. I go upstairs and put my clothes and toilet kit back in my bag and come down again.

'You're leaving?' Jasper says.

I squat down and give him a hug. I grab John's arm and pull him in. 'I had so much fun with you two this weekend.'

'Bye-bye, poppet,' Jasper says. It was from *Mrs. Doubtfire*.

I give Oscar a little wave and turn away.

My bike's in the garage, and when I wheel it out he's waiting for me.

'Where are you going?' He grabs my handlebars and puts the front wheel between his legs so he's facing me and very close. 'Please don't leave mad. I'm sorry. Whatever I've done I'm sorry.'

'*Whatever* you've done?'

'Being remote, cold, whatever.' He says it like it's an old and tired accusation, like we've been here many times before, in this boring cliché of an argument. 'I get jealous. I always have. When Sonya was dying, I knew everyone wished it were me.'

'Of course they didn't.'

'Of course they did. She was their *mother*. I was the dispensable one, the jerk who was always trying to get more time alone with his work. But there was this moment toward the end when I was hugging them on this terrible chair in her hospital room and I felt them turn fully toward me, like they knew it was over and it was just the three of us. It was awful and terrifying and heartbreaking, but it was exhilarating, too. I finally had their full attention.' He reaches out for my hand. I give it to him, and he pulls me in. He slides inside my shirt and puts his finger in my belly button. 'I like having people's full attention.' He kisses me. He circles my bare waist with his hands. 'So, I had some free time in Provo and I went to the library and happened to read an excellent story in the *Kenyon Review.*'

'No.'

'Yes.'

'I wrote that a long time ago.' I wrote it when my mother was alive.

'I had no idea you were so good.' He shakes me.

'Back in the eighties.'

Inside the house the boys have put the movie on again.

'We watched *Mrs. Doubtfire.*'

'PG-13 *Mrs. Doubtfire*?'

'They may have some questions.'

When we stop kissing, he puts my helmet on my head and fastens it under my chin, threading his fingers between my skin and the plastic so it doesn't pinch me.

'Give them a hug for me.'

'You already did.'

'Give them another.'

He waits for me to explain, but I can't. I'm not sure what I mean, either.

Muriel tells me she gave my number to her sister who has a friend who teaches at a school that has just fired their English teacher.

'High schools give me the creeps.'

'It's a cool place. Something like eighty percent of the students receive financial aid. Not your typical private school. The whole summer off to write.'

I figure I won't ever hear from them, but the next day I get a call from the head of the English department, Manolo Parker. He asks me to come in for an interview in three days, on the ninth of November, the day before my appointment with the oncologist.

Muriel lends me clothes, makeup, and her car for the interview. That morning I lie in bed feeling my lump. I can't tell if it's grown. The interview terrifies me nearly as much as the oncologist. I spend a half hour trying to fix my face, hide the deep gray-blue welts under my eyes with concealer, make my cheeks plump and rosy with blush, my eyes wider and more awake looking with an eye pencil. But my hands shake and the lines are crooked and there's no disguising all the fear.

I allow time for rush hour, and I need it. Traffic crawls out of the city, light by light. Driving is a luxury I've forgotten. There's heat, for one thing, and a radio. A guy is singing about taking his girlfriend to have an abortion. He calls her a brick that's drowning him slowly. He says this over and over. I have a moment at a long light when I partially nod off, and when I jerk back awake I think for a few seconds I'm pregnant, and then I realize it's not me, just the girl in the song, and it's a relief. I get disproportionately sad for the girl whose asshole ex-boyfriend wrote this song calling her a brick and is making money on those words now. I pass through stone pillars and up a long, wooded drive and park in the faculty parking lot.

There's a path from this lot up a steep hill to the school. Down below are fields marked out by white lines, goals at each end, and benches along the sides. It could be my high school. There's a guy on a tractor mowing. It could be my father. I can't work here. All the smells are the same.

The entrance is all glass, freshly renovated. Manolo meets me at the door.

His handshake is strong, not dialed back for a woman. He leads me down a glimmering hallway.

'I thought you should see how we start the day,' he says, holding open the auditorium door for a stream of students and their enormous backpacks. He greets them all by name. 'Ciao, Stephen. You liking *Sula* any better today, Marika? Becca, Jep, top of the morning to you.' They like him and his attentions. Becca points at me. 'You interviewing today?' I nod and she gives me a thumbs-up and keeps moving. Manolo leads me a few rows down, and we sit in plush fold-down seats with other teachers. He introduces me to the ones nearby, and a few others turn around and wave. They all seem to know why I'm here.

It's loud. The whole school is here, seventh through twelfth Manolo tells me. He gives me a quick history of the school: founded by three local suffragettes, all girls until '72, defunct from '76 to '78, rose from the ashes with the help of an anonymous donor whose only stipulation was that admission be need-blind.

The room quiets down. A gaunt woman with straight, gray hair to her shoulders has climbed up the steps to the stage and is standing at a podium in front of the closed curtain.

'Head of school,' Manolo whispers to me. 'Aisha Jain.'

'What I thought was love in me,' she says, 'I find a thousand instances as fear.' She looks up and around and back down. 'Of the tree's shadow winding around the chair, a distant music of frozen birds rattling in the—'

A hand shoots up in the audience, and she stops, points to it. 'David.'

'Amiri Baraka, also known as LeRoi Jones. I can't remember the title.'

'Title, anyone?'

Another hand down in front. She nods. 'Claire.'

'The Liar.'

'Good job, both of you. Bon appétit.'

'They get a free treat at the snack bar for getting it right,' Manolo tells me.

'Enjoy your education today,' she says and walks off the stage and takes a seat off to the side.

Students, lined up on the stairs, come onstage one by one to make announcements: photography field trip, green sneaker found on the roof (a large boy in back lumbers down the aisle to the base of the stage to retrieve it to much cheering), POC meeting after school here in the auditorium, Debate Club in 202, Gay-Straight Alliance in the library. When the announcements are over, the lights go down and the whole school starts screaming and stomping their feet as if we were at Fenway and the Sox had just put it over the wall. The curtain opens on two men with guitars, a woman on drums, and another woman with a sax at the mic.

'Mama,' she starts singing, low and slow, over the noise from the audience. It's 'Misguided Angel' by the Cowboy Junkies. A song Paco and I danced to in his kitchen in Central Square.

Manolo leans over. 'Math department band.' There's a makeshift piece of cardboard stuck on the front of the drum set that says: THE COSIGNS.

Next they play 'Ain't That Peculiar' and end with 'Try a Little Tenderness.' They're good. And they're having a blast. The whole school rises in a standing O, and we filter out of the room.

Manolo has a huge smile on his face. Everyone does, including me.

'Wow,' I say. 'What a way to start the day.'

We're walking more slowly than the rest, who are rushing past us to class.

'Aisha told me once that the number-one quality she looks for in a candidate when hiring is happiness. I thought it was cheesy when I first heard it, but you can tell. This is a pretty happy place.'

267

We go back through the glass entrance area and down a wide hallway, bright with sun pouring through a line of high windows. Honestly, I don't remember windows in my high school. Every memory is cast in dim tube lighting. Was anyone *happy* there?

Manolo points through an open office door and says that's Aisha's office, and we'll go in there in a bit. I follow him to his office, which he shares with another colleague who's in class. We chat in the middle of the room in matching chairs that spin before we cross the hall to my interview. He asks me what I read when I was in high school, and I tell him that I was assigned the standard fare of *The Catcher in the Rye* and *A Separate Peace*, Updike and Cheever stories, tales of boys being disillusioned by humanity, but on the side my mother was supplying me with Wharton and Didion and Morrison. I see a copy of *Macbeth* on a desk and tell him about this article I read recently about how Lady Macbeth has all the qualities of the tragic hero, but no one teaches it that way. He asks me if I've read Cormac McCarthy's *All the Pretty Horses*, which his seniors are reading, and I say I have and he asks me what I thought about it and I say I couldn't get past the writing to enjoy the story, that he seemed to be alternating between imitating Hemingway and imitating Faulkner. He looks disappointed, then a bell rings and he says he has to get to class. He grabs his book bag and says it was great to meet me and shakes my hand again, just as hard. He shows me to Aisha's office, and I realize that that was my interview with him. I thought we were just chatting, waiting for the real interview in Aisha's office to begin.

There's a receptionist at a desk in a small waiting area. She gets up and shows me in. Up close Aisha isn't as severe. She smiles easily and takes off her shoes as soon as she sits back down. She folds one leg under her. We're in green wing chairs near the window.

'What is amusing you?'

'Oh.' I can't think of anything to say but the truth. 'I was just thinking about this book that has a wing chair in it.' I touch the hard green wing by my head.

'Which book?'

'*Woodcutters*. By Thomas Bernhard.'

'German?'

'Austrian. Most of it takes place in this wing chair in Vienna.'

'The book takes place in a chair?'

'The narrator has gone to what he calls an artistic dinner at the house of old friends who disillusioned him when he was younger. He hasn't seen them in thirty years, and he sits in this chair by the door and ruminates about them and their *artistic dinners*. There are no chapters or paragraphs. It's just his thoughts, which are punctuated by the phrase 'as I sat in my wing chair.' It's a refrain. 'As I sat in my wing chair.' Many times a page. He's there because a mutual friend committed suicide and they've just been to her funeral and it's really a book about art and becoming an artist and all the ways it ruins people, actually.'

'How did it ruin her, the friend who committed suicide?'

I like the way she seems truly interested in this fictional world, as if it matters, as if she has all the time for it before she starts grilling me about my teaching background. 'According to the narrator, she started out as an actress and a dancer, but she met a tapestry artist and married him and channeled all her dreams of artistic greatness and international fame into him, he who would never have pursued it without her driving him on. And she succeeded. As he became more and more renowned, she became more and more miserable, and yet he was actually her work of art, so she kept having to work at it, and eventually she self-destructs. At least that's what I think it's about, as I sit in my wing chair.'

She has been smiling the whole time, which makes it hard to stop talking. And talking about characters in books is exciting and soothing to me at the same time.

'Have you always been such an enthusiastic reader?'

'Not really. I liked reading, but I was picky about books. I think the enthusiasm came when I started writing. Then I understood how hard it is to re-create in words what you see and feel in your head. That's what I love about Bernhard in the book. He manages to simulate consciousness, and it's contagious because while you're reading it rubs off on you and your mind starts working like that for a while. I love that. That reverberation for me is what is most important about literature. Not themes or symbols or the rest of that crap they teach in high school.'

She laughs hard.

Honestly, I forgot briefly why we were having this conversation.

'How would you do it differently in your English class?'

I think about this. 'I would want kids to talk and write about how the book makes them *feel*, what it reminded them of, if it changed their thoughts about anything. I'd have them keep a journal and have them freewrite after they read each assignment. What did this make you think about? That's what I'd want to know. I think you could get some really original ideas that way, not the old regurgitated ones like man versus nature. Just shoot me if I ever assign anyone an essay about man versus nature. Questions like that are designed to pull you completely out of the story. Why would you want to pull kids out of the story? You want to push them further in, so they can feel everything the author tried so hard to create for them.'

'But don't you think there *are* larger issues the author is trying to explore?'

'Yes, but they shouldn't be given primacy over or even separated from the *experience* of the story itself. An author is trying to give you an immersive adventure.' I throw out my hands, and I think this startles her.

She shifts away from me. 'The only trouble with your pedagogy is that our students have to sit for the SAT and the AP, and they would have to have some *familiarity* with those literary devices.'

I nod. 'Of course.'

It's over, I think in my wing chair.

On my way out I smell lunch. If it had gone better they might have invited me to stay and eat. It smells good. Eggplant Parmesan and cheesecake. I saw it written on the chalkboard outside the cafeteria. I wouldn't have turned down a free lunch.

Outside three girls are leaning up against the building in wool sweaters, faces to the weak November sun. A copy of *A Farewell to Arms* is facedown on the flagstones beside one of them. Imagine forcing girls to read about the fake and obsequious and self-immolating Catherine Barkley. 'There isn't any me. I'm you. Don't make up a separate me.' The only Hemingway I'd ever assign is *The Sun Also Rises* and only really for that passage when he goes into the church and prays for everybody and himself twice and wishes he felt religious and comes out into the hot sun on the steps of the cathedral with his fingers and thumb still damp and he feels them dry in the sun. I love that part so much.

I walk down the hill to Muriel's car. But it doesn't feel good anymore. I miss my bike. I'm not sure I can drive. I feel encased. I roll down all the windows. The driveway is shorter than I remember. I pull out onto the main road. I didn't know you could blow an interview by feeling too at ease. I didn't know that was a danger. I didn't talk about any of the things Muriel coached me on, the curriculum I developed in Spain and the undergrad classes I taught at grad school and then in Albuquerque. Instead I went off on that riff about Bernhard, and I remember as I get on the highway that it's not 'in my wing chair' but 'in *the* wing chair.' 'As I sat in *the* wing chair' is the refrain in *Woodcutters*, and I am awash in shame for having gotten it wrong. Plus she only hires happy people, so cross me off that list. I think of my conversation with Manolo about *All the Pretty Horses*, and it's clear now that he loved the book and I insulted it. I drive on the highway and absorb, one by one, all the ways the morning went wrong. *Your pedagogy*. She was humoring me. Then I remember the oncologist appointment tomorrow, and maybe none of it will matter because even if I get the job I'll just be the teacher who has cancer and dies.

I drop the car off at Muriel's and slip the keys through her mail slot. I have to walk through the Square and back across the river, which is fine. I have nothing but time now. In the Square I stop at Au Bon Pain. I'm hungry, and they have a chicken pesto sandwich for $2.95 that I like and is filling. In line I'm a little out of it. I keep remembering and forgetting the name of the sandwich I'm going to order. Sometimes Tony and Dana get food here, and I worry I'll see them, but it's too early. If they're working lunch today, they'll still be in the middle of the rush.

'Hey.' A tug on my jacket sleeve. A familiar rumble. 'Casey.'

It's Silas, in his motorcycle jacket.

Everything in me goes berserk at once. My face flames and my lips quiver, so I stretch them into a wide smile.

'Hey.' I give him a belated jerky hug. The jacket creaks and the kiss on the bridge comes back to me and my stomach pitches. He smells like his car. I hold on to him a bit too long.

'Are you ordering?' I ask, though I can see he has an Au Bon Pain coffee cup in his hand.

'No. Well, maybe I'll get something to eat.'

We stand in line together and I remember my order and he adds a turkey melt and pays for it fast, before I can get my money out of the purse I borrowed from Muriel.

We take our food to a table near the window. I can't eat. I take two bites and can't swallow them. When he slides out to get mustard, I spit it all in my napkin.

'Not good?'

I shake my head.

'What's going on? You look sort of . . . drawn.'

It's a kind way of putting it.

I tell him I got fired, and he's so sympathetic about it that I tell him about the lump and the bees and the no sleeping and the revision I can't write. I tell him about the interview and the math band and how I'd blown it by feeling too comfortable and how bizarre it was that I actually wanted to stay for lunch. I don't tell him about reading his story because it would mean telling him about being at Oscar's, but I want to. He is listening so carefully, nodding and fiddling with his coffee cup lid. He hasn't eaten much of his sandwich, either. He gathers up all our trash and throws it out and when he comes back I assume he's going to say he has to go, but he sits back down with both hands on the table now, close to mine.

'Remember when I asked you out then left town? It was because everything felt like it was coming loose and I'd have to get up and walk around the city at two in the morning. I couldn't stop walking. I felt like if I stopped walking I'd die. All last summer I kept packing my bags and not leaving. Then

I met you, and I knew I couldn't go out with you until I felt more normal. So I finally took off.'

'I don't have a Crested Butte.'

'You have something.'

'It's more like an abyss.'

'Something you need to get to.'

'Yeah. The rest of my life. It feels like the way is blocked.'

He smiles and takes a breath. 'Nel mezzo del cammin di nostra vita—' he stops and laughs at my expression. 'My accent is really bad.'

'It's atrocious. But go on.'

'Mi ritrovai per una selva oscura che la diritta via era smarrita. I took a Dante class in college, and we had the choice of reciting five pages in English or one page in bad Italian.'

'It's a beautiful first line.'

'I think of it a lot more than I ever thought I would.'

'I've really lost my cammin.'

'We all lose our cammin.'

'It's so physical. It feels like my body is rejecting me.'

He nods like he really knows what I mean. 'Have you tried, you know, concentrating on the top of your head then your forehead then—'

'It just makes it worse. The only thing that helps is clenching.'

'Clenching?'

I lift up my arm and squeeze my right fist. I count to ten and release it. I raise my left fist and squeeze and he copies me. I release and he releases. We do many muscles this way, arms, stomach, legs, feet. The last thing I show him are the face muscles, squeezing everything tight shut then opening our eyes and mouth wide. We look like crazed demons guarding a temple.

Afterward things feel smoother.

'That's good,' he says. 'I feel like I'm floating.'

We go outside. There are a few games going on at the chess tables.

'Hey,' Silas says, touching my jacket, 'Let's play.'

The guy at the last table is alone, waiting for a player. Silas asks him if we can play just ourselves and hands him ten bucks and the guy takes off. Silas lets me have the guy's seat, which is still warm and faces out to the rest of the courtyard and down Mass. Ave. toward Central Square. He takes the chair opposite. I haven't played in a long time. My father taught me on a small travel board with a magnetic bottom. We'd play on airplanes. This one is inlaid, black and tan, in the stone table. The pieces are marble, black and ivory.

'Ok, you're Adolf Anderssen and I'm Lionel Kieseritzky,' he says, straightening his knights. 'It's London, eighteen fifty-one. Bishop's Gambit. White opens.' He points to my pawn above the king and I move it up two squares and he nods. He moves his opposite pawn to face mine directly. 'I have this book about famous chess matches, and sometimes I play them.' He looks up at me. 'My version of clenching. Escaping into someone else's mind for a little while.' He taps the pawn above my king's bishop and I move it up one and he shakes his head and I move it up another, putting it directly and un-necessarily at risk from the only pawn he's moved.

'Why would I do that?'

'It's a risk.' He takes my pawn. 'But I think it gives you more control of the center of the board.'

I don't see why I have more control, having voluntarily lost a chess piece. He has me move a bishop, then he slides his queen across the board and says, 'Check.'

'Damn.' I move my king to the right, and he nods. 'Now I can't castle.'

'That's right.'

I get two of his pawns, and he gets my bishop and another pawn. We are reckless, Anderssen and I. When cornered, we go on the offense, sacrificing needlessly.

'The funny thing about this game—it's called the Immortal Game—is that they played it on a sofa during a break in a really intense seven-week world tournament. This was just a casual game, a game to relax between matches.'

'Maybe it's relaxing for you. But I'm getting crushed.'

He takes my rook, and his queen is poised to get my other rook and then my king. Instead of defending them, he has me move a dinky pawn one square in the middle of the board, threatening no one.

'Brilliant,' Silas says. And he takes my other rook with his queen. 'Check.'

I move my king up a square. It's all over. He's got his bishop and his queen after me, and I've got no one. But instead of going after my king he brings out a knight from the back row.

I study the board. I see why he feels threatened. I move my knight and take his pawn. 'Check.'

277

'Yes! That's what he did.' He slides his king over one.

And then I see it. I see it so clearly. I move my queen forward three squares. 'Check.'

He takes my queen with his knight. I move my bishop diagonally one. His king is pinned. Either way he goes, one of my knights will get him.

'Checkmate,' I yell at him. 'Checkmate!'

Silas whoops and raises both hands for me to slap.

'How did that happen?' I look at all the pieces I lost at the side of the table, two pawns, two rooks, a bishop, and a queen. 'How did he do that?'

'He didn't need them. He just had the guts to keep fighting.'

'I do feel kind of immortal now.'

He laughs. He looks happy and doesn't try to hide it.

I walk him to his car on Oxford Street. His school has early release on Wednesdays, but he has to tutor a kid at two and he's late. We walk close, my shoulder brushing against his upper arm like it did on the river that night.

'When I moved that pawn and you said brilliant, I didn't get it. But that pawn blocked your queen from coming back and saving you.'

'Yup,' he says, but he seems to be thinking of something else, too.

We reach his Le Car. I touch the hole in the passenger door. 'What happened, on our last date? Why didn't you kiss me?' It feels like liquid nitrogen coming out of me.

He's surprised by the bald question but not resistant to it. Something in his body relaxes. He leans against his car, props his heels against the curb. 'I felt like something was off that night. There'd been this ease between us, at least I thought so, and it was gone. You seemed sort of out of reach. I was still pretty sick, so I figured maybe it was me.' He's watching his shoe scrape the granite edge. 'I was going to bring it up the next time I saw you, but then I was at Oscar's and I heard his kid talking about the drawings on the fridge. He said one of them was Casey, his father's girlfriend. I called you a few times to see if that was true, and when you didn't call back I figured I had my answer.' He looks up and it feels like we're touching.

You know your horse, I hear Dana say.

My body starts clenching involuntarily, and I hope he can't see this.

'I get it,' he says. 'He's the full package. Three books, great house, cute kids.' He kicks the curb. 'He does have a bum knee, though.'

'Really?' I say, though I want to say other things.

'When he's been sitting for a while, yeah.' He pushes himself off the car and bends his legs a little and comes up. 'My knees are excellent.' He gets his keys out of his pocket and goes around to the driver's side and looks over the car's roof at me. 'FYI.' He starts the car and rolls down the windows. 'Good luck tomorrow.'

I don't know what he's talking about.

'At the doctor's,' he says.

He puts it into first. I remember the night when Lou Reed was singing and how horny his hand shifting gears made me.

'Can we do something sometime?' I say, desperate at the sound of the revving engine.

'No.' He eases the clutch. 'I can't get all tangled in your ropes.'

It sounds like something Star of Ashtabula would say.

He lurches into traffic and dips under the bridge, and it takes me a long time to walk away from that spot on Oxford Street.

The next morning I walk to my appointment at Long-wood. It's not far. I walk slowly and people come from behind and pass me with their coffee cups and their medical thoughts. Others come toward me from the hospitals in rumpled scrubs and drained faces.

I think about that time in high school when I was scared of killing myself in my sleep and I wonder if there is some part of me now that wants to die, wants to hoist the white flag and admit defeat. What if my body is done trying to make things work? What if it doesn't want what I want? I stop and stare at a strip of grass between the sidewalk and the street, the slender trunk of a small bare tree. What if this is all the life I get?

Muriel and Harry are in the waiting room. I don't know how they knew. I don't remember telling either of them the name of the doctor. They have me squeeze between them on a fake leather loveseat. The people around us are sick. Hairless heads, oxygen tanks, a caved-in mouth. Muriel picks up *People* magazine. There's an article about Joni Mitchell and her reunion with the daughter she gave up for adoption in Canada in 1965. Muriel and I have been following this story, but Harry barely knows who she is. He's never heard the song 'Little Green,' so we have to explain and sing parts of it for him, the part about icicles and birthday clothes and the part about having a happy ending. Muriel and I work ourselves into some tears about it, and Harry laughs at us.

'Camila,' a nurse says in a doorway.

Harry and Muriel are surprised when I stand up.

I sit on the edge of the examining table in the white johnnie with blue squares, ankles crossed, socks on, hands folded, begging for life. I'm aware of not having the strongest case. In the waiting room there was a woman with no eyebrows balancing a toddler on her knees and nursing a tiny baby tucked behind him. My disappearance from this earth won't make much of a ripple. But I beg anyway.

Two quick raps and the doctor comes in. He's very tall and very thin, a knife blade of intensity. He moves quickly, washing his hands and drying them as we speak, the knobs of his wrists raised and pointed like spurs. Where is the lump? How long? Is it sore? He lifts my right arm and feels around. He breathes through his sharp nose onto my shoulder.

'Where is it?' He's in a hurry. People are waiting. People are dying.

I find it with my fingers quickly. 'Here.'

I feel him find it. It's sore because of how often I prod it. His fingers make a quick circle around it and pull away.

'That's a lymph node.' He's at the sink again, washing in quick jerks. 'Regular size. Not much fat on you, so it's easier to feel.'

'But I can't find it on the other side.'

He shrugs. Pulls two paper towels from the dispenser. Rolls them around in his palm and tosses them out. 'Exit is to the left.' He yanks open the door and slides through.

Muriel and Harry are startled I'm out so soon. I signal to them across the room and push through the door. Then another door. Down a hallway and more doors. I wait for them outside in the sun. I didn't know it was sunny. Everything feels so much clearer, like I've gotten glasses. Above us is one thick square cloud that looks cut from marble. Traffic whips by.

'It's nothing,' I tell them. 'It's normal.'

'What?' Muriel is laughing. I am whimpering. Harry is hugging us both, dipping us from side to side. 'You little sod,' he says. 'You scared the daylights out of me.'

Oscar and Silas are on my machine when I get back.
'Now I have to make all kinds of *shapes* out of their hair when I shampoo it,' Oscar says. 'And it adds an extra forty-five minutes to bath time, which was plenty long enough before. When can I see you?'

'I'm sure it went okay, but let me know, all right?' Silas says.

I call Silas back and get his machine. 'It was nothing.' I pause, hoping he'll pick up even though I know he's at work. 'I'm fine.' I hang up and call Caleb.

'Oh. Oh. Thank the Lord. Thank the Lord.' He's imitating a televangelist. 'Oh Puritan Pilgrim Plymouth Rock miracle!'

'Praise be!' I say, laughing, but I feel the truth of it. Praise be.

'I'm coming back there. I decided that either way I should drive Mom's car to you.'

'I thought Ashley needed it.' Ashley is Phil's daughter.

'Ashley is an asshole who can go fuck herself. I'm quoting Phil here. I get along with her fine.'

'You're going to drive across the country by yourself?'

'I need some head-clearing me-time.'

This did not sound like Caleb.

'Adam said I could stay in his guestroom.'

He'd already run this by Adam? 'You're really coming?'

'I am.'

Four days later he's at my door.

I haven't seen him since the funeral. He looks different, taut. Hopped up, my mother might say. He reeks of Cheetos and maybe some Funyuns.

He doesn't think I look so great, either. 'You look like a rabid gerbil.'

'I haven't slept in so long.'

'Oh sweetie.' He hugs me hard. 'It's okay. It's gonna be okay.'

It's so much easier to cry when there are arms around you.

'Thirty years ago they would have said you were having a nervous breakdown and sent you to McLean's. Remember Mrs. Wheelock?'

I don't want to remember Mrs. Wheelock. I don't want what was happening to me to be called a nervous breakdown, a label from my childhood that scared me even before I knew what it meant.

He asks about my health insurance. I remind him I've been fired, and he says I probably have Cobra. I have no idea what he's talking about. He says I probably have full coverage at least until the end of the month and after that could pay to keep it going for longer. I tell him I've had enough doctors' appointments for the next ten years, but he means for a shrink.

'You probably have a certain number of visits per year. Maybe you could find someone who would be willing to schedule them all before the end of the month.'

'A nice rule-breaking shrink.'

I offer him a shower, and he peeks in my bathroom and says he'll be doing all his personal hygiene at the big house.

'I brought you something,' he says.

'I know you did.'

Out the window is my mother's car. It isn't the blue Mustang of my childhood or the white Rabbit of my teens. It's a black Ford I've only been in a few times. I'm relieved by how few memories I have of her in it.

But he reaches into a bag and hands me a round cookie tin.

'Yum, five-day-old cookies,' I say. 'You shouldn't have.'

'It's not cookies.'

I don't open the tin. I just shake it. Things swish around inside. 'We did this already. With Gil.' This friend of his had come with us up Camelback Mountain to the same spot where my mother had spread Javier's ashes sixteen years earlier, and we tossed into the wind the gray clumps of sand that were supposed to be my mother's body. I was mad Gil was there. Caleb had let him take a scoop.

'Not Gil. *Giles*. That was just half, remember? We agreed the rest should go in the Atlantic.'

I don't remember. I don't remember much about those days after she died.

'I thought we could go up to Horseshoe tomorrow.' Horseshoe Beach was where she always took us. 'Adam may take the day off and come.'

I give him a look.

'It's not the same,' he says. 'He knew her really well. She loved Adam.'

'Can't we just do this alone?'

'I think I need him there.'

'Be careful, Caleb.'

'That is not always my strength.'

I tell Caleb about the weekend with the kids and Oscar's mood when he returned from Provo, but how he's called me at least once a day since then.

'Invite him to dinner so I can smell him out,' he says. 'I have good instincts.'

'You have terrible instincts. He'll just charm your pants off.'

'Oh, I hope so!'

I smack him and pick up the phone.

We eat at Adam's. When we arrive, he pours us glasses of wine and we sit on the stools while he stirs a thick risotto on the stove. Adam quickly figures out that Oscar is Oscar Kolton.

He stops stirring. 'Holy shit. I am a big admirer of your work,' he says confessionally, as if it should mean more coming from him than from the regular admirer.

Oscar gives him his grateful humility dip of the head.

Caleb raises his glass. 'To Casey's armpit, which has brought us all together.'

Oscar is confused.

'I thought I had a lump. It was nothing,' I tell him.

I can feel Caleb looking at me.

'Why did you keep this little liaison a secret?' Adam asks, making circles with his finger between me and Oscar.

'It wasn't a secret. Caleb knew.'

'Caleb doesn't *read*.'

'I read your letters,' Caleb says. 'He writes long, gorgeous letters.'

'And you never write back.'

'I call. I'm good with the phone.' He has a little smile that Adam turns away from.

Adam gives the big pot a few more stirs then plates the risotto. We carry our servings to the table. I take the chair next to Oscar, and he points across the table to the seat next to Adam.

'Pairs part,' Oscar says, as if he's a dowager from another century.

Caleb takes my place and I go around the table and sit next to Adam. Oscar and Caleb start talking. Adam leans over and tells me about some lowball offers on his property. He says I have nothing to worry about yet.

'Case'—Caleb taps his fork on my plate—'you haven't told him our father was a Peeping Tom?' Our father is a party trick for Caleb. He has a whole routine of anecdotes he trots out.

I shut it down with a look, and he starts grilling Oscar about *Thunder Road*. Where and when is it set, who is the protagonist, what perspective is it told from? He's never asked me any of these questions about my novel. I didn't even know he knew about protagonists or perspective. Adam asks Oscar where he was when it all came to him. As if a whole novel comes to you in one great bolt of lightning instead of years of sustained concentration.

'I was driving home from a dentist appointment,' Oscar says. 'And I saw it all.'

Jesus.

'Fabulous,' Adam says. 'After the dentist no less.'

Oscar shrugs. Go figure. Genius will find you no matter where you are. He tells them about the new one he's working on and how he'll never make the deadline on his contract, that it's going to take much longer than he anticipated.

'Well,' I say. 'I find it *extraordinary* that you think you have something to *say*.'

They look at me with some alarm. I didn't mean it to come out with so much anger. I nudge Adam. 'Remember? Saying that to me? In the driveway?'

He shakes his head. 'Why would I ever say a thing like that?'

During dessert Oscar gets up to go to the bathroom. He sinks a bit with his first few steps across the room. The bum knee. I never noticed it before.

'Will you come with us tomorrow?' Caleb asks him when he comes back.

'Where to?'

'We're going to spread my mother's ashes,' I say. It comes out slowly, like my mouth doesn't want to make the words. 'At a beach.'

Oscar shakes his head without looking at me. 'Jasper has T-ball and John has a birthday party, so I can't swing it.'

He holds up his wineglass. 'Good Sancerre, Adam. Where'd you come by it?'

When we leave, Caleb gives Oscar a hug and Adam gives him his hand and says they should play some squash. Outside Oscar takes my arm and starts laughing. He's in a good mood. He won them over. He will always win people over. It will always be the thing he has to do.

He kisses me in the patch of light from the living room windows. 'I didn't realize you were the Jasper of your family.' Kiss. 'The charming brat.' Kiss. Kiss. 'The littlest provocateur.' All these small pecks interrupted by speech. They keep the flame low.

'I don't think we should do this anymore.'

'Do what?'

'Go out.'

He laughs and pulls me closer. 'What are you talking about?'

I don't normally have to break up with anyone. Usually they do it for me, or I leave the state or the country. I don't have to spell it out very often.

'Listen, Case.' He's never called me that until halfway through dinner tonight when he started copying Caleb. He steps us out of the window light, not wanting to be seen anymore. 'I know you're scared. It's scary. But I love you and we are good together. I feel so good when I'm with you. God, I *like* myself when I'm with you.'

'I'm not sure that's being in love with me, Oscar. That's being in love with you.'

'Is there someone else?' he says. I can tell he doesn't think this is a possibility.

'I think so.'

'Is it him?' He gestures toward the window.

'Adam?' Then I see that he's joking.

'Who is it?'

'It's not important who.'

'It is important. Do I know him?'

'No.' But I'm a terrible liar. So I tell him.

'That kid from my workshop? How old is he, fifteen?'

'He's my age.'

'Your age? He might be your age, but he's not in the same solar system, Casey. That guy lives on Jupiter.'

I don't mention that Jupiter is actually in our solar system.

He says a few more insulting things about Silas and Silas's writing, then he tries to tell me again why we should be together but with less conviction. It's starting to sink in.

'Well,' he says, taking his keys out of his pocket. 'Maybe I'll make that deadline after all.' He gives me one last peck. 'Probably the youngest lips I'll ever kiss again.'

I've forgotten what gets revealed right after you break up with someone.

'I doubt that,' I say.

He chuckles hopefully and walks down the driveway to his car.

We go in Adam's car to Horseshoe. It's a dismal day, a shredding wind, the water gunmetal gray and hard as stucco. There's a photo somewhere of my mother and baby Caleb on this beach. She's in a bikini, the bottoms big and square and rising up past her bellybutton. But she wasn't a swimmer and wouldn't want anything to do with this cold water now.

We walk against the wind on the firm sand to the shoreline. Caleb opens the cookie tin and takes a fistful of the silver rubble inside. The wind is coming too fast off the water for flinging, so he drops the coarse bits into a little wave that creeps up toward our shoes. I don't allow myself to believe it's her. I don't allow myself to believe that my mother's body—her hair, her smile, the two chords that made the sound of her voice, her heart, her good bum, her moisturized legs, her toes that tinkled when she walked— has been burned down to this rubble in my hand.

Still, I can't do it. I can't put these gray bits in water this cold on such a gloomy day.

'You do half,' I say to Caleb. 'I'll put the rest some- where else.'

I stand near him while he does it. Adam hangs back behind us. A lone seagull, the only one in the sky, flies low along the beach, close to our heads, then out to sea again, tilting hard left, one wing tipped toward the water, like a plane doing a trick. It rises and levels off then drops down, skims the surface, trailing its feet through the water, then lifts up again, raising itself in great wing-driven pulses, up, up, up, then a long glide and a few flaps then a long glide—up, flap, glide, until it's somehow no longer there at all.

I look around. I've been following the gull down the beach without knowing it. Caleb's done and leaning against Adam on the dry, white sand.

We were somber in the car on the way up, the cookie tin on Caleb's lap, but once back in the car, he tosses the remaining ashes from the front to the empty spot beside me in the back, cranks the radio, and starts teasing Adam about his driving.

We stop at the clam shack and eat at the window near the picnic tables that overlook the harbor where I sat with my mother the day she came back from Arizona and tried to explain, again, her year and a half of absence. I just nodded. I wish I had been awful to her that day. I wish I'd thrown my food and screamed vile things at her. I wish she'd dug all my feelings out of me. Maybe I'd be better at saying them now.

But Caleb has other memories. 'Do you remember coming all the way here after Gus's wedding?'

'Yeah,' Adam says. 'I remember that guy with the goatee tried to make out with you when I was right there in the back seat.'

Caleb laughs. 'He did more than that after you fell asleep.'

294

They're leaning over a dessert menu, pressing against each other.

'Can we go back now?' I say.

Caleb stays for five days. Adam doesn't go to work. I leave them alone. I drive my new car. I drive to Harry's and to Muriel's. I drive to the grocery store three blocks away. I answer ads in the *Globe* and get an interview at a school in New Hampshire. I drive up there, find the gothic, gloomy school, turn in the half-moon driveway, curve around the lawn and flagpole, pass the parking lot, and drive back home crying and clenching.

Phil leaves messages on my machine that Caleb doesn't answer.

He has a flight out on Thursday, but he doesn't get on it. He says Adam has tickets to a play and has asked him to stay.

That night I'm reading in bed, and I hear them come in the driveway and go inside Adam's house. I don't like what's going on. I want to call Mom. She wouldn't like it, either.

I go back to my book and try not to think of them.

I hear knocking and open my eyes. My light is still on, and my thumb is still inside the book, but I fell asleep. I *fell asleep.* I don't even care that I've been woken up, because I fell asleep like I used to, for years and years, my thumb in a book.

I unlock the door. Caleb is still in his suit from the theater, but he seems smaller in it. I've never seen him look so small before. Nothing is right about his face, either.

'Can I sleep here tonight, Case?'

295

He falls onto my bed, and I sit beside him.

'What happened?'

He shakes his head. He takes a deep breath. 'We consummated our flirtation.' And then he curls up and covers his face and a terrible whine comes through his hands. I didn't know how Caleb cries. I've never seen it before. It sounds physically painful for him. I rub his arm. I smooth his hair. The futon shakes beneath me.

'It's okay. It'll be okay. Phil will understand.' I don't know if Phil will understand. But I don't think he'll be as surprised as Caleb might think.

'I love him, Case. I think I've always, always loved him.'

'Adam? Gross.'

He whines. 'He *shoved* me off of him after.' He barely gets this out before he lets loose with a wild moan. Oafie starts barking from Adam's mudroom.

When the long jag is over, I pull his hands off his face. 'Listen to me. He wanted it. He wanted you. This whole week all he's done is talk about sex and the people you both fooled around with. He was working you all week. I saw it. He wanted you, then he wanted the satisfaction of pushing you away.'

'It was so awful. The expression on his face.'

'He's never going to allow himself the option of you or any other guy. He's not that brave. And I don't think you're in love with him. You just needed to play out an old attraction.'

He's lying there with his eyes shut, but he's listening.

'Go home. Tell Phil everything. See where it goes from there. Maybe you'll still want to leave him. Maybe you'll look at that gorgeous dining room table he made you and you'll think, "Is there anything sexier than an ophthalmologist who can make me a seven-foot table?"'

In the morning I drive him to the airport. He flips down the visor and sees the red hollows under his eyes. 'God, I look worse than you now,' he says. He looks out the window at the morass of highway construction. 'I hate Boston. Nothing but pain in Boston.'

At the terminal, he pulls his suitcase out of the back, and we stand close on the sidewalk.

'You going to be okay?' he says.

'Yeah, and so are you. Call me when you get home.'

He nods. We hug each other tight.

I feel like my mother, and I feel like my mother is hugging me.

He walks to the revolving doors. He waves. The doors spin him away.

C aleb left me the name of a doctor who agreed to see me three times before my insurance ran out at the end of the month. His name is Malcolm Sitz, and his office is in Arlington on the third floor of a brick duplex. He can only meet at five thirty in the afternoon. We've just lost daylight savings so it's already dark when I get there.

He's a slender man with smooth skin and a silver bob. He has a moustache he likes to touch. From my seat, a pilled wool armchair facing his ergonomic recliner, I can look out the window and down into the house behind his small yard. It's a contemporary house with walls of glass revealing a brightly lit kitchen. A girl of nine or ten is sitting at the table doing her homework.

He asks why I'm here, and I tell him about the buzzing under my skin, the ringing—

'You have ringing in your ears?'

'Not actual ringing. It's like my whole body is a bell, like a huge bell in a tower that's been struck and—'

He held up his hand. 'Let's skip the flowery descriptions. You're anxious. Why? When'd it start?'

I tell him about Red Barn and Luke and the night I first felt it. I tell him about my mother dying and leaving Barcelona and moving East and Iris and the potting shed and the revisions and rejections and EdFund and all the debt collectors catching up with me. He listens, his fat pen with the jelly grip hovering over a yellow legal pad, but he doesn't write anything.

'Anything else?'

I tell him about Oscar. I tell him about Silas.

'Did you ever hear the one about the donkey who starved to death between two stacks of hay,' he says.

Fucking, fucking Pilgrims.

Down in the bright kitchen a man is chopping vegetables, and a woman is measuring out rice and water in a pot. The girl is still doing her homework. Her legs are swinging back and forth under her chair.

I start to cry.

Dr. Sitz seems to know exactly what I'm seeing even though he cannot see it from his chair. It almost feels staged. Cue the stable family.

At the start of the second appointment I begin by talking about my parents, and after a few minutes he waves his hand at me.

'I don't want to hear those old soggy stories. Tell me what you were thinking about on the way over here.'

I tell him I was thinking about all the people I've pitied and scorned for 'selling out' or 'settling' and how none of them are alone or broke or driving to a shrink's office in Arlington.

'You're a gambler. You gambled. You bet the farm.'

'On this novel? That was a bad bet. I can't even finish it.'

'Not on the novel. Your success or failure is not based on what happens with that pile of papers. On yourself. On your fantasies. So what do you want now, at age thirty-one?'

'I want to finish the book.'

He nods.

'And start another one.'

He laughs. 'You're a very high roller.'

'So what are you scared of?' he asks me at our last appointment. 'I mean *really* scared of.'

I try to think about it. 'I'm scared that if I can't even handle this right now, how will I be able to handle bigger things in the future?'

He nods. He scrapes his moustache against his thumbs. 'Bigger things in the future. What's bigger than this? Your mother dies suddenly. It echoes her previous abandonment of you thus making her death a double whammy. Your father proved to be incapable of being your father. You owe money to several large corporations who will squeeze you indefinitely. You spent six years writing a novel that may or may not get published. You got fired from your job. You say you want a family of your own but there doesn't seem to be a man in your life, and you may have fertility problems. I don't know, my friend. This is not nothing.'

Of all his strange responses, this is the one that helps me the most. This is not nothing.

M anolo calls and offers me the job. Two sections of
ninth grade, two sections of juniors, and a creative
writing elective starting next semester. Full-time salary,
Blue Cross Blue Shield health insurance. No more Pilgrims.

'I don't understand.'

'What don't you understand?'

'The interview with Aisha didn't go well.'

He laughs. 'Trust me. It went very well. She wouldn't
hear of anyone else after you came in.'

He asks me to come in that afternoon to fill out some
paperwork and pick up the books I'll be teaching, the school
handbook, and the English department curriculum. He asks
if I can start the next Monday.

'Also, I don't know if you saw the posters but we're
hosting a writing festival in two weeks. Would you be
willing to make some introductory remarks? You're the
one in the department who can speak to a real commit-
ment to the writing life. Aisha liked whatever it was you
said about that.'

What had I said about that?

'Sure,' I say. 'I can say something.'

There's a particular feeling in your body when something goes right after a long time of things going wrong.

It feels warm and sweet and loose. I feel all that as I hold the phone and listen to Manolo talk about W-4s and the study hall schedule and my mailbox combination and faculty parking. For a moment all my bees have turned to honey.

I have a week to finish the revision for Jennifer and prep for my classes.

I get out my manuscript and start reading. I take notes. A few things she said come back, but when I push to remember more, I can't. I start the rewrite anyway. I look up and it's dark. I look up again and it's past midnight.

I work like that for five days and nights. I eat spaghetti with red sauce and apples with peanut butter. I don't even go out for a run. When people skulk around my window with the realtor I pull down the shade. I luxuriate in the time, the endless time. No doubles, no shifts at all. The Iris smell is gone permanently from my hair. My body still zings. But it isn't all bad zinging. Some of it is good energy. Some of it is a strange excitement.

On Friday afternoon I stand in line at the post office.

'Still at it,' she says, punching in the numbers.

'Yup.'

'Well, can't shoot you for trying.'

Over the weekend I reread *Siddhartha* and *Their Eyes Were Watching God* and make lesson plans. Muriel and I go to a consignment shop in Davis Square. If I had gone alone I would have found nothing, but she sets me up in a dressing room and brings me treasures: a gray cashmere sweater with buttons down the back, a knee-length suede skirt, black boots with a bright red zipper.

On Monday morning I wake up at five. I need to establish a routine right from the start: an hour and a half of writing every day before work. I sit at my desk and collect my notes—on dupes from Iris, in the backs of a few books, in a small pad I keep in my knapsack—about an idea I have for something new. At the back of a new notebook I make a rough timeline of what I have so far. I turn to the front of the notebook. I already know the first line.

My first class is juniors. They come in and slough off their heavy backpacks with a thud. I try to say hi to each one as they come in, as if it is normal for me to be teaching a high school class. I haven't been around this age since I was this age. Just looking at their faces—the zitty one, the shiny one, the worried one, the pissed-off one—makes me grateful I'm not back there still. Before they came in, I was nervous, but now that I see them I just want to help them get through the day. I learn their names quickly—it's a lot easier than memorizing apps and entrées for a six-top—and ask them to catch me up on their semester so far, what they liked and what they didn't. I realize I'm sitting up on the left corner of the desk just like Mr. Tuck used to, and even though I'm still mad at him, I'm channeling him right now.

They're halfway through *Their Eyes Were Watching God*, but I go back closer to the beginning and read them several pages out loud and end on the part about Nanny on her knees in the shack, praying about her mistakes. Afterward I ask them to write about a time they felt like that. They open their notebooks slowly. They're wary, like when you try to feed a squirrel.

I call Muriel from my office on my free period. I spin in my chair and tell her about the beautiful paragraph a junior named Evelyn wrote about her little sister being born and all the compliments I'd gotten on the boots. Two teachers walk by talking about the New Deal. It's lasagna for lunch and the smell travels the hallways.

After we hang up I feel good enough to imagine calling Silas at Trevor Hills where he works—I imagine him on break, too, in his office—but my heartbeat picks up and I need to be calm for my next class.

High school classes are short and fly by. I never get through half my lesson plan. After months of talking about lamb shank and lemon rind reductions, it's a relief to talk about books.

At the end of each day that week I remember my own novel but with more curiosity and less panic. I wonder if Jennifer is reading it. I decide not to worry about not hearing from her until next month.

But she is on my machine when I get home from school Thursday afternoon. It's a brief message, and she is talking very quickly. I have to play it a few times. The revision did the trick, she says. She's going out with it.

I call Muriel and play it for her to make sure she is saying what I think she is saying.

She screams.

Saturday night I meet her, Christian, Harry, and James at a Thai place in the Square. Muriel draws a picture of my book in hardcover on a napkin and has us all pile our hands on top of it.

'On the count of three we are going to raise our hands high and let out a barbaric yawp.'

Everyone has their own version of what a barbaric yawp is, but our collective yawp is loud and the management comes over. Muriel shows him the napkin drawing and points to me and explains, and he comes back with a yellow cloth.

'Yellow is our very lucky color in Thailand,' he says.

We lift our plates and he spreads it out. I don't think I ever did anything so kind for a customer at Iris.

Harry makes a toast and our glasses clink and it feels separate from me, the book, momentarily, like it's on its own path.

The next week of school is shorter—only four days of teaching then the writing festival on Friday.

Monday, washing my hands in the faculty bathroom, I'm smiling. I don't even know why. The gray bruises under my eyes are fading. My face is filling out. The food at the school is as good as it smells, and I eat a lot of it. It's already a joke with my ninth graders, how much food I put on my tray at lunch.

Wednesday Jennifer calls in the late afternoon. I'm home from school, making some notes for the speech I have to give at the festival. She gives me names of the publishing houses she sent my book to. I write them all down, these names from the spines of the books I've been reading all my life. It doesn't seem real that my novel has actually been delivered (by messenger, she tells me) to editors at these offices. My pulse is hammering and I worry that it won't slow, but it does, like a normal heart.

'I'll check in with you when I hear something.'

I give her the number at school, and we hang up. Oafie has gotten out and is scratching at my door. I let him in.

'That was my *agent*,' I tell him. He sniffs under my desk and steps onto my futon, makes a few rotations on my comforter, and sinks down. I stroke his head. He has a new blue collar with pink letters on it. Ophelia, it says.

'Ophelia?' I say aloud and the dog lifts his head. Her head. Ophie. 'All this time you've been a girl?' She lays her big head back down on my thigh.

When I get to school on Friday, Manolo is out front waiting to greet the three visiting writers. I wait with him.

He looks down at the folded pages in my hand. 'Nervous?' he says.

'I think you hired me just so you didn't have to make this speech.'

The writers arrive all together in a beat-up Volkswagen. I recognize a great black cape coming up the path.

'Victor Silva?'

'Casey Peabody?'

He envelops me in his cape for a hug. It smells like Iris—garlic and Pernod. I introduce him to Manolo, and Victor introduces us to the other two, a young man with a shaved head and packed arm muscles and a woman in her fifties with an Irish accent. We bring them inside to Aisha and all go to the library where there is coffee and pastries and a place for their coats, though the muscular playwright is only wearing a black T-shirt and Victor Silva has no plans to remove his cape.

The students start arriving, not just ours but buses from other schools. This is another thing I haven't understood: students from five other schools have been invited. They swarm in and are directed to the gymnasium. When I get there with the writers, the bleachers are full, and the overflow of kids are sitting cross-legged on the basketball court in a wide ring around the podium in the middle. We have to step through them to get to it. The writers sit in the chairs beside the podium, and Manolo steps up to the mic and welcomes everyone. He introduces each writer with brief summaries of their careers. Victor Silva, it turns out, has published four books of poetry and a collection of personal essays. How did I not know this?

'I'm going to turn it over now to the newest addition to our English department,' he says and gives me an introduction, too. Somehow he has taken the information from my resume and made it sound good, my paltry publications and grad school prize.

There's a bit of clapping, and I walk up to the podium. I see a few clusters of students I teach and many others I don't know. Their faces are lifted up at me. I think of Holden Caulfield, wanting to catch children before they fall off the cliff, and I get it now. I take a long breath. A kid from eleventh grade gives a little whoop.

'Thank you, Brad,' I say into the mic. 'Your grade just went way up.'

There are so many more people than I had imagined. But it can't be that much harder than reciting the specials to an impatient ten-top at Iris. Plus, I want to tell these kids the things I've written down. My lips tremble and my voice hops around a bit, but I get it out.

I tell them the truth. I tell them I am thirty-one years old and seventy-three thousand dollars in debt. I tell them that since college I've moved eleven times, had seventeen jobs and several relationships that didn't work out. I've been estranged from my father since twelfth grade, and earlier this year my mother died. My only sibling lives three thousand miles away. What I have had for the past six years, what has been constant and steady in my life is the novel I've been writing. This has been my home, the place I could always retreat to. The place I could sometimes even feel powerful, I tell them. The place where I am most myself. Maybe some of you, I tell them, have found this place already. Maybe some of you will find it years from now. My hope is that some of you will find it for the first time today by writing.

It's disorienting, walking back to my seat. The room is loud with clapping. People are looking at me. And when I sit, the girl next to me says that was cool, and Manolo is still clapping at me from the podium. He repeats the workshop topics and the rooms they are in. He points to the table where there are extra program schedules and tells everyone to have an inspired day.

I go to Victor Silva's workshop. It's full of the students who are not put off by a waxed mustache and a black cape. He has us draw a floor plan of the first place we ever remember living. 'The rooms, the closets, the hallway,' he says as he draws one himself on the blackboard. He turns back to us and says, 'Now add the significant details: the couch, the bourbon bottle, the slot between the wall and the fridge.' He laughs. 'You see? I've already told you my whole childhood in three details.' He jogs to the left and writes in block letters:

NO IDEAS BUT IN THINGS.

'William Carlos Williams. Live by that, I tell you.'

Once we have our details—our white-hot places of experience he calls them—we have to choose one and write about it. 'Not in sentences but in bursts of feelings—phrases, words, don't worry how they relate just get them out. You are vomiting here.'

I circle my mother's bathroom and start writing about it—the greasy face lotion, the dry shampoo spray, the heavy razor, the amber bottle of Chanel No. 5—and all the things that became mine the day she left.

'Casey.' The school's receptionist, Lucille, is squatting beside my chair. 'I'm sorry. She said it was urgent.' She hands me a blue Post-it. 'Jennifer,' it says. 'Line 2.' I follow her out of the classroom to the office.

She shows me into the development office, which is glassed-in like Aisha's but cluttered with stacks of brochures. I pick up the phone.

'So Amy Drummond has offered thirty North American.' Someone else has offered twenty, and someone else has come in-between with twenty-five for world. She goes on to mention other editors and subsidiary rights, but I'm still stuck back on her first sentence. And the word 'offered.'

'I've let the other houses know we're receiving offers. Some of them had blown it off, and now they're speed-reading.' She guffaws. She is giddy, in her own way. 'You there? Your book is going to be bound and sold, Camila. We're in an auction. Start practicing your signature.'

'Everything okay?' Lucille says when I came out.

'Yes. Thank you. Thank you so much.' I love her and I love that office and I love that phone.

I float like a balloon back to the classroom. Everyone is writing. I mouth an apology to Victor Silva who raises his middle finger very slightly at me from his desk in front. I return to my mother's bathroom, the Pantene shampoo, the green velour bathrobe she left behind and that I wore until my father told me not to.

Victor asks us to find the moments of heat in the writing we have done, has us circle and isolate those words, and with them we write a poem. We read them out loud. There's one about an ashtray, a sequined dress, flour on a kitchen floor. Victor says something about each one. The feeling in the room is beautiful, wide open.

The hallway is crowded when we change to the next session. The boy ahead of me has on a green-and-white athletic jacket. TREVOR HILLS it says across his back.

In the workshop with the Irish essayist, I sit next to our librarian.

'Trevor Hills? Are they here?'

She nods.

'With their teachers?'

'Usually one or two come along from each school.'

My heart is pounding Silas, Silas, Silas.

The Irish essayist has us close our eyes and listen to the words she says without trying to control our thoughts.

I keep mine open a crack, to scan the packed room. He's not here.

312

'A rainy day,' she says.

My mother and me running from the Mustang to the house.

'The sound of a musical instrument.'

Caleb playing the guitar.

'An act of love.'

My father cleaning my golf clubs in the kitchen sink.

She has us write about one of these moments that come up unbidden, unforced. I'm writing about the golf clubs when Lucille taps me on the shoulder.

'Line 1' it says on her blue Post-it.

On the way back to the office I find out she's worked here fourteen years and her son is in my ninth-grade class.

Jennifer tells me about a new round of offers. 'Let me ask you,' she says. 'Is there a line you want to cross? A number you need to get to? You mentioned you have some outstanding student loans.' Did I? 'Give me your wildest dream number.'

There is a calculator on the desk. I punch in a year's rent for that top-floor apartment with the window seat and bookshelves and add my debt. I tell her the number. We are not even close.

I head back to the essay class, but the halls are packed and it's over. The one I want to go to next is on the second floor. The stairwell is jammed, and I move up slowly.

'I guess you didn't bomb the interview after all.'

I look up. Silas is on the landing in a tie. People are pushing past us. I climb a few steps closer.

'They'll come to their senses soon,' I say.

313

'I liked what you said this morning,' he says. 'About writing. Good for them to hear those things.'

His fingers are on the railing a few inches above mine. My legs start to wobble. 'Do you want to eat lunch with me?' I say.

He looks like he's going to say no.

'I don't have a lot of friends yet.'

'I don't—'

'Please?'

He grimaces. 'All right.'

'I'll wait for you at the big doors.'

He nods and drops past me.

Lunch is back in the gym, bag lunches at round tables. The room is thundering with talk. I stand in the doorway as kids stream past, waiting for Silas. But it's Lucille who comes first.

'I told her you were probably at lunch, but she said it was urgent.'

She's irked, understandably, so I explain about the book and the agent on the way back to the office, and she gives me a hug and hurries me to the phone.

Three editors are still in the auction. Jennifer thinks I should talk to them. I try to tell her I'll be free in an hour, but she says they're in their offices now. They've canceled their lunch plans to talk to me.

I hang up and Lucille is through the glass, asking me with her arms what happened. 'I have to talk to editors!'

She does a dance in her office chair, and I do one in mine.

I call each of them. I talk to the last one a long time. She has read it so carefully and has a good idea about adding a small bridge between the first and second parts. Like the 'Time Passes' section of *To the Lighthouse*, I say, and she says that's what she was thinking of. It's exhilarating, this conversation. But I miss lunch. I miss Silas.

The last session of the day has already begun. I peek in a few classrooms, but I can't find him. In the muscular playwright's class, they are already writing. He sees me and points to a chair down front and I have to take it.

'Write down your biggest fear,' he says quietly and hands me a slip of paper. On the other side of the room a student is already starting to collect the folded slips of paper in a wool hat.

We're in one of the bigger classrooms with tall windows. On the sills there are a few books: *Sula, Jane Eyre, The House on Mango Street*. I have never let myself imagine my own book being published. When I was a kid I used to expect to win tournaments and often did, but I stopped having expectations about achieving anything long ago.

The wool hat comes closer. I hold my pencil over the blank strip of paper. The wool hat is in front of me. 'I have no fears today,' I scribble, fold it up and drop it in. I'm stunned by the truth of it.

The student hands the hat to the playwright, and he cinches the opening and shakes it up and down. I try to think how I can leave the room to find Silas. But I'm up front, and the playwright is only a few feet away, blocking my exit.

'All problems with writing and performing come from fear. Fear of exposure, fear of weakness, fear of lack of talent, fear of looking like a fool for trying, for even thinking you could write in the first place. It's all fear. If we didn't have fear, imagine the creativity in the world. Fear holds us back every step of the way. A lot of studies say that despite all our fears in this country—death, war, guns, illness—our biggest fear is public speaking. What I am doing right now. And when people are asked to iden- tify which kind of public speaking they are most afraid of, they check the improvisation box. So improvisation is the number-one fear in America. Forget a nuclear winter or an eight point nine earthquake or another Hitler. It's improv. Which is funny, because aren't we just improvising all day long? Isn't our whole life just one long improvisation? What are we so scared of?'

No. I will not be doing any improv. I put my pencil back in my bag and shift closer to the edge of my seat. As soon as he moves away I'll escape.

'You,' he points to a girl two rows behind me. 'You,' he points to the boy at the end of my row. 'And you.' He points to me. 'Stand up.'

We stand.

He holds out the hat to the boy. 'Pick a fear, any fear.' The boy picks.

'Show it to your partners, but do not say it out loud.'

He holds out the piece of paper, and we read: 'I am scared of the blue giraffe.'

Jesus.

'Okay,' he says to the boy, 'you possess this fear. It is overwhelming and relentless. And you,' he says to the girl, 'need to talk him out of it. In whatever way you can.' He turns to me. 'And you'—I have a bad feeling about this—'are the fear itself. Start now.'

They both look at me. The blue giraffe. I stand up straighter and pull my shoulders down and start gnashing my jaw and ripping leaves off trees with sideways jerks of my head. I keep doing this as I get closer to the boy.

'Talk to him,' the playwright tells the girl.

'You know this isn't real,' she says to the boy. 'This is just something you made up a long time ago when you were a little boy and scared that night your parents were fighting, but she doesn't exist and she's not going to hurt you.' She is good. But the more she tells him I don't exist the more real I feel. The boy moves away from me, and I follow him to the blackboard, around the desk, and back closer to our seats. I stand up on my chair and bend over him and start making a loud and terrible sound, a combination of my father's snoring and Clark's awful heavy metal singing. The girl keeps talking, and I start howling as loud as I can to stop him from hearing her, tilting my long neck back to get the loudest sound and thrashing my head and people are laughing and also a little scared of me and I am scared of nothing.

In the hallway after the bell rings, you can tell who's been in improv for an hour and a half. Our bodies are looser, and everything is funny. We're all moving in the same direction:

to the front doors where the buses are idling in the circle. Lucille appears beside me with a Post-it.

'We crossed the line.'

I hug her hard and feel her laughing. 'Thank you, thank you, thank you.'

Then I burrow into the crowd to find Silas.

Outside I spot three Trevor Hills jackets getting onto one bus. Through the tinted window I can see a figure standing with a clipboard counting boys. Not Silas.

'Casey!'

Victor Silva swoops over. 'I have something for you.' He hands me two tickets. David Byrne at the Strand in Providence, Rhode Island. 'Mary Hand gave me a bunch of them.'

'You were fantastic today,' I say.

'I liked that line about your mother's outline in the bathtub.'

'Thanks.'

'See you in Rhode Island.'

The buses pull away. The circle empties. But down in the faculty parking lot something bright shimmers. Just a little green. A little green Le Car.

I run down the hill. His back is to me. I flail my arms. I howl his name. I am a fearless blue giraffe.

He turns and I am beside him. Despite my new long neck, he is still taller. And lovely, in his white shirt and loosened tie.

But he is withholding the chipped tooth.

'I'm so sorry I missed lunch, Silas.'

He holds up his hand. 'It's fine. I know how it goes with you.'

'No. *No!*' I holler. 'It *doesn't* go like that with me! I wanted to have lunch with you. I did. So much. I needed to tell you things.' My voice breaks. I swallow. I have to get it out. 'First of all, your story about Star and the tree is very beautiful. I stole it from Oscar's house, and I read it before bed most nights. I got my heart broken last spring, and I was scared of it happening again. I liked you so much, but you were risky. Oscar had this big hole that I thought maybe I could fill, but I kept thinking about kissing you. My whole body would go *zing-zing-zing*'—my hands run up and down my sides spastically—'every time I thought about it. I broke up with him and I wanted to tell you that at lunch but I had to talk to these editors because we're in an auction and we just crossed the line.' I hold up the Post-it and start to cry. I start to sob, like a fearless blue giraffe.

He takes the Post-it. 'Your book?'

I nod.

'Casey.' I feel his hand on my hair. I step closer to him. Slowly his arms pull me in. 'I'm so happy for you.' He squeezes more sobbing out of me. He doesn't let go.

'Will you come see David Byrne with me?'

He laughs. 'David Byrne?' He pulls back to look at me. The beautiful sliced tooth.

I show him the tickets crushed in my hand.

'Sure.' He's so close and not moving away. He unsticks some of my hair from my cheek and bends down to whisper, 'I think your boss is coming down the hill.'

'It's okay.' His face is still close. 'I'll just be the new teacher making out in the parking lot.'

And I kiss him. A long uninterrupted kiss that goes straight through my body, ringing it in the very best way.

When we get to our section at the Strand, we are in a sea of Iris employees. Gory and Marcus are at the beginning of the row with Fabiana between them, then Dana and Tony and Yasmin. Dana is talking about her date the night before and how the guy put a clove in her mouth before kissing her. 'What am I, a ham?' she says as we slide past. Angus and Yasmin are arguing about how to pronounce 'mischievous.' Silas and I take seats next to Harry and James, who look like they've been making out, red lips and chafed cheeks. Mary Hand is in the row ahead of us, with Craig, Helene, and Victor Silva—the old guard. Thomas and his wife are there, too, with their baby girl who's sound asleep.

We sit during the opening act but when David Byrne walks onstage in a bright pink mohair suit and says quietly into his mic, 'I can't seem to face up to the facts,' Mary leaps up and we all follow her down to the small dance pit in front of the stage.

The crowd shrieks for the whole song. Next he sings 'Making Flippy Floppy' and 'The Gates of Paradise' from his new album, then 'Take Me to the River,' which makes people go crazy all over again. He makes quick costume changes, each time coming back onstage with fresh energy. He doesn't speak to the audience until he picks up a guitar, slips the strap over his head, and steps up to the stationary mic in the center. He's just performed 'Miss America' and is still wearing a kilt and black combat boots with knee socks. He starts picking out a slow melody I don't recognize. 'Hello, Pro-vi-dence.' The crowd roars at the sound of his speaking voice. 'I'm not known for love songs.' He has to wait for more cheering to subside. 'But I wrote this one a long time ago. A heartbreak song. Everyone has written at least one heartbreak song, haven't they? This is for you, Mary.'

Everyone screams, but we from Iris scream the very loudest. She is in front of me, a little to my right, sandwiched between Victor and Craig, who both have their arms around her. I can see half her face. I look for regret or yearning, but she is just smirking her regular smirk at him, purple and red stage lights flashing across her skin.

We sway to his guitar. The words are cryptic, flights of stairs and hamburgers in brown boxes. The song turns faster halfway through, and we pull apart and dance in front of the stage like he wrote it for all of us, about our heartbreaks and recoveries and our friendships that might just last.

Afterward in Silas's car our ears are blaring, and when I ask him in the driveway to come in, he doesn't hear and I have to ask again. And when he comes in he flops on my futon like he belonged there all along.

The geese are all asleep. A few tip their heads out from under their wings as we approach. I open the cookie tin and a few more sway slowly over to us. It's cold, and Silas has wrapped the green blanket around me so I feel like I have wings, too. I shake the tin and walk backward in a circle around them. The ground is warmer than the air and warmer still where the geese have been sleeping. The ashes fall out evenly onto the grass.

They peck at the silver flakes, their beaks moving like machines, faster than the eyes can register. More join them. They don't fight. There's enough to go around.

I hold the blanket open for Silas, and he slips beside me and pulls it closed.

'Is this weird?'

'Yeah,' he says. He puts his lips in my hair. 'I love weird.'

They peck and gnaw for a long time. There's not much left when they're done. They putter around for a while on their wide rubber feet. Their necks look made of fur, not feathers. A few return to sleep, curtseying to the ground and burying their heads between the folded wings on their backs.

I'll miss them when they take flight. I won't be there. Their fast excited chatter, their wings finally spread wide, their feet tucking in behind them. Wheels up. I'll miss it. I'll be in class or at my desk or in bed when they cut across the sky.

'I want them to go right now.'

'I know,' Silas says. 'They'll go when they're ready.'

A book in the library said that some Canada geese may travel as far as Jalisco, Mexico. My mother will like that, the long exhilarating trip, the foreign landing.

But others, the book said, will stay where they are for the winter. Those geese are already home.

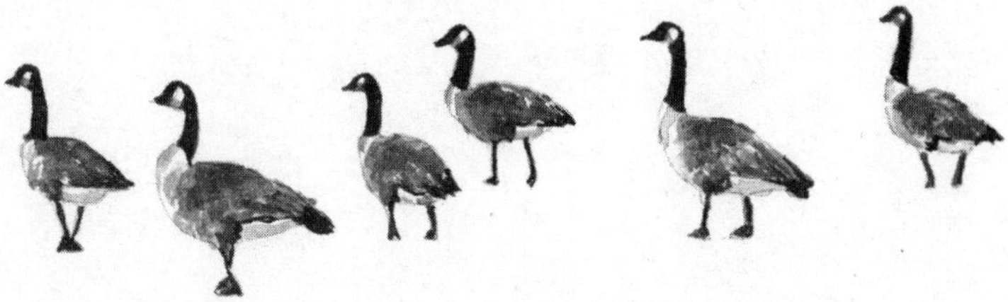

Read on for
book club discussion questions
and an essay by the author.

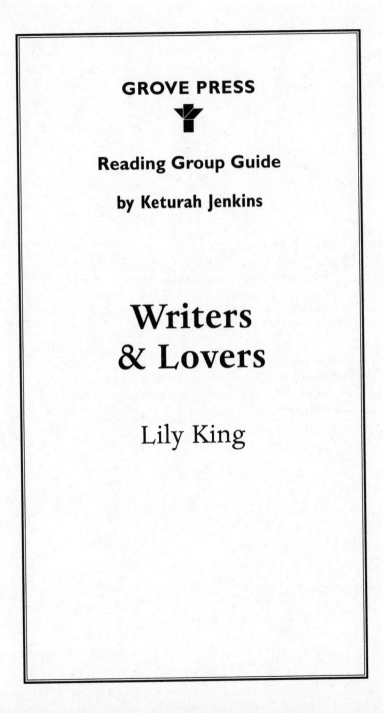

GROVE PRESS

Reading Group Guide

by Keturah Jenkins

Writers
& Lovers

Lily King

ABOUT THIS GUIDE

We hope that these discussion questions will enhance your reading group's exploration of Lily King's *Writers & Lovers*. They are meant to stimulate discussion, offer new viewpoints, and enrich your enjoyment of the book.

More reading group guides and additional information, including summaries, author tours, and author sites for other fine Grove Atlantic titles may be found on our website, groveatlantic.com.

TOPICS & QUESTIONS FOR DISCUSSION

Set in Boston in 1997, *Writers & Lovers* is a transitional moment in a young woman's life as she struggles mightily to pursue a career in writing. Talk about Casey's character, her personality, her ambitions, and her thoughts on marriage: "It was nothing I ever aspired to" (p. 72). Is she relatable? How or how not? Then discuss how your perspective of the protagonist changed over the course of the novel.

———

Geese are prominently featured in the novel and are known to be very loyal birds that mate for life and protect their young. Talk about how the geese are used as symbols in the story. Why do you think Casey chooses the geese to honor her mother's memory? Did you also think her tribute was "weird"?

———

How do the city of Boston and the restaurant, Iris, function as characters? In what ways are the worker's lives influenced by their place of employment? Casey comes to consider members of the staff such as Harry, Mary Hand, and Victor Silva as part of her extended family. Observe how they, in turn, affect Casey and their importance to the story.

———

Casey's mother and father have given her plenty of reasons to mistrust them. Compare Casey's relationship with her mother with that of her father. To which parent is she closest and why? If she hadn't discovered her father's voyeurism (p. 278) do you think she would have forgiven her mother and moved in with her? Explain your answers.

———

On several occasions during the novel Casey suffers extreme anxiety attacks. Persistent thoughts of her mother's death, her father's betrayal, crushing debt, and recent medical scares, leave Casey feeling like her "whole body is a bell" (p. 287). Speak about the ways her anxiety hinders her life and how she copes.

Throughout the novel, Muriel is often the calming voice of reason and the most stable relationship in Casey's life. Talk about their friendship and how the author avoids the trope of toxic female friendships.

We're introduced to Luke early in the story, but the repercussions of that failed relationship linger. Consider Luke's role and how his actions affected Casey's relationships with Oscar and, especially, Silas.

Take a closer look at how King uses Casey's novel, *Love and the Revolution* to explore the grieving process. Think of a time in your life when writing helped you to overcome a difficult period and share what you learned from that experience.

When Casey decides to commit to just dating Oscar, she says, "I'm done with the seesaw, the hot and cold, the guys who don't know or can't tell you what they want" (p. 199). How does your opinion of Oscar change after they start dating? Compare Casey's relationship with Oscar to that of her relationship with Silas; what draws the couples together and what tears them apart? Do you agree with her choice of partner at the end of the novel? How would your decision have differed from that of Casey's?

A major theme of the book is Casey's past and current lovers and how those relationships impacted her. On page 239, Paco, her ex from Barcelona, says to her, "You hate men" (p. 239). Do you agree with him? Examine if King successfully addressed this one way or the other. Give examples to support your views.

———

Discuss the role of the patriarchy in this novel. How does it affect Casey's life and relationships? What differences does she observe about the behavior and reception of male versus female writers?

———

On page 223, Casey says, "My father had this kind of drama in him, sudden surges of despair about life and wasted chances and breaks he never got. I figured that an actually successful man like Oscar would have outgrown all that crap." What should we make of this comparison to her father and what does it say about Oscar's character? Do you think she was being fair? Why or why not?

———

Casey remembers, "It's Star of Ashtabula who reminds me of my mother" (p. 241). Why do you think Silas and his story come to mean so much to her?

———

We discover later in the novel that Casey isn't her real name her father started calling her that after his favorite poem, "Casey at the Bat." On page 213, she tells Oscar, "That's me. Named for a guy who struck out when it mattered most." What does this say about her self-esteem and how she views herself? Why do you think Casey shared this part of herself with Oscar when she kept so many other things a secret?

———

Take the discussion a step further and consider why, after years of estrangement from her father, she still chooses to identify by that name? Reflect on the significance of the author revealing Casey's real name, Camila, in the very next chapter when she is contacted by an agent hoping to represent her. What might King be trying to say about identity?

———

The theme of having a room of one's own, the privacy to write to her fullest potential is always on Casey's mind. In what ways does she compensate for not having an ideal place to write? How did learning about Casey's writing process impact your reading and connection to the character? What do you think inspires Casey to write?

SUGGESTIONS FOR FURTHER READING:

A Room of One's Own by Virginia Woolf

Days of Distraction by Alexandra Chang

Track Changes by Sayed Kashua

Girls Burn Brighter by Shobha Rao

My Name Is Lucy Barton by Elizabeth Strout

Dept of Speculation by Jenny Offill

Woodcutters by Thomas Bernhard

Normal People by Sally Rooney

Leaving Atocha Station by Ben Lerner

Clever Girl by Tessa Hadley

Commonwealth by Ann Patchett

How Should a Person Be? by Sheila Heti

Autumn by Ali Smith

Worms, Eggs, Sperm, and Other Thoughts on Writing

A few years ago I gave a reading at an Ivy League university and after the reading there was a Q & A. It was a very organized Q & A, with a microphone in an aisle and people standing in line to ask their questions. I thought it all was going well until the last person in line asked me, "What factors determine your authorial distance from your narrator?"

I am paraphrasing badly because that's what I remember the meaning to be. What the person actually said was a series of theoretical, jargony words all strung together and I remember standing there at the podium having to translate it to myself very quickly.

I answered with complete unjargony honesty: "I don't think when I write," I said. "I don't make those kinds of decisions cerebrally. I am like a blind worm on the ground." (Only later did I suspect that all worms are blind.)

The person at the mic looked so disappointed that I tried to go on. I said writing was an intuitive process for me, not an intellectual process. If I actually asked myself a question like that, I'd never write a word. That kind of thinking would stop me in my tracks. "I am just a blind worm on the ground," I repeated.

The questioner stood there, unsatisfied, frustrated, possibly angry, but to my relief did not press me further and sat back down. Later I learned this was the head of the creative writing department there at that university.

I love English literature classes. I loved them in middle school and high school and college and grad school. For years I was a high school English teacher, in Spain and in Massachusetts and on an island off the coast of Maine. But I cannot approach any kind of writing with my English teacher brain. That's the brain that wants to analyze, find themes and metaphors and motifs and irony and resonance, to deconstruct and reify and measure authorial distance. That brain expects perfect and immediate cohesion (or deliberate disruption) of all fictional elements. That brain needs to be banished from the process—or at least from writing the first draft.

Because that brain cannot *create* a thing. All it can do is dissect and evaluate and criticize. When you are writing something new, when you are in the blank-page stage, what you need, *all* you need, is your creative, sensual, wide-open brain. Your creator, not your critic. Your worm on the ground. Later on, the creator and the critic can work hand in hand to rewrite and overhaul and buff everything up nicely, but for that first draft, you need to get him (my critic is male—yours may be female or non-binary) out of the room. When I am writing something new, I get up to my study in the morning and often say aloud to the critic: You, out, and slam the door. Because when I am writing first-draft, blank-page stuff, I need to be wide open. My imagination needs to be wide open. I need to allow myself to write *whatever* comes out, however it comes out. A lot of times I put things in parentheses because it's not quite right but I don't want to get bogged down. I want to keep moving, keep feeling. I don't judge it, not as I'm writing it and not when I'm done for the day and not the next day either. I don't look back. I know the critic will deal with it later.

A few months after that Q & A, I stumbled on Robert Olen Butler's book *From Where You Dream*. There are parts of this book in which he articulates exactly what I was trying to say that day.

He writes, "Art does not come from ideas. Art does not come from the mind. Art comes from the place where you dream. Art comes from your unconscious. It comes from the white-hot center of you." I've been in many writing workshops and never have I heard anyone talk about writing this way. Other art forms, Butler says in this book, lend themselves to this kind of discussion because they are purely sensual—painting, music, dance. Our medium, the written word, is not inherently sensual, of the senses. But in fiction, and in poetry and creative nonfiction, we are using it for that end, to create a sense experience for the reader.

After I published the novel *Euphoria* about three anthropologists in Papua New Guinea between the world wars, I was invited to an anthropology conference. I gave a reading and during that Q & A these anthropologists asked me what I was trying to teach the reader about women at that time and what did I want people to learn about that stage of anthropology and what exactly did I want people to know about the impossibility of scientific objectivity.

I kept having to say that I wasn't trying to *tell* the reader anything. I was just trying to create *an experience*. The reader could take from that whatever they liked. Experience comes to us through the senses, through emotion, and emotion comes to us through the senses. It doesn't come in through thought. And you access the senses through what Robert Olen Butler calls the unconscious and what I call the blind worm on the ground.

I'm not so comfortable calling it my unconscious because to me it is a conscious process. I am awake. I'm drinking my tea. I'm getting up to pee. But I'm accessing some receptive part of me that on a good day can hear and see and smell and nearly touch my characters and their surroundings.

When I get close to the end of a first draft, the critic starts pressing against the door. I can feel her. (Funny how when I'm ready for the critic she turns female.) She wants to get her hands on that hot mess. And that is a great pleasure, when you finally have something to let the critic loose on. I write by hand, in notebooks, for my first draft, so for me the next step is to get it onto the computer. That's when I let the critic in. We work together, shaping, creating new stuff and cutting out the crap. On a good day it is a fun process. On bad days the critic roughs me up a bit. But mostly it's joyful. It's my favorite part.

The blank-page stage can be scary and stressful. The unknowns too great. And afterward, when you are many revisions in, there are too few unknowns, and things feel rigid and small changes can unravel too much fabric. But in this stage it's still fluid, not yet set, still receptive to reshaping. When I type in that rough draft I can hear it like I did not hear it as I was slowly, day by day, writing it, and like I will not hear it again as I read it over. I can hear it and play with it—it is both a fully creative process and a fully editorial one. It is the one time when the critic and the creator are both working full steam and in harmony. They are in balance. They are a team, passing the ball easily up the field.

Then when I have a full draft on the computer I print it out and set it aside for as long as I can bear it. After a week or two I try to approach it as a reader, read it like a novel I didn't write, and really try to feel what's wrong with it. Feel. Like a reader feels.

I take notes. I make big and little overhauls. I write scenes in pencil and type them up and put them in. I print it out again. I wait as long as I can, I read it like a reader. I make notes.

I start understanding the book as a whole. The English teacher brain has been let fully in by now. We notice the themes, the motifs, the power of small objects. And together we enhance what's already there. But we like subtlety. We are not trying to rewrite John Steinbeck's *The Pearl*.

And this printing and setting aside and reading and note-taking and revising happens many times. Over and over. Until I feel I can do no more alone, and I show it to my husband and then my writers' group and then my agent and finally my editor.

Years ago I worked for Planned Parenthood and went into middle schools to teach kids about sex and birth control. Before I could do that, I had to study the process and the facts so I could be ready for their questions. I learned that in ovulation, when the egg has traveled through the fallopian tube and is waiting in the uterus to be fertilized, its surface is in a sort of open and porous state. The sperm race to it and when the first one gets all the way in, the egg locks down, becomes impenetrable, and all the other hundred million sperm bounce off it. After so many drafts, the novel can feel a bit like that, and fresh edits can make me feel like a sperm after the egg has locked shut. But you have to have patience and push your way in.

When *Euphoria* was finished and I'd given it to my writers' group and sent it to my agent, I was in my car, going to meet a friend for lunch. I was late, a little stressed, and as I put my blinker on to turn off the highway, I saw my narrator in a museum nearly fifty years after the events in the novel. It was the last scene. I hadn't been searching for a last scene. I thought I'd already written the last scene. But there it was. And I was open to it. I let that sperm in, the blind worm crawl—whatever weird metaphor you prefer.

The first scene in *Writers & Lovers* is based on something that happened to me years ago when I was writing my first book and living with my sister and her boyfriend in a carriage house in Brookline, Massachusetts. I was broke and they let me stay in their tiny extra room for free. My one duty was to walk their dog while they were at work. One morning a neighbor was out in the driveway when I was coming back from walking the dog. I'd been writing all morning, and was still in my sweats and hadn't brushed my hair and was wearing these old slippers with the stuffing coming out.

He asked if I was still writing a novel and I said yes and he said, "It's extraordinary that you think you have something to say."

I went back to my little room like I'd been shot. Of course I didn't think I had something to say. He wasn't trying to be mean. I think, like a lot of lawyers, he wanted to be a writer. But he was inhibited by this fear that he didn't have anything new to say.

When you are writing your blank-page first draft, you don't know what you have to say, and even if you think you know what you have to say, you end up saying something different. And you might think you are saying one thing and then someone who reads it thinks you are saying something else.

I knew, standing in that driveway in Brookline, that I wanted to tell the story of a young woman named Rosie who, after making a great sacrifice for her sister, moved to France and made a mess of things. That's all I knew. I didn't know what that first novel, *The Pleasing Hour*, was trying to *say*. I just knew it was inside me and had to come out. I knew that I felt better after I had written each day. That's all I knew. What you need to be true to, what you need to abide, is what you hear inside you, what wants to come out.

Listen to that. It has a story to tell.